GRIFF MONTGOMERY, QUARTERBACK

First & Ten Series, 1

Jean C. Joachim

Moonlight Books

ABOUT THE E-BOOK YOU HAVE PURCHASED: Your non-refundable purchase of this e-book allows you to only ONE LEGAL copy for your own personal reading on your own personal computer or device. **You do not have resell or distribution rights without the prior written permission of both the publisher and the copyright owner of this book.** This book cannot be copied in any format, sold, or otherwise transferred from your computer to another through upload to a file sharing peer to peer program, for free or for a fee, or as a prize in any contest. Such action is illegal and in violation of the U.S. Copyright Law. Distribution of this e-book, in whole or in part, online, offline, in print or in any way or any other method currently known or yet to be invented, is forbidden. If you do not want this book anymore, you must delete it from your computer.

WARNING: The unauthorized reproduction or distribution of this copyrighted work is illegal. Criminal copyright infringement, including infringement without monetary gain, is investigated by the FBI and is punishable by up to 5 years in federal prison and a fine of $250,000.

A Moonlight Books Novel

Sensual Romance

Griff Montgomery, Quarterback

Copyright © 2015 Jean C. Joachim

E-book ISBN: 978-1-62622-802-3

First E-book Publication: February 2015

Cover design by Dawné Dominique

Edited by Tabitha Bower

Proofread by Renee Waring

All cover art and logo copyright © 2015 by Moonlight Books

PUBLISHER

Moonlight Books

Dedication

To Rick Regan

A great football fan, news editor, and special friend. He supported my writing with kind words of encouragement every time we met. We miss you. Gone so soon, way before your time.

Acknowledgment

Thank you to the following people for their support:
Tabitha Bower, my editor, Renee Waring, my proofreader, Ariana Gaynor, David Joachim, Marilyn Lee, Sandy Sullivan, my publisher, with *special thanks* to Larry Joachim and Steve Joachim, for providing guidance and insight about football.
A special "thank you" to Cheryl Trodella,
a pug owner and lover, for providing the name "Spike" for the pug in this book.

Other books by Jean C. Joachim

<u>FIRST & TEN SERIES</u>
GRIFF MONTGOMERY, QUARTERBACK
BUDDY CARRUTHERS, WIDE RECEIVER
PETE SEBASTIAN, COACH
DEVON DRAKE, CORNERBACK
SLY "BULLHORN" BRODSKY, OFFENSIVE LINE
AL "TRUNK" MAHONEY, DEFENSIVE LINE
HARLEY BRENNAN, RUNNING BACK
OVERTIME
<u>THE MANHATTAN DINNER CLUB</u>
RESCUE MY HEART
SEDUCING HIS HEART
SHINE YOUR LOVE ON ME
TO LOVE OR NOT TO LOVE
<u>HOLLYWOOD HEARTS SERIES</u>
IF I LOVED YOU
RED CARPET ROMANCE
MEMORIES OF LOVE
MOVIE LOVERS
LOVE'S LAST CHANCE
LOVERS & LIARS
His Leading Lady (Series Starter)
<u>NOW AND FOREVER SERIES</u>
NOW AND FOREVER 1, A LOVE STORY
NOW AND FOREVER 1, THE BOOK OF DANNY

JEAN C. JOACHIM

NOW AND FOREVER 3, BLIND LOVE
NOW AND FOREVER 4, THE RENOVATED HEART
NOW AND FOREVER 5, LOVE'S JOURNEY
NOW AND FOREVER, CALLIE'S STORY (series starter)

<u>MOONLIGHT SERIES</u>
SUNNY DAYS, MOONLIT NIGHTS
APRIL'S KISS IN THE MOONLIGHT
UNDER THE MIDNIGHT MOON
MOONLIGHT & ROSES (prequel)
<u>LOST & FOUND SERIES</u>
With Ben Tanner
LOVE, LOST AND FOUND
DANGEROUS LOVE, LOST AND FOUND

NEW YORK NIGHTS NOVELS
THE MARRIAGE LIST
THE LOVE LIST
THE DATING LIST

SHORT STORIES
SWEET LOVE REMEMBERED
TUFFER'S CHRISTMAS WISH

GRIFF MONTGOMERY,

QUARTERBACK

First & Ten Series

Jean C. Joachim
Copyright © 2015

Chapter One

GRIFF PICKED UP THE last dinner plate and drew back his arm to hurl it against the wall when the doorbell interrupted him. It was the police. Two officers stood on his front step.

"Mr. Montgomery. We had a complaint about noise coming from here. Caller said it sounded like a fight." The policeman looked apologetic. "Your family still here?"

"They moved to California two days ago."

"Mind telling us what's going on?" The cop shifted his weight, clearly uncomfortable.

"I dropped a stack of dishes. Made a huge mess, too. Would you like to come in, officer?" Griff stepped away from the door.

"No, sir. I'll take your word for it. Would you mind signing an autograph for my boy, Billy?"

"Not at all." Griff wrote on the paper the policeman provided. Then he smiled as the two men tipped their caps and returned to their squad car.

Pays to be a celebrity in a small town. He remained on the stoop, peering at the neighboring houses. He figured the sound must have carried. Folks would be home at four o'clock on a Saturday, too, out gardening and mowing the lawns. They would have seen his sister, her two kids, and her new husband drive away. *Hell, you couldn't miss the moving van. Damn thing carried away half my house.*

So, what had the neighbors pushing their noses into his business? *Can't a guy let off a little steam his own way in his own house?* Anger bubbled up again in his chest.

He had one more plate left, but now, he had no excuse for the crash. If the police returned, they wouldn't believe his bullshit story a second time. He returned to the kitchen and cringed when he saw the size of the mess he'd made. Sharp pieces of china in all sizes scattered across the floor and into the dining room. He'd even managed to nick the paint on the wall in several places. And he was the only one there to clean it up.

He hated cleaning, a job his sister, Kathy, had taken on when she was living there. *Fuckin' A, Kathy. Why aren't you here?*

In his heart, Griff knew that he wasn't mourning the defection of his sister to Los Angeles. Sure, they were close, but he was glad she'd found Wes, her new spouse. It had been ten years since her first, Dan, had died in a fire in his office building. He'd left Kathy with two young children. She had needed a husband. Even with his helping out, Griff couldn't fill that role. His biggest gripe was the children, who had become like his own. He missed them.

When he was twenty-three, he'd moved in to help his sister. It was supposed to be temporary. The kids were little, Joey was five, and Missy, three. The grandparents were too old, they said, to take on the responsibility of such young children. So Griff had become their new father figure.

At first, he had been uncomfortable. He didn't know how to care for little kids. But the children hadn't known that. They'd loved him right away. It wasn't long before Griff had become a true family man, going to parent/teacher conferences with Kathy and reading bedtime stories. Joey and Missy were sweet and charming, like his big sister. He couldn't help returning their affection.

It had been the least he could do for the woman who'd helped raise him. Kathy was seven years older than Griff. A menopause surprise baby, she always teased. She had been there to shepherd him through the ins and outs of life when his parents had been too tired or preoccupied to find the time. He owed her, he'd figured. And this had been the perfect payback.

Griff made a boatload of money as the star quarterback for the Connecticut Kings. He paid the bills, and Kathy had signed over the house to him in return. At thirty-three, he was ready to think ahead to retirement, and increased family time, but his had flown the coop. Now, he was left alone with a big home and no kids. His life, brimming over with activity for ten years, had ground to a halt.

No more soccer games, little league tournaments, or scout troop overnights. No more camping out or playing catch in the yard. No board games on Saturday nights. No trips to Frosty Freeze for ice cream. No birthday parties. No kids' movies with popcorn and soda.

He was not a happy man.

Griff pulled out the broom, but had to hunt for the dustpan. After several curses, he located it under the sink. *Who puts a fuckin' dustpan under the sink? It can get wet under there.* Sweeping took time. He was careful, not relishing the idea of ending up with tiny shards of glass in his foot. When he finished, he returned the dustpan to its home, frustrated he couldn't find a better spot.

Then came going over the floor with a wet paper towel to pick up the bits too small to see. When he was finished, he ripped off his now-sweaty T-shirt and hopped in the shower. Even the refreshing water on his body couldn't remove the thoughts from his head. His ready-made family, his neat, cozy, compartmentalized life was over. How could he fill the empty space in his heart?

Sure, he still had his women. A girl in every major city shared his bed on road trips. And his local bed-buddy, Carla, the bartender at The Savage Beast, was still here. Griff took an occasional night at The Savage. Betty, a retired Broadway star, played piano and sang on Friday and Saturday nights. He enjoyed her music and the convivial atmosphere.

Maybe Carla's ready to make it permanent with me. The sex is good. I'm sure we can find other common interests besides The Savage Martini, playing pool, and singing along with Betty.

Stuffing his frustration down inside, Griff dressed in his casual best for a Saturday night at The Savage and his plan to get closer to Carla. After sliding his long legs into new jeans and pulling on a light blue T-shirt that hugged his muscles, he combed his mahogany-brown hair. He wore it slightly long, shaggy around the ears, at Kathy's suggestion. His smile was dazzling, and his dark eyes, sexy.

He plucked the keys to his silver Jaguar XK convertible off the dresser and roared into downtown Monroe, the small town that was home to The Kings.

IN AN OLD VICTORIAN house across town, Lauren Farraday lugged a suitcase to her small car. Her newly ex-husband, Bob Decker, stood on the front porch, watching.

"That's a big suitcase for a couple of days."

"I don't know how long I'm going to be there," Lauren said, taking the steps one at a time.

"Linda doesn't want the dishes, so I'm leaving them for you."

"Good." She returned to the porch, plopped down on the loveseat, and took a sip of iced tea.

"But she does want the vacuum. I thought that was a fair trade." He took a slug of beer from a can.

"Whatever."

"I want to be fair."

"I don't care." She struggled to keep anger out of her voice.

"But I do. I don't want you to feel dumped or anything." He shifted his weight.

"I don't," she lied.

"Fine. You know we only got married because of...that and so, I mean, it's only fair—"

"Shut up, Bob. I get it. I didn't argue with you about the divorce. I didn't fight you for stuff. Let it be, okay? It is what it is. I've accepted that."

"It's not like you were madly in love with me."

She sat up. "Don't go there."

"I mean, just saying—"

"I know exactly what you're saying. We've said it a thousand times in the last three months. Can you please let it go already?" She crossed then uncrossed her legs.

"Okay. As long as you're all right."

"I'm fine."

"Sure got over me fast," he mumbled.

"You can't have it both ways, Bob. Me crying my eyes out over losing you and then being cool when we split up. Make up your mind." Her brows knitted, as a note of irritation crept into her words.

"You're right. I feel a little... Well, I left a few extra thousand in the savings, in case you need it."

"Thanks." *Guilty, maybe? Damn straight, you feel guilty. Bastard.*

"Linda and I'll be shoving off in the morning."

"Here's a list of things you need to do before you go," Lauren said, pulling a piece of paper from her pocket.

Bob glanced at it then balled it up. "Honestly, Lauren. Don't be insulting. I know how to close up the house."

"There's more on there."

"Yeah, yeah."

"I hope you and Linda'll be very happy."

"I bet you do."

Lauren couldn't ignore his snide tone. "Trying to be civil here. At least it's not like you're leaving me for someone new."

"That would be worse?"

"In a funny way, yeah. It would." She took a gulp to moisten her throat.

"Guess there's nothing left to say except…good luck." He opened the screen door and went inside.

Lauren let out a breath. The barking of a small dog caught her attention. A pug slipped out the front, circled her legs, and jumped up. "Zander," she whispered, bending down so the canine could lick her face. She smiled and muttered affectionate words to the enthusiastic pooch.

"Where the hell is that mutt?" Bob shouted.

"Out here. And he's not a mutt," Lauren said.

Bob joined her and fastened a harness and leash on the panting dog. "Little monster won't stay inside."

"He likes to ride in the car with me."

"So take him to Rhode Island."

"He's not allowed in the hospital, Bob. Please close the door. I'll be leaving in a minute, and he'll be fine."

Bob dragged Zander, straining at the lead to stay with his mistress, away and slammed the door behind him. She jumped at the loud sound and swore under her breath.

Time to get on the road. She pushed to her feet and picked up her cell. There was a missed call from her brother. She dialed.

"Don? I'm getting in the car now."

"What time will you get here?" Her brother's voice sounded edgy.

"Hmm, four thirty, now. Tell Dad I'll be there by dinnertime."

"Need directions?"

"What? No. I've been to the hospital plenty of times."

"I hate hospitals."

"Yeah. I know. Me, too."

"Dad's asking for you."

"I'm on my way. I'll be there in a little over two hours. Did you tell mom?"

"She's in the Caribbean with her flavor of the month."

"Nothing you can do, then. See you soon. Love you."

"Love you, too."

She took a deep breath and got behind the wheel. The moving truck was parked at the curb, awaiting her departure so that it could take over the driveway. She grabbed one last look at the house and spied Bob carrying luggage. She sighed as a shudder passed through her. Her eyes watered. *What am I getting sentimental for? I can't wait to be rid of that bastard.*

For a split second, the image of what might have been in this wonderful old house danced before her eyes. Her vision, her dream of a loving husband and two kids, vanished like mist under a hot sun. A quick shake of her head returned her to reality. *Can't change the past. Lose the dream and move on. Dad needs you.*

Lauren put the car in gear and headed toward the highway that would take her to Providence and the bedside of her ailing father.

GRIFF MONTGOMERY STOPPED on Elm Street in front of The Savage Beast. The sign said "Open." Creaky hinges announced his arrival as he entered his favorite watering hole. Carla was behind the bar, setting up.

"Not open yet," she called out.

"Sign says you are."

"Griff?" She looked up. "Come on in." She beamed a thousand watt smile at him.

He looked her over with appreciation. *Carla's got it all. Amazing body. Great personality.* Her long, black hair swung down to cover her ample cleavage. She tossed it back with a snap of her head. His gaze rested on her breasts as the memory of their last tryst in her apartment upstairs lingered in his mind.

"You're early."

He preferred not to explain that he had no reason to be at home. "Got anything special today?"

"Yeah, Roddy's new drink, the Savage Sunrise."

Griff lifted an eyebrow. "What's in it?"

"Same as a Tequila Sunrise, only papaya juice instead of orange. He says it's healthier. I think it's bullshit."

Griff laughed. "Now I have to try it. Bring it on."

She peeked at him as she mixed the drink. "Got a lot of free time nowadays?"

"You might say that," he replied, avoiding the question, staring at the suggestive painting behind the bar.

She placed the glass in front of him. "When are you gonna fix me up with one of your hot teammates?"

"What's wrong with me?" He took a sip and gave her a thumbs up.

"We've been bed buddies long enough to know it's not happening beyond that."

He seated his tall, rangy body on a stool. "Don't know 'till you try."

She wiped her hands on a towel and fixed him with a stare. "You gonna stop running around, whoring across the country and back, just for little ole me?"

"Whoring? Wait a minute..."

"That's what I thought." She turned her attention to a dozen wet wine glasses.

"Give me a chance, Carla."

"To break my heart? No way. Besides, I'd hate to ruin a good friendship." She dried some of the stemware.

He shot her a one-sided grin. "I knew you were gonna say that."

"Burger tonight?" She raised an eyebrow.

"With blue cheese, please."

"I know. Well done. Coming up." She disappeared into the kitchen.

Griff looked around. He was usually at the bar after dark, when the kids were in bed or at least busy with homework. During the day, it looked different. The soft lights at night gave the wood a rich patina that faded under the harsh, afternoon sunlight. The floor looked like it needed refinishing. The barstools needed repainting. But at night, everything looked better, finer, and the atmosphere was warm and friendly.

Carla brought out his burger and poured herself a Coke. "Family took off for the West Coast?"

"They did." He took a big bite. *No one makes a blue cheese burger like Carla.* "This is great, as always."

She smiled at him. "So, now you're looking to settle down?"

"I guess."

"I don't want a traveling man."

"One big injury and my career's over, Carla. Time to put down roots."

"Yeah? Tell me you don't have a girl in every port, sailor." She chuckled.

Griff blushed. *Might have to get rid of them if I'm gonna do this.*

"That's what I thought," she said, wiping the bar down with a wet rag.

"What about my teammates? They're no different."

"Oh? You telling me they're all man-whores like you?"

"Maybe not all, but most."

"Damn. Then bring in the few who aren't. Let me look them over."

He laughed. "Kinda like a cattle call?"

"More like a…a…beauty pageant."

Conversation slowed down and ended completely in an hour when a crowd began to form. The Friday after-work folks stopping for a quick cold one before home blended with the single people who came by for a drink, dinner, and some companionship. Some made connections for the night, some only came to eat, drink, and sing.

Griff knew the regulars. He'd hung out here when Kathy and the kids had lived with him because he didn't feel right bringing women back to the house. It was a comfortable place where he was accepted and not bothered too much for being well known. Tonight, though, it took on a different feel. No matter what happened at The Savage Beast, he wouldn't be going home to his family.

Carla was right. They couldn't turn a casual sexual relationship into a marriage. Still, Griff remembered the soft feel of her flesh and the raucous laughter they'd shared. But he wouldn't want his wife working in a bar, and Carla wouldn't want him telling her what to do.

And he wanted someone who wanted kids. Had to have kids. They were an absolute, non-negotiable part of the equation. He'd had so much practice that being a dad for real should be a piece of cake.

He chuckled to himself, knowing fatherhood was never simple, even with practice. Then, he remembered Carla making a face whenever he'd mentioned his niece and nephew. *"Spoil this body to produce another fucked up human being? No way."* Nope, Carla was not in the running.

After two more Savage Sunrises, Griff left her a generous tip, slipped off the stool, and drove home, alone, for an evening of unbearable quiet and inane television.

GRIFF ROSE WITH THE sun, even on Sunday. He had coffee and read the paper on the back deck, overlooking his tranquil swimming pool. He wore a wife-beater tank top and shorts, as he was planning to run a couple of miles then work out in the gym at the stadium. He needed to keep in shape, and the exercise helped ease his loneliness.

In the past, these few weeks after school ended and before training camp began at the end of July had been golden. Griff and Kathy had shared family vacations. Griff had taken his sister and her kids to Disney, of course, but then on more sophisticated trips. One year they had gone to the Galapagos, another to the Baseball Hall of Fame, and then the Maine coast. This year, now that the children were older, he had planned to take them to London, Paris, and Rome. But the plans had gone up in smoke when Kathy had announced her move to San Francisco.

He was restless with too much time on his hands. So, he arrived at the stadium by eight o'clock. Pete Sebastian, or Coach Bass, as he was known to the team, was already in his office. Griff chuckled to himself and waved as he passed the glass wall. Since the Coach's kids had gone off to college, he rattled around his big, empty house, too. Griff expected him to show up at The Savage Beast any Saturday night now.

He met up with his best friend, Elroy "Buddy" Carruthers, in the gym. Fast and smart, Buddy was Griff's wide receiver. Shorter than Griff by a couple of inches, Buddy was lean and hard. He was on the treadmill and gave Griff a wave.

Griff went to the small weights and began pumping iron to strengthen his arms. Buddy was drenched in sweat, indicating he'd been on the machine for a while. After fifteen minutes, both men took a break.

Unmarried, Buddy tied for the worst reputation as a man-whore with Devon Drake, a cornerback. The two men were always on the lookout for new women, often taking single rookies along on their quests. Buddy swore he'd never take a married player out to get laid on the road. Griff had laughed when his friend had made that pronounce-ment and called him "a man-whore with principles."

Griff had brought Buddy home to dinner with his family often. They'd had touch football games in the backyard with the kids and their friends. He'd noticed how relaxed and comfortable his teammate was with Kathy and her children and wondered why Buddy wasn't married. But Griff never pushed. Buddy didn't talk much about his past, college days, or anything personal. Griff wondered if his friend had been such a big seducer back then, too.

Whenever he asked, Buddy would make a joke and avoid the question. Finally, Griff took the hint and stopped asking.

At one point, he'd thought Buddy might be interested in Kathy. Griff had made it clear that he was not an acceptable date for her. Buddy had backed off, saying, "Hey, if I had a sister, I wouldn't want her dating a guy like me, either."

The two men prowled bars together on the road. Tempting young women were never in short supply. Occasionally, they would zero in on the same girl. Then they would make a silent bet as to who would win her. From time to time, their target would leave the bar by herself and the men would shrug, laugh and go to bed early, alone. Buddy never drank nectar from the same flower twice and appeared content with his life choices.

When Griff hit bumpy roads with his niece and nephew, he'd go to Coach Bass for advice. Coach always made time for his star quarterback. Times like those, the team became extended family for Griff.

His life had been perfect. Now, it was shattered like a glass breaking into smithereens after landing on a stone floor. What's more, he wasn't sure where to go to patch it back together.

Coach suggested renovating his house. With the family gone, Griff bounced around like the last pea in a pod. He hired an architect, who made drawings and suggestions, like a gigantic bedroom suite for him with a new, lavish bathroom. She recommended tearing down walls and redesigning everything—including a complete renovation of the kitchen. The house wasn't old and wasn't new. It was nondescript, but functional. Her ideas enticed him.

The entire project would cost about two hundred grand. But when he was done, it would be a palace. He signed the papers, made the first payment, and looked for a place to live until the place was ready.

Chapter Two

GRIFF PULLED UP AND parked his car on the street next to the small, Victorian house. Kids were playing kickball in a yard next door. He could hear them yelling and the sound of the soft ball being whacked. He'd played kickball with Kathy's kids a thousand times when they were growing up. It was the easiest sport to use to get them started. They'd loved it and so had he.

His mind flew back to the day Kathy, Wes, and the kids had left. He didn't want to remember, but the memories came nonetheless.

"It has to last you a long time, young lady," Griff said, giving his niece a hug.

"Aren't you coming to visit soon, like you promised?"

"We'll see."

She made a pouty face. "You always say that when you mean 'no.'" She stamped her foot, crossed her arms, and glared at him.

"Missy Marie Thomas, have you walked Pookie and given your suit-case to Wes?" Kathy shooed the thirteen-year-old outside.

"Where's Joey?" Griff glanced around the living room. Quite a few pieces of furniture were on their way to San Francisco, making the room feel naked. Kathy's new husband, Wes Emerson, had taken a position with Global Tech and was taking his new family with him.

"It's Joe, now, Uncle Griff."

"Oh, yeah. Sorry, sorry. I forgot." He ruffled the fifteen-year-old's hair. At six four, Griff stood almost a whole head taller than the teen. He pulled the boy to him for a quick squeeze. Tears stung at the back of his eyes.

"Please check on your sister. She's supposed to be walking Pookie."

Joe nodded, waved to his uncle, and left.

"Now, you, mister." His sister rested her hands on her hips.

"I'll be fine, Kathy."

"I want you to have your own life, for a change. Get married. Have kids."

"Wave your magic wand and make Miss Perfect appear." He chuckled.

"Mom! Come on. We're ready," Joe called.

Blinking rapidly, Kathy embraced her brother. "'Thank you' doesn't cover it, Griff. I...I..."

"I know," he said, patting her on the back.

In an instant, she was down the stairs, tucked safely in the front seat while Wes maneuvered the overloaded car out of the driveway. Griff stood at the window. He raised his hand and rested it on the glass. A pain shot through his chest. His breathing became shallow as a lump in his throat cut off his air. Silence overwhelmed him.

The same pain returned as he watched the children play. *As if it were yesterday, not a month ago. How long before I get past it? Maybe never.*

"You must be that new fella looking to rent my place." A small, slightly round woman with short, brown hair stood on the lawn, wiping her hands on an apron.

"Yep. That's me. This your place?" He turned his gaze to the neat, quaint house, painted dark teal blue with cream trim. The small porch had a rocking chair, and the pointed roof added charm.

"It is. Rent's three thousand a month. Due on the first. You got kids?" She looked him up and down.

"Nope."

"Good. The house is full of antiques. My husband and I collect. We have a shop, too. Wouldn't want kids running around breaking stuff. Any pets?"

Griff shook his head.

"Perfect. Come on in." He followed her inside. The little bell on the front door took his attention, but only for a second. The mouth-watering aroma of baking bread engulfed him. *I'll take it.*

"What are you making?"

"Pullman loaf. My husband's favorite."

"You own this, but live somewhere else?"

"Yep. We have a bigger one with a shop on the ground floor. It's nearer the turnpike. You've probably passed it. Amy's Antiques?"

He nodded, not sure he remembered, but wanting to be polite. The small living room had a fireplace with a screen and andirons. The furniture was antique and delicate. His brow furrowed. *Can I put my ass on that sofa without breaking it?* He joined Amy in the kitchen, where the smell was so strong it made his stomach rumble. She took two pans out of the oven and placed them on a rack.

"Do you need a hand?" he asked.

"Nope. Got it. I'm used to it. Do it all the time."

The bread had a beautiful, light brown crust on top. Amy gently turned the loaves out onto the counter. "They'll need a bit to cool. Maybe after we look upstairs, they'll be cool enough to give you a slice. Would you like that?"

"Are you kidding? I've never had homemade bread before."

She smiled at him. "That's fine, then. You look awfully familiar. Should I know you?"

Griff cast his gaze to the floor. "I play pro football. Sometimes, I get in the local papers."

"That's it! Now, I recognize you. You're the guy who wins all those games for the Kings."

"I don't win the games. It's the team. I'm just the quarterback."

"Crap, don't be modest. Isn't the team's picture I see. It's yours." She narrowed her eyes for a long look at him. "And I can see why."

That made Griff blush. "Maybe we should see upstairs?"

"Of course, of course." She took off her apron and hung it on a hook then entered a tiny, winding stairway from the kitchen.

"Not sure I can fit in here," he said, ducking his head.

"These are the back stairs, used by the maid and butler. Yeah. They are kinda small, aren't they?" She eyed his broad shoulders before she backed out and led him to the front staircase.

They walked through a formal dining room with dark, antique wood furnishings, including a highly polished, oval table and six chairs. Griff glanced at the delicate legs and decided they wouldn't hold him. But the room had charm, like stepping back in time, and he approved.

The bedrooms upstairs were adequate, though he had serious concerns about the length of the bed in the master suite. *It's only for a few months.* Lace curtains, rag rugs, wood floors shined to perfection, and unique, hand-made quilts added the flavor of the period the house was from. Griff thought of it as a giant dollhouse when he had to duck to get through the doorway of the maid's room in the back.

In the kitchen, Amy sliced off two thick pieces of warm bread. She pulled European butter from the fridge and spread it liberally before offering the plate to Griff. He accepted gladly. He closed his eyes as the first bite melted in his mouth. Amy tore hers in half and took a delicate nibble.

"This is amazing," he said.

"Thank you. What do you think of the house?"

"It's beautiful. You've got every little detail. I'll take it."

She clapped her hands once and grinned. "Great! You're our first renter. And no worries about you being able to afford the place."

Griff plucked his checkbook from his back pocket.

"One month's security and one month's rent, please."

He nodded and wrote the check.

"I hope you'll be very happy here."

"I'm sure I will."

Amy took the money and handed him the keys. "You can move in on Monday. Good luck, and I hope you keep winning."

"Thanks, Amy." Griff shook her hand. When he got back to the car, he turned and stared at the house. The beauty of and meticulous care given to the little Victorian impressed him. He was looking forward to living in this small, museum-type place so different from his own. Only for a second did he doubt the plans he'd agreed to for a modern renovation.

He shook his head slightly. *I'll be like Alice, after she took the growth pills, squeezing myself into this mini-house. Its charm will be gone by the time my place is done.* Still, he viewed it as an adventure and a detour from his usual style. *Kathy would approve.*

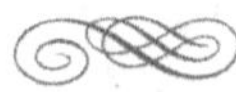

RHODE ISLAND

"I'm sorry, Annette, I don't know when I'm coming back. We're moving my dad to a nursing home. I can't do that overnight."

"The Carpenters need you to work with the architect this week. I don't know what you want me to do."

Lauren took her lower lip between her teeth. "Do what you gotta do."

"Della is available. I have to give it to her. I hope you understand."

Lauren sighed. "I do. I get it."

"I'm sorry. Hope everything goes well with your dad."

"Thanks." Lauren put her cell back in her purse. *So much for that commission.* She returned to the waiting room at the hospital.

Her big brother stood up and stretched. "How'd that go?"

"Not great."

Don tilted his head and raised his eyebrows.

"No, I don't want to talk about it." *Can my life get any worse? I hope Bob left me enough money to pay the mortgage for a couple of months.* Anxiety gnawed at her stomach, making her queasy.

"Let's get something to eat. I'm starved," Don said, moving toward the hallway.

"You go ahead. I'm not hungry."

He extended his arm, reaching for her hand. "Come on. You don't have to get anything, but I hate to eat alone. Besides, enough moping."

Lauren pasted a grin on her face for her brother's benefit. His warm, dry hand squeezed hers, sending comfort through her. Whenever they'd had to get shots when they were kids, Don would always hold her hand. He'd kid her that she couldn't make him say "ouch." She'd focus on squeezing him so hard he'd have to yelp. The shot was over before she could panic. Afterward, he'd feign pain, moaning and groaning, gripping his hand. His antics made her laugh.

Don had always been there for her.

But adult problems couldn't be handled so easily. Don was married with three sons and a daughter. He had his own stresses and strains. Besides, Lauren knew he couldn't fix her life, no matter how hard he tried. Still, she was grateful for the concern he showed and the time he carved out of his tight schedule to devote to her and their father.

They sat down to two burgers and Cokes in the hospital cafeteria and talked about the options for their dad, looking over the pamphlets and discussing the advice from the social worker. Next step was visiting the recommended places, picking one, and trying to get him accepted.

That burden would fall on Lauren's shoulders. Don had to get back to work. He sold cars and couldn't miss so many days. He had a family to feed. Lauren only had herself and her pug, Zander. Now that she was losing the fat commission on decorating the Carpenter's house, money would be tight.

She and Bob had been married such a short time that they had agreed to forego alimony. Lauren had gotten the house, Bob had gotten whatever furnishings he had wanted, and they had called it quits. Clean and easy, he had said at the time. She frowned, remembering that conversation. *Clean and easy for you, maybe.*

There'll be other commissions. Annette's place is well known. I'll survive, even if I have to sell the house. Dad needs me now, and I've got to do this right. After lunch, Lauren took her notes, hugged her brother, and met with the social worker one more time.

She spent the next several days listening to doctors, visiting the homes, and reminiscing with her dad. After one week, the hospital gave her the green light to move him. Lauren had filled out the paperwork and waited to hear if the place she liked most would take him.

While she relished the time she spent with her father, looking at him, so shrunken and weak, was upsetting. He had played professional baseball, used to be strong and handsome. Now, he was a shadow of the man she had known, and it made her sad.

She rose early on Wednesday, the day she was to move her dad into the Springfield Residence. She hated the idea. Facing a plate of bacon and eggs at the diner down the block from her motel, her appetite went south. A lump gathered in her throat, closing it to food.

Don breezed through the door, his brows furrowed, his face grim. He slipped into the booth across from her. "Today's the day." He motioned to the waitress. She brought a pot of coffee over and filled his mug.

"Yep." Lauren's eyes filled.

Don reached over and squeezed her hand before he lifted his cup. "I know, Ferret," he said, using his childhood nickname for her.

"Don't call me that."

He smiled. "Knew I could get a rise out of you. Finish and let's get this thing over with. Then, let's get blasted."

Lauren took a forkful of eggs, finished the bacon, and wiped her lips with the napkin. "Sounds like a plan."

Don grabbed the check. They piled into his car and drove to the hospital.

AFTER FOUR SAVAGE SUNRISES, Griff forgot where he was living and walked back to his old home, which was all sealed up. He turned around and headed to Mott Street, where the little Victorian rested. On the way, he passed a dark house and spied something moving by the back door.

A groundhog? A large rat? Curiosity coupled with alcohol emboldened him to move closer. The figure shifted, turning to face him. It uttered a low, threatening growl.

Griff stopped short. As his eyes adjusted to the darkness, he made out the form of a small dog. He took another step, and the pup started to bark. He peered into the shadows and made out the stubbed nose of a pug. By now, the canine was barking furiously. Griff backed up. As he continued on his way, the animal quieted and lay down, still watching him.

The next morning, he threw on his running gear and returned to the empty house to see if the pooch was still there. Curled up next to the back steps was the pug, which jumped up and began barking at Griff again. He looked in the windows and didn't see any signs of life. There was little furniture, and no car in the driveway.

He frowned. "Went off and left ya, did they?"

The racket continued then the little creature sat and panted.

"Bet you're thirsty." Griff ran back to his place for a bowl and a bottle of water. He approached carefully, stopping about halfway to set up the dish. The pug eyed him with suspicion. Griff filled the bowl and backed up. The dog sniffed and took a step toward the offering. The quarterback stood frozen, completely still, watching as the canine approached slowly and took a long drink.

"Probably hungry, too." He tossed a piece of bread at the bowl and laughed when it bounced away. *Not exactly a bullet pass.* The wary pooch took another drink then carted the bread in his mouth to a corner by the back steps. He scarfed it down, keeping his large, brown eyes trained on the footballer.

"Who leaves a dog outside to fend for himself?" Griff muttered under his breath. He shook his head and went back to his run.

Later that day, at the grocery store, Griff added dog food to his cart, determined to keep the feisty pug alive. He showed up at the house with more water and some food. This time, he didn't back away, but filled the bowl and crouched down. The starving dog approached cautiously, sniffing the air. When he got to the feast, he chowed down quickly.

Griff inched closer until he could reach out and touch the pooch. The animal lifted his gaze and growled. The football player put his hand out. The pug sniffed it then went back to eating. When he finished, he licked his chops and looked up at the quarterback, allowing the human to creep closer. Griff stretched out his hand and touched the furry head, then petted the dog. The creature sat up, allowing the man to continue.

After two meals, the dog, who Griff named "Spike," came right up when the man arrived with food. After a couple of days, since there was no owner in sight, Griff decided to take him. Spike allowed the man to put a harness and leash on him and trotted along behind the football player home.

After a bath and a good meal, man and dog settled down on the sofa to watch television. Spike rested his head on Griff's leg and closed his eyes. The quarterback smiled and petted his new friend. *This is what I need. A dog.* Although the animal couldn't replace a family, he saw Spike as a first step toward having the life he wanted.

When Griff told Buddy about the new companion, his friend raised his eyebrows in surprise. "A dog? Really? You got a dog?"

"A pug. Named him Spike. I rescued him. I can't believe he was abandoned."

"How the hell are you gonna take care of a dog when we're on the road?"

Griff put down the weight he was lifting and frowned. "Hadn't thought about that. Guess I'll have to board him."

"What a fuckin' pain in the ass. What were you thinking, man?"

"I couldn't leave him there to starve, could I?"

"Toss him some food and call the A.S.P.C.A."

"I didn't think of that. He's a good dog."

"He's still a pain," Buddy said, shaking his head. "What's happening to you? You're getting domestic on me."

Griff laughed. "Maybe you're right. Man whore no more?"

"Damn! Don't say that."

When Griff got home after his workout, he was greeted with ferocious barking. When Spike identified his new owner, he quieted down, licking Griff's hand and trotting behind him into the kitchen for dinner.

AFTER A TEARFUL FAREWELL with her father at the nursing home, Lauren slipped behind the wheel of her car and headed home. She tried to concentrate on the road, but sadness welled up inside her. *That may be the last time I see Dad.* The idea was too upsetting to think about. *I'll have to come up here more often.* She focused on the road, sweeping disturbing thoughts from her mind.

Lauren chewed her lip as she wondered what would be waiting at her office. *Is there any work for me?* Annette set up her company differently. Everyone brought in business and used her resources. She also parceled out accounts and paid her decorators as consultants instead of employees. This arrangement meant Lauren didn't receive a salary or health insurance.

When she had been married to Bob, it hadn't mattered. Now, the tenuous work situation preyed on her mind. She needed to get back and check her bank balance. Anxiety made her depress the gas pedal.

All at once, it hit her. *Why am I rushing? There's no one at home. No one will miss me or wonder if I'm dead if I'm an hour, or ten hours, late.*

Loneliness engulfed her. To get rid of the silence, she switched on the radio. Lauren loved quiet time to read, sketch, or think. Now, she dreaded filling the empty hours. *Thank God for the Girls' Night group, or I'd have nothing.* Her last conversation with Don came to mind.

"Are you dating anyone?"

"Dating? Really, Don. I'm divorced a couple of weeks."

"So? Never too early to get back on the horse."

"Wonderful analogy."

He grinned and shrugged.

"I'm not dating anyone, and just the idea makes me want to throw up."

"You're pretty, Laurie. Go for it. Get a real guy this time. Not some jerk."

"Nice to know you approve of my taste in men."

"Am I wrong?"

"Oh, shut up."

Don laughed at her remark and took her hand in both of his. Then, he changed the subject, leaving her relieved.

In the car, every song screeched about love—unrequited love, unspoken love, great love, sexy love, lost love—until she wanted to scream. *Doesn't anyone ever sing about anything else?* She turned off the radio. Love wouldn't be high on her list for some time. Maybe never. *Once a man finds out about me, he'll run for the hills.*

Lauren decided to channel her energy into her work. *Build up a clientele. Work my butt off. Then, maybe I can open my own company and not need Annette anymore.*

It was four o'clock when she rolled into her driveway. Feeling buoyed by her decision to become a workaholic, Lauren stopped on the threshold of the house. She put her suitcase down and took a deep breath. *It's empty. Bob said he'd leave the bed and the couch. Be prepared.*

Warm summer air caressed her face. *Why rush in? There's no one there, anyway.*

She sank down into a wicker chair and propped her feet up on the small table. Moving her dad had been exhausting, draining her emotional, as well as physically.

Picking up her cell, she dialed Canine Condo, where her Zander had been staying. *Thank God Bob agreed to let me keep him. Maybe it's not too late to get him tonight.*

"No, Lauren. Zander's not here."

"What? You sure? Bob was supposed to drop him off."

"Nope. We have room. Is he coming now?"

"No, thanks. I'm home." She closed the phone. Tears pricked at her eyes. *He lied. He took Zander. Why am I surprised?* She pulled out a tissue. *Don't be a wimp. Call him. Get your dog back!*

"What's up?" Bob sounded preoccupied.

"Why did you take Zander? Was telling me I could have him just another lie?"

"I don't know what you're talking about. I don't have the dog. You dropped him at Canine Condo."

"What? You were supposed to do that. It was on the list, remember?"

"What list?"

"The one I gave you. That you balled up and refused to read."

"Well, if you saw I didn't read it, why didn't you drop him there?"

"I couldn't do everything, Bob."

"He's your problem now." Her ex-husband hung up.

Her heart beat quickened. Adrenaline pumped through her veins. She opened the front door and called the dog's name. No answer. She ran outside and repeated the action. No answer. Panic rose in her chest, her pulse thumping in her ear. No whimpers or barking broke the quiet of the summer day. *He's gone.* A sob broke from her throat as tears cascaded down her cheeks. *Zander, where are you?*

Chapter Three

AFTER THREE DAYS OF leaving a crying dog at the door, Griff tucked Spike under his arm and strapped him in the backseat of his fancy car. Once he got to the gym, he wasn't sure what to do, so he fastened the leash to a machine by the door.

The pug curled up and was snoring, until three teammates walked in. Spike jumped, barking at the men, startling them. They laughed at the little dog, with the fur on the back of his neck standing up and his little legs stiff.

Griff put down the barbell and took hold of the lead. "Whoa, Spike. These are friends."

"You can't have a dog in here," Bullhorn Brodsky, offensive lineman, said.

"What's the matter? Don't you like dogs?" Griff asked.

"Hell, yeah, I like dogs. Not in the training room. What if he takes a shit in here? It'll stink up the whole place." Bullhorn wrinkled his nose in anticipation.

"He just did, Bull. Not likely he will again."

"You'd be surprised. My dog takes a dump three times a day."

"You've got a Rottweiler. Big dogs, big shit."

Devon Drake, the cornerback, crouched down and extended his hand to Spike. The dog sniffed it then gave him a lick. "He likes me. I say we keep him. He can be our mascot."

"Just so he doesn't shit in here, Montgomery," Bullhorn said.

"Speaking of shit, ever smell yourself after a game, Bull?" Griff made a face. "Makes Spike's smell good."

The men laughed as they chose their machines. Buddy joined Griff in the weight area.

"You're keeping this dog, eh?" Buddy asked, adjusting the weight on the apparatus.

"Yep. Gives me a reason to go home."

"How about a warm, naked, female body under the covers?"

"Got someone in mind?"

Buddy chuckled. "I wish. I guess a pooch is better than nothing."

After working out, Griff took Spike out to the field to run with him. The small dog sprinted for a bit then trotted over to the cool grass that had recently been watered and lay down, panting.

"Is that a dog or a rat? He's got no stamina," Brodsky said, as he started a lap.

"He's a little guy. Leave him alone, Bull."

"You're worried about me hurting his feelings? Bullshit! He's an animal, Griff."

"I know, I know." Griff couldn't account for the protective feelings he had for the pug. Maybe it was the fact the canine had been abandoned and starving that touched the quarterback's heart. Whatever it was, he had become insanely attached to the creature, quickly. Although he'd never admit it, he guessed that he and Spike had an understanding about loneliness, about being deserted, and had formed a silent pact to have each other's backs.

Spike needed Griff, and it felt good. Maybe only in a small way, but it was a beginning, a tiny step back to the life he had lived.

"He's full grown. Where did you get him?" Bull asked, approaching the snoozing pup.

"I found him, starving, hanging around an empty house."

"So, he's not yours?"

"He is now."

The footballer picked up the pug and headed for the showers. Spike slept on the floor of the locker room until his master was dressed. They

got in the car and drove to town to get some errands done. Griff intend-
ed to check out the local dog-boarding place. He needed to arrange for
doggie daycare when he went to training camp.

After spending more time than he cared to in the pharmacy and
the grocery store, Griff cursed out Kathy for leaving, for the umpteenth
time. *She used to do all this shit. Fuck. Why couldn't she find a guy who
lived here?*

The downtown section of Monroe was quaint. Some of the build-
ings had distinct New England flavor, with colorful shingles, white
trim, and black shutters. He made his way down the street with Spike
trotting alongside. They stopped at Canine Condo. A pretty redhead
sat at the front desk. She greeted Griff with a broad, warm smile. He
had to ask for information on their services twice, as her attention shifted to Spike.

She was crouched down, talking to and petting the dog, which
licked her face. When she stopped giggling, she turned her gaze on
Griff. While he considered flirting with her, he picked up on her lack
of interest quickly. He figured it out when he spied her wedding ring.
He pocketed the boarding information and guided the reluctant pooch
out to the sidewalk.

LAUREN WALKED DOWN Main Street in Monroe, past cute
shops. Barb's Boutique, Monroe Gift Shoppe, and the Love-to-Read
bookstore, sporting a poster announcing a signing for one of her favorite authors, but Lauren didn't see it.

She'd been in a daze since she had lost Zander, staring out at the
world with unseeing, green eyes. A week later, pain still flowed in her
veins. Her feet ached from trekking to every lamppost and telephone
pole in her neighborhood to tape up lost dog flyers. Exhaustion and de-
pression weighed her down. The unbearable quiet at home drove her to
take long walks. While out, she called Zander, but got no response.

On her way to Sandy's Salon to get a trim, a familiar bark drew her attention. Her head snapped up. There, coming down the sidewalk on the other side of the road, was a pug who looked an awful lot like Zander. He was on a leash held by a tall, good-looking man. Lauren's heart rate doubled. She whispered to herself, "Zander."

"Hey!" she called out, but the man didn't look her way. "Zander. Zander!" she hollered, her voice getting higher each time. The dog turned and barked. That was all Lauren needed.

She raced into the street. A car making its way to the south end of town screeched on its brakes. The man holding the dog dropped the lead and leapt in front of her. He snatched her arm and yanked her out of the way. She fell to her knees on the pavement, but didn't feel the pain because the pug was licking her face. She kept repeating his name as tears flowed.

"You okay, lady?" the man asked, grasping her elbow and easing her to her feet.

Lauren clutched his arm while her knees trembled. She narrowed her eyes. "You stole my dog," she said, before bending over to pet the pooch.

Lauren sensed his stare. She swung her head and caught him looking at her nicely rounded bottom. Their gazes met. She noticed the lusty light emanating from his chocolate brown eyes, and it made her shiver.

She stood up and turned to him, flipping her hair over her shoulder, pursing her lips. Flashing green eyes threw a cold look his way as her shoulders straightened, attempting to reduce the view of her cleavage. She rested her hands on her hips as he stared at her, frozen.

He snapped to attention. "What?"

"You heard me. You stole my dog. This is Zander. And he's mine." She reached for the pug's leash.

As he raised it above her head, his eyes narrowed. "So, you're the asshole who left this dog to starve and die? No way are you getting him back. I should call the cops."

"Who the hell are you, and what the hell are you talking about?"

"I'm Griffin Montgomery. I found this dog, starving, guarding an empty house. Your house? Did you conveniently forget you had him? And now, you want him back? Go to hell." He gritted his teeth. His eyes darkened, and his hands fisted at his side. He pulled Zander closer to him and moved his long legs forward.

She tugged on his arm. "I'm Lauren Farraday. That's my dog. Give him to me." Her jaw tightened, her lips compressed into a thin line, and her arm outstretched.

"On a cold day in Hell. If you were a man, I'd take you behind that store and beat the shit out of you, Miss Lauren Farra-I-don't-give-a-shit-what-your-name-is." He took a menacing step toward her.

Fear coursed through her, forcing her to retreat, as she closed her fingers around the lead and opened her mouth. "Help! Police!"

A policeman strolled over. Griff Montgomery made a face and shifted his weight. The officer tipped his cap at the quarterback and scowled at Lauren. "What seems to be the trouble here, Mr. Montgomery?"

"Him? You're asking him? I'm the one who screamed," Lauren said, puffing her chest out, until she saw Griff staring.

"Mr. Montgomery is the quarterback for The Connecticut Kings, miss."

"Oh? And that makes him God? He stole my dog!"

The officer laughed. "I seriously doubt that, miss."

"Lauren Farraday, officer."

"Miss Farraday. Griff, what is this about?"

Shit! He's on a first name basis with the police. I'm doomed.

Griff related his side of the story.

"Zander is micro-chipped, officer. Can you read those?"

"I'm afraid you'll both have to come down to the station, so we can investigate her claim. Sorry, Griff. We'll get this straightened out. I'm sure there's nothing to her story, and if she neglected this dog, we'll call Animal Care and Control. We'll look her up. See if there have been other complaints." The cop gave Lauren a stern look as he returned to his car. "Follow me," he instructed.

"We'll see, Mr. Football Player, just whose dog this is," she sniffed.

"Come along, come along. Leave Mr. Montgomery alone. He hasn't broken the law, lady, and maybe you have."

Lauren stuffed her outrage down and slipped behind the wheel of her car. When Griff loaded Zander into his vehicle, the pug barked. The sound tugged at her heart as she drove the short distance to police headquarters. *I have to get him back. He's my life now.*

WALKING FROM THE PARKING lot to the courthouse, Lauren looked up at the sky. *Do I still have an umbrella in the trunk?* She chewed her lip. *This silk suit will be ruined.*

She had come to fight for custody of Zander against Griff Montgomery. Griff claimed to have saved his life. Told the police she had neglected the dog. But that was all wrong.

Bob was to blame. In his rush to move to L.A., he had forgotten about Zander, an animal he had never liked anyway. Tears gathered in her eyes as she considered the possibility of losing the case. Zander and a half-empty house were all she had. She sighed, a deep shuddering breath, as she approached the building.

When she turned the corner, she almost ran into Griff Montgomery. The six foot, four inch, football player stood on the steps, looking devastatingly handsome in a perfectly tailored, navy blue suit and white shirt.

Cameras clicked and reporters swarmed around the charismatic quarterback. Her heart sank as she watched him smile with confidence.

Even his stance shouted, 'winner'. *He's famous. I'm nobody. I don't stand a chance.*

A loud boom interrupted her thoughts. The clouds moved in swift, angry bunches then the heavens opened up. She ran inside in time to avoid being drenched. Her shoulders drooped. She blinked rapidly as her gaze connected with Griff's. His eyes narrowed when she brushed away a runaway tear before she turned her back and escaped into the ladies' room. *I'll be damned if I'm gonna let him see me cry.*

She rinsed her face and cracked open the door. Griff was nowhere to be seen. She crept out and took a seat in the back of the courtroom. Griff was in the first row with Zander on his lap. Lauren ached to pet her pug, but sat quietly, her hands folded in her lap.

She looked around for another woman sitting alone. Don had hired a lawyer for Lauren, as she didn't have the funds. They had conferred on the phone, but had never met in person.

When Lauren's name was called, she stood up.

A woman sitting across the aisle from her also rose. She whispered in Lauren's ear, "I'm Marcy Chase. Nice to finally meet you."

Don, bless you.

Marcy squeezed Lauren's hand. "Don't worry. We'll win."

"But he's so popular," Lauren said, as Marcy opened the gate. She motioned her client to be quiet as they took their seats behind the table.

Lauren peeked over at Griff, sitting at the other one. He had a lawyer, too, who shot a nasty look her way. She swallowed, her mouth suddenly dry. She studied the quarterback. The planes of his face suggested high cheekbones and a chiseled jaw. His lips looked firm, but full enough to promise a sensuous kiss. His piercing brown eyes connected with hers. They were cold and confident. She shivered.

Marcy squeezed her hand again then motioned for her to stand as the bailiff announced the arrival of the judge.

After everyone sat, the official spoke. "I've read the papers from both sides. Why don't you each tell me your version of the story, in fifty words or less? Mr. Montgomery, would you like to go first?"

"Objection." Marcy rose to her feet. "Doesn't the plaintiff usually have the right to go first?"

"If you want to stand on ceremony. Go ahead, Ms. Farraday." The judge made a face as he waved his hand at her.

His reaction made Lauren more nervous. *No way am I winning.* She went up to the witness stand and was sworn in. As she told her part, she noticed Griff Montgomery's glare soften. He looked at her with curious eyes. His presence filled the room and made her stammer. "My instructions to Bob were clear. But he often didn't follow what I said. One reason why we're not together. But that's another story."

"So, you thought your dog was in daycare?"

"Yes. You can ask the people at Canine Condo. I called them as soon as I got home."

"And what did you do when you found out the animal wasn't there?"

"I cried."

"And then what?" the judge persisted.

"I put up signs all over the neighborhood." She opened her purse and pulled out a wrinkled piece of construction paper. *How feeble is this? I sound ridiculous.*

"I see. Thank you, Ms. Farraday. You may step down."

Lauren's legs wobbled. She grasped the railing around the box and took a deep breath. One peek at Griff's mocking expression made her mad. *He thinks I'm faking for the judge.* She marshaled her strength, straightened up, and marched to her seat with a confidence she didn't feel. He raised his eyebrows. *Dognapping bastard.*

"Now, Mr. Montgomery. If that's all right with you, counsel?" The judge shot a derisive look at Marcy, who nodded.

Griff strode to the witness stand. His confident swagger annoyed Lauren. *Thinks he's hot shit. So does the judge and every guy in this courtroom.* She frowned as she listened to his tale. It opened her mind to the truth.

As he went on, taking much more time than she had, she realized that the real villain was Bob, not Griff. Although she despised him for refusing to give up the pup, she was glad he had taken Zander in and fed him. The pug might have died if the footballer hadn't found him. She had to be grateful for that. If she had found a helpless dog with no food or water, she would have assumed the same thing about the owner that he had about her.

Shame filled her. His account of the facts would have put her in a terrible light, making her appear to be an animal abuser, if she had not already explained. She wondered if her version had been wiped out by the athlete's side. The judge frowned when he looked at her, and her hope to get Zander back grew dim.

The justice asked no questions and dismissed Griff when he'd finished his recounting. The magistrate shuffled through papers on his desk, stopping to read, and then turning to another. The courtroom was silent.

"Okay. Seems obvious to me. While the microchip and vet documents verify Ms. Farraday's claim to this dog, her actions cast doubt on her ability to provide for his welfare. On the other hand, Mr. Montgomery's papers and veterinarian documents substantiate his ability to keep the dog in good health."

"I object. The health of the dog was established by the care given by Ms. Farraday first. Mr. Montgomery only had the dog for two weeks. His overall health could not have deteriorated that fast."

"Overruled."

Marcy sat down, and Lauren's confidence sank.

"As I was saying...this is an easy case. I'm putting the dog in joint custody for six months. At that time, Mr. Montgomery will report back to the court, with vet testimony, as to the care of this animal. If the dog receives quality care from Ms. Farraday during her time with him, then the court will return Zander to her. If he does not, then Mr. Montgomery will retain sole custody. At that time, I would entertain the possibility of visitation for Ms. Farraday."

"I object!" Both lawyers jumped to their feet at the same time.

"What? Why?" As they started to squabble, the judge banged his gavel. "I've given my ruling. Objections are overruled. You two work out the schedule. Share the dog. Court is adjourned."

Lauren let out the breath she was holding. *At least I didn't lose him. But share him with that...monster?*

Griff's face was stormy. He strode over to her with Zander under his arm. "I'm keeping him."

Lauren pushed to her feet and steeled herself. "You heard the judge. He's mine. You can share him for six months then find yourself a new pet."

"That's what you think."

"What's the matter? Did you expect to win? Did you think that because you're some hot shit athlete, the judge would just give you Zander and ignore the fact that he belongs to me? Well, you were wrong."

"I thought the judge would give him to someone who cared for him. Not an animal abuser."

"Weren't you listening? Bob is the one at fault here. Not me."

"You married that asshole. So, it's your fault."

"Really?" She cocked an eyebrow at him. "That's faulty logic. All brawn and no brains. You're an idiot."

Griff stepped toward her, his fist raised, until his attorney pulled him away.

"Come on. Let's go outside and discuss the schedule."

"I'LL TAKE HIM DURING the week. You can have him on weekends," Griff said.

"Wait a minute. That's not fair."

"Fair enough for someone as irresponsible as you."

"The judge said joint custody. I get equal time."

Griff's lawyer shot him a warning look.

"What's your idea?" Griff shifted his weight. *She's gonna be a pain in the ass.*

"Every other week."

"Nope. Not gonna work for me."

"Why not?" She looked up, her mouth pouty, distracting him.

"Saturday nights are my late nights. Sometimes, I don't get home until two or three...or not at all." He sensed heat rising in his face as Lauren stood quietly, blushing. "Of course, if that's your late night, too..."

"It isn't, no. I'm home. Every Saturday night," she blurted out.

"No social life? Hmm. I can see why."

"What does that mean?" She fisted her hands and planted them on her hips.

"Nothing."

"Nothing? Try again."

"All right, every other week, but we make the exchange on the weekend."

"Don't want you to miss your night out whoring," she sneered.

"If you were a man..." Griff clenched his fingers at his sides, his temper barely controlled.

"If I were a man, what? You'd punch me?"

"Damn right."

"Bully."

Griff laughed. His gaze swept over Lauren's curvy body. "I take it back. It's a shame you're home on Saturday night. Could be making some man happy."

"Oh?" Her tone was warmer.

"Some man who's a glutton for punishment and likes to screw bitches."

Her hand came up and slapped him so fast even Griff couldn't react quickly enough.

"Holy shit. Did you just assault him in the courthouse?" his lawyer asked.

Lauren's attorney gasped, grabbed her by the wrist, and escorted her out and down the front steps. "What are you doing?"

"He...he...he called me a bitch."

"You can't hit people."

"I didn't hurt him. He's twice my size."

Griff rubbed his cheek, glaring at her, as he descended the stairs.

"Look, if you two can't agree to a schedule, we will," his lawyer said, looking at Marcy.

"Okay. I drop him off with you on Sunday afternoon. You give him back to me on Saturday morning," Lauren said. "I'm sorry I hit you."

"Fine," Griff agreed, through gritted teeth.

"Can I say goodbye to Zander?"

He lowered the dog to the sidewalk. Lauren knelt down. When he wagged his tail and licked her, she buried her face in his fur. Griff saw her shoulders move. *Oh, no. Shit. Don't. Don't cry. Please don't cry. I can't take it.* Within seconds, Lauren was clutching the pug to her chest, sobbing. People leaving the courthouse stopped to stare. One or two came over to Griff for his autograph.

He scribbled something quickly then took her firmly by the arms and raised her to her feet. "Don't cry. Okay? I can't stand it." Griff's heart melted as he watched her cling to the canine. Memories of comforting his niece and nephew during their bouts of tears after a bad day tore at his guts. Tempted to let her have the dog, he remembered the lonely nights made better by Spike's presence.

She fished a tissue out of her purse and dabbed her eyes and nose. "I don't care."

"Come on, lady. Please."

"My name is Lauren."

"Okay, Lauren. No tears. All right?"

She sniffled twice, blew her nose, and then nodded. "I'm okay. He's been mine for three years."

"He's a great little guy."

"Warm on a cold night. Cuddles with me when I watch television. Always by my side."

"Me, too."

She looked up at him with full eyes. "You love him, too, don't you?"

"I wouldn't say love...maybe 'like a lot.' I'm used to him. That's all."

"You wouldn't fight so hard to keep him if you didn't love him."

Though she spoke softly, out of earshot of the crowd forming, her words stripped him bare. She saw through his façade, saw how much the little pooch meant to him. He looked at the ground and shuffled his feet.

Two more people approached for autographs, and he was relieved to have the distraction.

"Drop him at my house," she said, scribbling on a piece of paper. "On Saturday morning."

He took the address and picked up the dog. "Deal."

Lauren gave the animal one last pet and hurried to the parking lot, her cheeks wet. Griff watched until her car pulled out.

"Hey, Griff, what was that about?" a spectator asked.

"Just a misunderstanding," he said, shrugging his shoulders. He shook hands with both attorneys and headed for his car. After fastening the pug in, Griff rested his forehead on the wheel. He took a deep shuddering breath and blinked rapidly. *I'm gonna lose him, too. He belongs to her.*

The idea of another loss squeezed his heart. He'd grown attached to Spike and didn't know how he'd be able to let him go, even six months from now. He sat back, turned the key in the ignition, and put the vehicle in gear. *Gonna have to ramp up my search for a wife and a new life. I've got six months to find her. I can't let him go until she's in my life.*

The tightness in his chest loosened a little. A woof from the backseat made him smile as he rounded the corner and pulled into the driveway of the little Victorian.

When Griff opened the door, Spike ran into the house, right to his water bowl. The quarterback followed his dog into the kitchen and filled his dish with food. He straddled a chair to watch the pug wolf down his meal. *At least he needs me.* The thought eased the pain in his heart a little.

Chapter Four

WITH SPIKE TUCKED SECURELY under his arm, Griff pushed open the door to the workout room at the stadium.

"No dogs allowed, Montgomery. And that includes your girl-friend," snickered Aloysius "Trunk" Mahoney, defensive linebacker.

"Very funny. I'm gonna die laughing."

"What if he shits in here?" Mahoney cocked an eyebrow at Griff.

"He already took a dump in your helmet, asshole."

The half dozen players working out stopped. They laughed as Trunk's face got red, and the pug barked. The linebacker mumbled something under his breath as he made his way to the treadmill.

Griff parked Spike on the floor by the door and plopped a weight down on the leash. The dog curled up and closed his eyes halfway. The quarterback warmed up on the treadmill.

His pal, Buddy, doing biceps curls, moved closer. "Still got that mangy mutt?"

"He's not mangy. Yeah. He's still with me. Sort of."

Buddy raised his eyebrows, and Griff explained the court's decision to his teammate.

"You've got to share him with some bitch? Why don't you just give him up?" Buddy asked.

"I like having him around." Griff increased his pace to a fast walk.

Trunk snickered. "In bed with a dog? You're slipping."

"He's better looking than anything you've slept with."

"Are you referring to my wife?" Trunk's tone turned belligerent.

"Oh, you're married? Gee, I didn't think so when we were in Miami, San Francisco, and Dallas last year," Griff shot back.

"Fuck you, Montgomery," Trunk muttered under his breath.

Griff upped his speed to a run. After a few minutes, he turned off the machine, downed a bottle of water, and approached the weight benches. The door opened and an attractive blonde entered. She waved to the men before she posted a sheet on the wall.

"New roster," Trunk said, eyeing the list.

The men gathered around. It included last year's team members plus the February draft picks. Griff spotted a rookie quarterback. *Tony Hastings. From Kensington State.* Griff ground his teeth. Kensington State University was a major rival of his alma mater, Wellington College. *Are they planning to replace me? Who is this guy? Is he backup?*

The blonde turned to Griff. "Coach Bass would like to see you for a minute, Griff," she said.

He grabbed Spike, nodded, and followed her up to the administrative offices.

"Come in," Pete said.

Griff sat down, placing the pug on the floor.

"Whatcha got there?"

"New member of the Montgomery family. This is Spike."

The dog perked up, giving a short bark at the mention of his name.

The coach grinned. "Kinda cute in an ugly sort of way."

"What's up, Coach?"

"I wanted to explain about Hastings."

"I saw his name on the roster."

"We got lucky he wasn't picked before we got our turn. He's good, but he's green. I want you to take him under your wing. Teach him."

"Train my replacement?" Anger bubbled up inside Griff.

"He's not your replacement. Unless you retire or get injured."

"You're not putting me out to pasture?"

"You're only thirty-three, Griff. Not exactly over-the-hill."

The quarterback let out a breath. "No, I'm not."

"We haven't found anyone in the last few years we thought would be a good back-up. Until Tony. Talk to him. Make friends. You're his idol, you know."

"Idol? I'm too young to be anyone's idol."

"Well, you're his. So, be nice to him. And don't worry. I hope you'll be leading us to a couple more Super Bowls."

"Thanks." Griff pushed to his feet.

"By the way. Leave the dog out of the training rooms, okay? Don't want him to get hurt."

"Really?"

"Yeah."

"Anyone complain?"

"A couple of guys. Department of Health. Codes and all that shit." Coach glanced down at some papers on his desk.

"I get it. Fine."

"Sorry. But you can bring him to the games. Have him sit with your girlfriend."

"Would do, except I don't have one."

Coach looked up. "No girl?"

"Not yet."

"Good luck."

Griff smiled, shook the Coach's hand, and left. Opening his cell, he dialed Lauren. She agreed to pick up Spike.

"Griff's new girl is outside," Buddy said, his face plastered to the locker room window.

"She's only picking up Spike," Griff countered, tucking the canine under his arm.

"Woo hoo! She's hot. Let's go meet her." Buddy hustled to the door.

The other men yanked on pants and followed. Lauren stood in the sun, shading her eyes and blinking. Griff put the dog down, and Spike ran to his owner. Lauren crouched down to greet the wiggly pug, who licked her face.

"Aren't you going to introduce us?" Buddy asked, all innocence.

"Are you kidding?"

"If you're not interested, hell, I sure am."

"That's the point," Griff said. He headed for Lauren, who picked up the pooch's leash then faced the quarterback.

"Quite a welcoming committee. Aren't you going to introduce me?"

"To these animals? Never. Come on." He took her arm, turning her toward the parking lot and escorting her to her car.

"Some of them are kinda cute. 'Specially the one with the blond hair," she said, fishing around in her purse.

"Buddy? He's the biggest man-whore of them all."

She chuckled as she pulled out her car keys. "Bigger than you?"

"He leaves me in the dust."

Lauren stopped, her eyes wide. "Wow."

"Hey, you don't know anything about me. Why are you making these judgments?"

"Reputation. I thought all male athletes were after only one thing—a bed partner for the night."

"Not all. Maybe some. Maybe some of the time. Not all the time. Crap. I'm getting all tangled up here."

"Yeah. Forget it. Doesn't matter what I think of you, anyway." She opened the back door and bent over to fasten Spike's leash into the seatbelt.

"Oh? Why?"

She squared her shoulders, put her hands on her hips, and faced him. "Let's get this straight. We hate each other..."

"Hate is a strong word."

"Dislike, then?"

"Well, yeah, maybe."

"We're in the middle of a custody battle. Don't be a jerk. I know what you think of me."

"Do you?"

"You telling me we're best friends?"

"No, but we don't have to be mortal enemies, either. We both like Spike. Can we be civil?"

"Civil? To a man who's trying to take my dog away? He's my life. And you want me to be happy about it?"

"Your life? That's too bad." He looked her over, his gaze taking in all her luscious curves. "A woman who looks like you should have more going for her than that."

"I should slap your face."

"For giving you a compliment?"

"That's not a compliment. It's...it's...it's a...never mind!" Her green eyes blazed at him.

"There are plenty of women who'd love to hear that from me."

"Yeah? Well, tell it to them. You can't sweet-talk me. I'm not giving up Zander."

"I never said you should."

"Oh? That's not what you testified to in court."

"That's before I knew the whole story. Your ex is an asshole."

"That's the first thing you've said that I agree with." She slid behind the wheel and turned on the ignition.

"I get him back Sunday morning?"

"That's the schedule. Don't get any STD's this weekend."

"Thanks a lot."

"You're welcome." He could have cooled three drinks with the amount of ice in her voice.

She hit the gas pedal and zoomed out of the parking lot. He got the message. She didn't want to have anything to do with him, and that was a first. He was intrigued. He'd never met a woman who wasn't falling all over him, especially since he'd started playing football in high school. He had to admire her independence, even if she was a bitch.

He laughed to himself. *Never been attracted to a bitch before. Guess there's a first time for everything.*

When he returned to the locker room to grab his gear, he was pelted with questions.

"What's her name?" Buddy asked.

"She dumb enough to go out with you?" Trunk Mahoney piped up.

"We're just sharing the damn dog. So, shut the hell up, okay?" Aggravated by Lauren, Griff needed to clear his head. He did what he always did when he needed to think—he went for a run. *I've got to have the best year ever. Show that asshole Hastings I'm not ready for a nursing home.* Anger fueled his body as he pushed himself to run farther and faster.

For the next two weeks, he extended his workouts at the gym to stay in shape. On Griff's time, Spike was left home alone for hours. On Friday, he returned at three. Spying another car in the driveway, he entered the house cautiously. When he opened the door, the smell of something wonderful baking greeted him. *Amy.* He smiled, and his stomach rumbled at the thought of her warm bread with melting butter.

She stood in the living room, hands fisted on her hips, a scowl on her face.

"What?" he asked.

"Dog. He peed on my heirloom rug and chewed on the leg of my sofa. He's got to go, or you do," she answered.

"Damn! Spike. How could you, buddy?"

"This is gonna cost a fortune to have fixed."

"Send me the bill."

"I will. You're a great guy, Griff, but you didn't have a dog when I rented to you."

"I know, I know. It's my fault."

"I'll be back tomorrow, and either it's no dog or no Griff. Okay?" He nodded.

"I left you a loaf," she said, as she closed the door behind her.

Shit! My house isn't ready. But I can't give up Spike. Saturday morning, he was due to deliver the pug. Griff hatched a plan and packed his bags. By nine, he and the pooch were on their way to Lauren's. He admired her lovely Victorian, painted yellow with white trim, as he climbed the steps.

She was waiting and flung open the door as soon as they hit the top step. She embraced the dog and kissed him. He licked her face. "Thanks for bringing him." She moved to go back into the house when Griff took her arm.

"Wait. A new wrinkle."

"What?" Her brows knitted.

"Nothing bad. It's just that I've been kicked out of the house I'm renting. Spike's fault. And mine is being renovated. Spike and I have nowhere to live."

"Get a motel." She turned her back to him.

"You live alone in this big place, right?"

"So?"

"How about renting me a room?"

"Are you crazy?"

"That way you can be with Spike all the time," he said.

She stopped for a moment, a small smile playing at her lips. "How much would you pay?"

"Name your price."

"Three thousand a month."

"Including two meals a day?" he asked.

She looked him up and down. "Bet you eat like a horse. Add five hundred."

"Deal." *She's not Kathy, but a hot meal and a room is better than nothing.*

WHAT THE HELL HAVE I done? She chewed her lip as Griff returned to the car for his luggage. *I don't want that monster living in my house.* But Bob had only left three thousand dollars in their checking account. Lauren knew that wouldn't go far, with the mortgage, taxes, water, electric, vet bills, and food. She'd been avoiding the truth. She needed funds. *Maybe by the time that money is gone, I'll have another customer from Annette.*

She guided the pug into the living room as Griff climbed the front steps.

"Where do you want this?"

"This way." She unsnapped the dog's leash and headed toward the back of the house. At the end of the hall was a magnificent room. Painted a light, grayish blue with white molding, it had two floor-to-ceiling windows facing the backyard. Gauzy, white curtains swayed slightly in a gentle breeze. A smaller window faced the side of the property. A vintage quilt in a blue, green, and white print covered the queen-size bed. A white dust ruffle bordered the bottom.

An antique roll top desk took up one corner of the room and a comfortable, wing chair and dresser the other two. The room was light, airy, and totally charming. She noticed him smile. "This is the guest room."

"Bed's a little small," he said.

She shot him a sharp look.

"What do you want? I'm a big guy. It's okay. Nice room." He moved to the windows. His large frame dwarfed the spacious chamber. Lauren put her hand over her chest to cover the spreading blush of embarrassment. She'd moved in here, giving Bob the master bedroom, after they had agreed to a divorce. Standing in what had been her private place, with the sexy quarterback, sent a shiver down her spine.

"The kitchen," she said, turning on her heel. Griff followed her into the well-equipped space with fine, wood cabinets, black granite countertops, and an old, oak table and chairs.

"Nice," he repeated, looking around.

"You're welcome to use everything."

"I don't cook."

She cocked an eyebrow at him. "Really? How do you eat?"

"Take out. I used to live with my sister and her family. Kathy was an excellent cook."

"Spoiled rotten," she mumbled under her breath. "I can cook, but I'm no Iron Chef."

"I'm sure it'll be fine."

She took him on a tour of the rest of the house—living room, den, three bedrooms upstairs, and even the attic. The master bedroom had a brick fireplace, white marble mantle, and plank floors.

"Ever use the fireplace?" he asked.

"Nope."

"Guess your ex wasn't a romantic."

"Nope." *Too much work to haul wood up here,* he'd complained when she'd asked. But she wasn't about to admit that to Griff. She'd take a small log up to bed with her from time to time. Though she now had a nice stash, the idea of enjoying a fire by herself only depressed her.

The queen-sized bed had a carved oak headboard, ruffled duster, and a pink, quilted bedspread. There was a dressing table, chaise longue, and antique, oak dresser. After Bob had moved out, she'd spent a weekend furiously redecorating, painting the walls herself. The pink, mauve, and white color scheme was decidedly feminine, which pleased her. The footballer made her uncomfortable, looking ultra-masculine standing in her boudoir.

"This is a very girly room."

"Of course. It's my room."

"Figures," he said, moving toward the staircase.

The pug was curled up on a small bed in the living room, snoring.

"Zander, treat!" Lauren called. The dog cracked an eye, stretched, and then trotted into the kitchen.

"We've got to iron out this name thing, or the dog's gonna get confused."

"His name's Zander. I don't see the problem."

"What kind of pussy name is that?"

"What?" Her eyes widened, and her mouth fell open.

"Sorry, sorry. I mean, that's a sissy name. Spike is a man's name."

"A man? A serial killer. A bully, maybe. Not a sweet pug."

"I can't take him into the locker room with a dumb name like Zander. Where did you come up with that? It stinks."

"So, don't go in the locker room with him. Leave him with me."

Griff smiled. "Good try. He's half mine for the next six months."

"So?"

"So, I'm not calling him Zander. Spike, it is."

Lauren let out a breath. "Fine! Spike, then."

His face lit up, and he grinned. "Knew you'd see it my way."

"It's Saturday. My time. He sleeps with me tonight."

"Too bad Spike's all the company you've got upstairs."

She raised her hand to slap him, but he was quicker this time and caught her wrist. He squeezed. "Ow. Ow. Let go."

"No hitting. Promise?" He squeezed again, more gently.

"Okay, okay. I promise. Let go. You're killing me."

"Now, if I really wanted to hurt you..."

She rubbed her wrist. "You did. You did."

"That was nothing."

"Don't do it again."

"Don't slap me."

"I won't. Watch what you say to me. I'm not a whore, like you are."

"I'm not a whore. Just popular."

She snorted a laugh at him. "That's one way to put it."

His gaze traveled her length, stopping at each curve, its heat piercing her clothing. She shifted her weight under his appraising stare. His sexy grin gave her the chills.

"You're not bad looking. I'm surprised you're up there all alone."

"I'm not alone. I have Spike."

"Same difference," he muttered.

But she heard him. "Some people sleep alone by choice," she sniffed.

He snorted. "Who would choose that?"

"Me." She turned her back to him, fastened the harness and leash on the dog, and headed for the door. "Time for our walk, Zan...er...Spike."

The pug's tongue lolled. He appeared to be grinning at her.

WHEN THE DOOR LATCH clicked closed, Griff returned to his new digs. He unpacked his clothes then took his shaving kit into the adjoining bathroom. He opened the door to a large room. *Formerly two closets?* A purple, green, and white iris print wallpaper graced the top section of the wall that wasn't tiled. Pretty flowered tiles appeared scattered among the solid white. The room had a window right above a small vanity.

Griff hesitated to sit on the flimsy dressing table chair for fear his weight would break it. He eased down slowly, until he knew it could take him. Delicate, feminine colored glass bottles piqued his curiosity. He uncorked one and held it to his nose. A fresh, sweet fragrance greeted him. Each bottle had a different subtle, floral scent.

He opened one drawer after another and discovered new female treasures. He rubbed a bit of peachy powder between his rough fingers, enjoying the silk-like softness of it against his skin. *Kathy never had stuff like this.* He explored every inch of the room, smiling at each lotion and oil he discovered. *Must have been her bathroom. Maybe she stayed in this room when they broke up.* He lifted each bottle of nail polish and studied the colors. *Brazen Red. Lady's Pink. Crazy Coral.*

He imagined each on Lauren's fingernails before deciding he'd like "Crazy Coral" best. *This lady takes care of herself.* He pictured her rubbing oil and lotion into her skin after a bath. He tried to imagine her naked, but didn't have enough details. *What are you doing? This is bitch-on-wheels. Dog neglector. Stop thinking about her body.*

But he couldn't. Her clear eyes were a beautiful shade of green, even if they were flashing in anger at him. Her long, dark hair called to him. Her curvy figure made his fingertips tingle as he thought about touching her. *Forget it. This is just somewhere to stay until my place is finished. Besides, she hates me. But what if she comes in to get this stuff, and I'm in the shower?* He swallowed, ignoring the twitch between his thighs at the sexy idea.

He put his things on the counter in the bathroom and returned to the bedroom to hang up his suits and shirts. When he heard her voice, he jumped.

"Let me show you where the dog stuff is." She headed for the kitchen.

Seeing all her emollients and scents had been like seeing her undressed, like peeping at her. Private knowledge of what she rubbed on her body turned him on. Searching for control, he pushed the lusty feelings from his brain and joined her. Lauren was bent over, giving Spike a treat. Griff's gaze zeroed in on her enticing rear end.

She stood up. "He gets a treat after every walk."

He crouched down to rub the pooch behind the ears. "Yeah?" Temporarily controlled by his groin, he was incapable of stringing together words to form a decent sentence.

"That's what I've been doing," she said.

"Okay. Was that your room?" he asked, easing his butt onto a stool at the counter.

She blushed.

"I don't mean to pry. You don't have to answer. I'm just a boarder here. You don't owe me anything."

"I moved there when Bob and I decided to separate."

"Thought so." He nodded.

"And you do mean to pry. You're in every aspect of my life, threatening me, taking something that's mine. Now, you're in my house. I feel...I feel...I feel invaded." He saw her flush of embarrassment turn to one of anger.

He raised his palms. "Whoa. I don't mean to. I'm just sharing the dog. Your life is your life. I'm sure it works for you, and it's none of my business if it does or doesn't."

"That's right. It isn't." She huffed out of the room with the harness in her hand.

Griff followed her, concerned. Her eyes filled and a few tears ran down her cheek. She swiped with her hand across her face as she hung Spike's leash on a peg by the front door. He shoved a handkerchief between her fingers "You know what tears do to me. Please...," he explained, when she glanced at him.

She laughed. "Now, I know how to get back at you."

"Waterworks do it every time." He grinned. "How about I take you out for dinner?"

"I have some stew I made yesterday. I like to give it an extra day. It tastes better that way."

"Lamb stew?"

She nodded.

"My favorite. A rain check, then. Tomorrow night?"

"What about your hot date?" She looked up at him.

"Later. Lamb stew comes first." He licked his lips.

"Tomorrow it is."

"Got any booze?" he asked.

She led him into the living room and opened a cabinet door. A fully stocked bar faced him. "Beer in the fridge, if you prefer."

"What do you drink?"

"Vodka and tonic."

"Coming right up." He pulled out a bottle.

"I'll put the stew on to heat."

She had a couple of his favorite brands of liquor, along with whipped cream vodka. Memories of a steamy night with Carla and a bottle of the sexy stuff made him grin. Griff mixed two drinks, leaving room for ice. His worries about moving were melting away. His stomach rumbled, and his mouth watered at the promise of a home-cooked meal.

The aroma of the stew permeated the kitchen. Griff opened the freezer and added ice cubes to the glasses. Lauren pulled placemats from a drawer and plates from a cabinet.

"You can set the table," she said.

Griff handed her a drink before he set about the task. "Forks and stuff?"

Lauren pointed to another drawer as she stirred the pot. She took a piece of meat and tasted it then put the spoon back. "Oops. Sorry about that. I'm used to cooking for Bob and me. He never minded when I did that."

"Neither do I. It's fine."

She ladled out two steaming bowls and placed them on the plates. She plucked a couple of hot rolls from the toaster oven before retrieving the butter from the fridge+

He raised his drink before speaking. "To Spike."

"To Spike," she repeated.

He took a healthy gulp before tucking into the meal.

"Best stew I've ever eaten," he said, between mouthfuls.

"Thanks." She continued eating, but a spot of color in each cheek revealed her pleasure at his remark.

They ate in silence. The taste of homemade food brought memories of Kathy and her children. Emotion tightened his chest. He missed the loud dinners with great food, differing opinions, arguing, and laughter. Being the big cheese to the kids had made him eager to return home. Their greetings after a game, especially a loss, had buoyed his spirits, turning his attention away from his shortcomings and onto what was most important in his life—his family.

"This was a fantastic meal. Thank you," Griff said, when they had finished.

He rose from the table and headed for the sink. "If you cook, you don't clean up." He picked up the sponge and turned on the water.

Lauren smiled and threw her hands up. "If you insist."

When he was done, he went to his room. After a short shower and a quick shave to reduce his scruff to where he wanted it, he applied aftershave and dressed. He passed Lauren and Spike curled up together on the sofa as he headed out. She was reading a book and petting the dog. At the front door, he turned to wave at her.

"Have a great night," he said.

"You, too."

The crowd at The Savage Beast had already thickened. He could barely reach the bar. Carla shot him a lusty grin as she prepared a Savage Sunrise for him. People recognized him and scooted over to make room. Griff rested his elbows on the counter. He grinned at her.

"Your lucky night."

"Yeah?" He raised his eyebrows. The low cut of her top, revealing plenty of cleavage, called to him. He stared, thinking her breasts looked a little too large then shook his head. *They're never too large.*

"No date tonight?" She shot him a saucy smile.

He reached for her hand and kissed it. "Yeah, my lucky night." His groin twitched, as desire flowed through his veins. He had four more drinks before the crowd left. Carla took him by the hand and led him upstairs. They undressed without ceremony. She pulled the covers down on the bed, slid in, and beckoned him.

He followed, taking her into his embrace. It wasn't long before they were making love. Griff's climax quickly followed hers. But shame filled him. He lowered his sweaty forehead to hers to whisper, "I'm sorry."

She pushed on his chest, and he rolled off so she could light up a cigarette. After blowing out smoke, she folded her arms across her breasts and turned her head. With an angry glance at him, she spoke.

"Who's Lauren?"

Chapter Five

RESTLESS, LAUREN PACED the living room. After a few minutes, she leashed Spike and took him for a walk. The exercise energized her. *I could do five miles easy.* But the pug pulled her back toward the house. She gave him a treat then sank down on the couch. Channel surfing didn't turn up any programs she wanted to watch, so she opened a book.

Spike curled up next to her. She shifted position several times, unable to get comfortable. The pug shot her a sleepy, dirty look then jumped down and circled in his bed before plopping down. He was asleep quickly.

Although she had been engrossed in her reading before dinner, now she couldn't concentrate. The story appeared slow, not capturing her mind, which was centered on one person—Griff Montgomery. Try as she might, she couldn't get him out of her head. She pushed to her feet, pacing to the window to peek out, and then back to the sofa.

"He's not so bad. Was actually nice," she said to Spike. The dog cracked one eye open and snorted at her. "I know. I didn't expect it, either."

She chewed on her thumbnail before going to the kitchen. In the freezer, she found a container of mint chip ice cream. It had barely been touched. She scooped out a generous portion and returned to the couch. Spike sniffed the air, his little nostrils moving in and out. He opened his eyes then closed them again when he realized the food wasn't for him.

"He liked my stew. Ate it all. No leftovers. I'm gonna have to buy a lot more food."

Spike ignored her. She stared fondly at him.

Curiosity poked at her. She washed her dish then tiptoed down the hall to Griff's room. *What if he comes home while I'm snooping? Nah. He's not coming back tonight.*

She pushed the door open slowly then laughed at herself. *No one here but me.* She turned on the light and looked around. The first thing that drew her was a picture on his dresser. She took a closer look. It showed a smiling woman and two adorable children. The resemblance between the woman and Griff was striking. *They look alike. Is she his sister? Are those his kids? None of my business, right?*

She opened the closet and saw a neat row of sweatshirts and work-out pants followed by six suits and a dozen dress shirts. A tie rack was the dividing line between his casual and dress clothes. A nice scent wafted to her nose. *Is that him or his aftershave?*

She closed the door again and headed for the bathroom. He had a hot lather machine on the counter. His razor was laid out next to an electric. *Two razors?* A bottle of expensive aftershave, La Nuit, stood next to them. She sniffed. *It's him.* She gulped air as his scent turned her on. Lauren touched the damp towel that had dried his skin earlier. Her breath hitched as she wondered what he looked like naked.

The slamming of a car door brought her back to life. *Griff! Shit!* A glance at her watch told her it was midnight. *What the hell am I doing up so late? Waiting for him? I thought he'd be out all night. Damn.*

She switched off the light and scurried out of the room like a mouse being chased by a cat. When his key turned the lock, she was in the kitchen, trying to catch her breath and putting away the dishes from the dishwasher.

"You still up?" Griff tossed his keys on the kitchen table.

"Midnight isn't late. It's Saturday night," she lied. "You're home early."

He cocked an eyebrow. "Were you waiting up for me?"

"Of course not. How could you think...? No. No way." She tried to control the tremor in her voice, but wasn't successful. A deep breath calmed her nerves.

"I know how to lock a door. You don't have to wait up."

"I know that." She cast her gaze to her hands.

They stood in awkward silence for a moment. The dog stretched, yawned, and padded into the room.

"Hey, Spike. Oh, wait. I can't pet him, can I? It's your time." He chuckled.

"Don't be silly. Of course, you can."

Griff crouched down to scratch the dog behind the ears then straightened. "Time for bed."

"I thought you already did that?" The unfiltered words flew out of her before she could stop them. Lauren clamped her hand over her mouth, but it was too late.

He threw a stern look her way.

"I'm sorry. I don't mean to pry. It's none of my business," she prattled on.

"Damn right, it's none of your business."

"I'm sorry. Really. It's just that you said...indicated...implied you wouldn't be home 'til morning and I...well, I mean, here you are. And I wondered...okay. I'm shutting up now."

"Good night." He turned his back to her and headed toward his room, stopping in the doorway. "And 'no,' I'm not going to tell you about my date."

Embarrassment choked her. She scrambled up the stairs, wishing she could disappear.

SUNDAY MORNING, THE ringing of the doorbell woke Griff. He rolled over, cracked open an eye, and spied the clock. *Ten o'clock. What*

the hell? It's Sunday. No practice. Who's at the door? He crawled out of bed, slightly hung over, and pulled on a pair of boxers. He scratched his face, his chest, and then his crotch and yawned as he made his way to the front door.

When he entered the entry hall, a loud gasp jerked him awake. Facing him was a group of ten women, different sizes, shapes, and ages, but all fully dressed. As they stared at him, smiles slowly spread across their faces. Griff felt naked. Sputtering, he backed into his room and slammed the door. The buzzing of female voices carried to him. Griff washed his face, combed his hair, and threw on pants and a T-shirt before rejoining them.

When he inched the door open, they were not visible, but he heard voices drifting from the living room. He tiptoed to the kitchen, poured himself a mug of coffee from the full pot on the counter, and peeked around the corner.

"There he is," said one blonde, pointing at Griff.

He wanted to run.

"It's Griff Montgomery. From the Kings," observed another.

"Lauren, you didn't tell us you were living with Griff Montgomery."

"I'm not. I'm not."

Watching Lauren turn bright red, Griff chuckled. *Serves her right for being so nosy last night.*

"He's renting a room here. We're sharing the dog. I told you about the court thing last time."

"Yeah, but you didn't tell us it was Griff Montgomery."

"Come on in, Mr. Montgomery," the blonde said, motioning to him.

Griff grinned and stepped into the room.

"I'm sorry if we woke you up," Lauren apologized.

"That's okay. What a nice surprise to find a group of beautiful women waiting outside my door."

The ladies giggled.

Lauren jumped up and grabbed his arm, turning him around. "You don't have to stay and be polite, Griff. I'm sure you have something you need to do." She steered him back to his room.

At the door, he turned a suspicious gaze on her. "What don't you want me to know?"

"Nothing. Nothing." But her darting eyes, unwilling to meet his, gave her away.

"Who are these women?"

Lauren straightened up. "My...uh...book club."

"A book club?"

She nodded. "Yeah. Just don't want you to think I'm a snob. I mean...you probably don't read much."

"What's that supposed to mean?" He rested his hand on his hips.

"I mean, with all the working out, and the women, and the late nights..."

"I read. I read plenty."

"I'm sure you do."

But he could tell by her face that she didn't think he read anything at all, ever. And she was right. Couldn't remember the title of the last book he'd picked up. Shame stole into his chest. *Damn it. I'll read. I'll read as much as you do.*

"The group only meets for about an hour or two once or twice a month. I hope it won't bother you."

"Won't bother me at all." He slammed the door in her face.

Griff threw himself down on the bed. He laced his fingers behind his head and stared out the window. *She's the most infuriating, insufferable, condescending, and annoying woman in the world. And I have to live under her roof. Damn it.*

Until the women left, he was trapped. He flipped on his laptop and Googled Amazon. He typed in bestsellers. Up popped a list called "Book Club Picks." *She can have a book club, so can I.* He clicked then scrolled. *Romance, thriller, fiction.* Griff bought a book from each category that looked interesting, including romance. *Hell, maybe a dirty one?* He snickered. *I can hope.* After picking out six novels, he entered in his credit card number and his new address and hit "submit."

Restless, he paced then cracked open the door to listen. He heard the sound of crying. A mixture of low voices blended together, preventing him from identifying sentences. After creeping out into the hallway, he caught a word here or there, but couldn't make sense out of it. *I've heard of sad books, but this is ridiculous.*

He retired quickly to his room when he heard footsteps rounding the corner. *Best not to get caught eavesdropping. In two days, I'm gonna be reading plenty of books. But I'm not gonna cry when I talk about 'em.*

His phone dinged, signaling the arrival of a text. He winced when he read it—

We're done. Why don't you give Lauren a tumble? Carla.

All the years he'd been tomcatting around, he'd never done that before—never called the woman underneath him by another one's name. Until last night. The memory made him restless. He grabbed his keys and headed for his car. *I'm outta here.*

The women looked up as he stormed out the door. Griff didn't care. He needed air. Once behind the wheel, he entered the highway. With the windows open, he drove to Evergreen Mountain. At his favorite perch, he pulled over and got out. Standing on a ledge with a view on three sides of the small mountain range, he took a deep breath.

No woman had ever bothered him so much before. He'd be damned if he'd let Lauren Farraday get under his skin. She'd already cost him the greatest dog and the best lay ever. He had to get her out of his mind.

So, she has a body that won't quit. And those eyes. Yeah, they see into my soul. So what? She isn't the hottest chick I've ever seen. Well, maybe close. Okay, the hottest and the best cook...maybe. But she's a bitch, and she's hiding something.

When he arrived home, the last of the book club ladies was getting in her car. He stopped a little ways away and watched the blonde hug Lauren and whisper in her ear. Lauren wiped her cheek and nodded. *Maybe she's gay?* Once the woman was backing out of the driveway, Griff returned.

His presence startled Lauren. She jumped.

"How about that dinner out?" he asked, leaning against the archway to the kitchen.

"I didn't hear you come in."

"Sorry. How 'bout it?"

"Okay. When?"

"An hour?"

She nodded then climbed the stairs to her room. Griff took a shower, wondering what it was about Lauren that made her stick in his mind. *Tonight, I'm gonna find out.*

LAUREN PRESSED HER hot cheek against the cold, bathroom tile. She took a deep, shuddering breath, fighting tears. It had been months, but she still couldn't get past it. Her support group helped, but after they left, loneliness engulfed her.

Trying to cope with her loss was bad enough. Adding the annoyance of having dinner with an arrogant womanizer made things worse. All she wanted to do was cuddle up with a book, her pug, and forget her life.

Now, she'd have to put on makeup, change clothes, and pretend to be cheerful. *Ugh. Why did I ever let him in here? Oh, yeah. I need the money.* She washed her face, applied makeup, and searched her closet.

Nothing sexy. God forbid! This man doesn't need any encouragement. Why do I say that? He hasn't come on to me. In fact, he said I wasn't bad looking. Really? I'll show him.

She picked out a peach colored jersey dress that crisscrossed in the front, hugging her hips and showing plenty of cleavage. A pair of black, patent leather slides set off her slim calves perfectly. She pirouetted in front of the full-length mirror, tossed her glossy locks, and smiled. *We'll see who's 'not bad looking,' Mr. Jockstrap.* Laughing at her own joke, she plucked a white shawl off a hanger and grabbed her small, black purse.

As she descended the stairs, she called out, "Did you feed Spike?"

At the sound of coughing, she looked up. Griff was choking on a drink, his eyes tearing as he stared at her.

"Are you all right?"

He nodded, sputtering a few times and coughing twice before speaking. His voice was raspy. "Fine. Didn't expect..."

"What? Didn't expect a woman who isn't 'bad looking' to dress like this?"

He nodded. "I didn't mean to insult you. It was a compliment, actually."

"Not in my book. Did you feed the dog?"

Griff moved his gaze to her face. "I can't find the dry food."

"I don't feed him dry food. Wet food."

"Wet food? That's not good. He should eat dry food."

"He's eating wet food, has been, and is doing fine. It's here," Lauren said, pointing.

"I'll pick up a bag of dry."

"You will not! I gave in and let you call him Spike. But I'm putting my foot down on his food. This is special. I buy it at the vet's office and that's what he's getting." Her brow furrowed, her lips compressed into a thin line, and she crossed her arms over her chest.

Griff raised his palms. "Okay, okay. Don't throw a hissy fit. Feed him any shit you want."

She unfolded her arms and blew out a breath. "Fine," she said, picking up Spike's empty bowl. "I give him about a third of a can each meal."

"Got it." Griff stepped back and let her fill the dish.

"Where are we going?" she asked, rinsing the food off the spoon after placing the dog's dinner on the floor. Spike came trotting in to gobble down the mush.

"I was going to take you to The Clam Shack. But dressed like that? Nothing less than The Sweet Magnolia will do."

Lauren smiled. She'd heard about the restaurant, the finest, most expensive in Monroe, but she'd never been. When Griff offered his arm, she curled her fingers around his biceps. *Big mistake.* The flexing of his muscle sent a shiver down her arm. She let go as if he was a hot coal. *Don't let his looks get to you. He's a snake.*

She glanced up at his broad shoulders barely contained by the fine fabric of his navy sports jacket. The white shirt set off his dark hair and brown eyes. Her pulse kicked up a bit when she realized she was going to the toniest restaurant in town with the best-looking, most sought-after bachelor in the entire state. *Relax. He's just a guy, like any other guy. Yeah, sure.*

"Fantastic. Thank you," she said, a broad grin on her face.

"I'll have the prettiest girl in the county at my table." He opened the door for her.

Is he sweet-talking me? Probably. Does he mean it? Doubt it. Still, I could get used to this. She hadn't ever had this type of attention, even when she was dating Bob. With a toss of her head, she threw out the doubts and self-pity. *Tonight, I'm going to be a princess and have fun.*

He held the car door open for her, too. The buttery softness and rich scent of the finest, saddle-colored leather surrounded her, like an elegant sable cape. *Cinderella for a night. I'll take it.* She snuggled down into the luxurious seat and threw a sexy look at Griff. His eyebrows shot up for a second before he matched her flirtation with one of his own.

The vehicle roared to life, carrying Lauren to a charming, old building attached to a mill. The maître d' showed them to the best table, outside on a stone patio, a bit secluded, overlooking the mill wheel and the water that made it turn. The soft sound of the rushing brook soothed her frazzled nerves, as did the champagne cocktail the waiter brought.

Griff sat back and narrowed his eyes as he sipped his whiskey and soda.

Before he could speak, she jumped in, firing off the question most on her mind. "So, Mr. Quarterback, have you ever been married?"

"Nope. Not yet. Still waiting for the right woman."

She gave a short laugh. "With the hundreds who have passed through your life, you haven't found the right one yet? Maybe she doesn't exist."

"Hundreds? You mean thousands, don't you?"

She choked for a moment on her drink. "Thousands? Really?"

"Just teasing. I don't know how many. Never kept count. Women aren't cattle."

She arched an eyebrow.

"You sure have a low opinion of me, and you don't even know me. Why?"

"You're a professional athlete, a synonym for 'man-whore.'"

"How do you know that?"

"Unlike you, I read. Newspapers, online articles..."

"You mean gossip columns and rumors. You're right. I don't read shit like that. Do you actually know any pro athletes?"

"I don't. I admit it."

"Most of them are family men."

"You expect me to believe they aren't playing around on the road?"

"They're human. Maybe some of them have stepped out once or twice, but not most of them. They're good guys. They go home to their wives, support their kids, and give a shitload to charity."

Lauren opened her mouth then closed it. She sat back, looking at Griff, then took a sip from her glass. "Okay. Maybe I've been unfair. I don't know them."

"They're men. Some good. Some bad. And they eat, sleep, breathe, and make love like other men. Their needs are the same."

"What about you?"

"Except for being single, I'm no different."

"Single. That means you don't have to follow the rules?"

Griff sat up and leaned closer to her. "What rules?"

She laughed. "Gotta love your honesty."

"Don't judge me. Maybe I'm not as bad as you think."

"And maybe you're worse."

He chuckled. "You've got balls. I'm taking you to the best place in town, and you insult me. Maybe I should skip out on the check and let you wash dishes."

Lauren shifted in her seat. The waiter returned, and Griff signaled for another round. She avoided the quarterback's gaze as the busboy removed their empty glasses.

"You wouldn't do that, would you?" she asked, when they were alone.

"Of course not. I invited you. My treat. But you were worried, weren't you?"

She shook her head.

"Oh yes, you were. Even if only for a second. What's happened to you? You have no faith in men. Who did this to you? Your ex?"

Lauren took a deep breath. Tears threatened. *Don't cry. Don't be a wimp. Stop it.* "Life. Life did this," she whispered. "Marriage. I'll never marry again."

"That's a bit harsh, isn't it?"

"Not harsh. Safe. For me, it's safer."

"Boy, he must have done a number on you."

"You could say that."

Griff reached across the table and squeezed her hand. "I'm sorry. But it wasn't me. It wasn't every man you'll meet. You've got to let whatever it is go."

"Easy for you to say."

"I've had my own...challenges."

"You? How could you have any...hard times? You lead a charmed life."

He gave a rueful chuckle. "You don't know how ridiculous that sounds."

The server arrived with their drinks. Griff indicated they were ready to order. She chose the medallions of beef with mushrooms, and he selected the sirloin steak. Griff added salads with walnuts and bleu cheese to both. The waiter bowed and left. The gentle swishing of the water through the mill wheel was the loudest sound as they tasted their beverages and eyed each other.

"So, tell me about your...challenges, as you call them." Lauren crossed her legs and sat back.

Griff cleared his throat and shifted in his chair. His gaze lowered to his glass then lifted it to her face. "This is personal stuff. I don't want to see it on the front page of a tabloid."

"You think I'd blab to the press?"

"You never know."

"I wouldn't. I promise. Should I pinky-swear?"

He chuckled. "Okay. You promise?"

"I do."

He took a gulp and began, starting with the death of Kathy's spouse. Lauren sat up, leaning in toward him as he spun his tale. She watched his facial expression change from happy to sad. The tone of his voice and the pace of his words started out matter-of-fact and slow, but gained in speed and intensity. She noticed him blink rapidly at a few parts.

He stopped when the food arrived, turning away. *Hiding his feelings from a stranger? I get it. Can't trust just anyone not to call the press.*

"When she left, she took my family with her. Three thousand miles away. My life hasn't been the same. So, when Spike came along...well, you know him. He's amazing at plugging up a hole in your life." Griff sliced off a piece of steak and put it in his mouth.

His story touched Lauren. "I don't know what to say."

"Tell me how your food is."

She tasted her beef and made a cooing noise. "This is the best ever."

"It's a great restaurant."

She put down her fork, reached across the table, and squeezed his hand. "I'm so sorry for all you've been through. What you've lost."

"They're not dead, but might as well be. I call Sundays. Sometimes, they have time to talk, but more often, they don't. Teenagers!" He shook his head.

"Do you want kids of your own?" she asked, trying to appear nonchalant.

"Hell, yeah. Got a ton of practice being a dad. It's a deal breaker for me. Gotta have my own."

Lauren's chest tightened. Her hand shook, dropping her fork on the floor.

Chapter Six

LAUREN WAS SHOCKED that he wanted kids. *Idiot! All men, even womanizers, say they want kids. So, he wants kids. He's not interested in you, anyway. And you can't stand him. So, what's the problem?*

But she didn't hate him anymore. He'd ceased to be a cardboard cutout of a shallow, egotistical athlete. Empathy with his pain and loneliness opened her heart. She'd never known a man who would make those sacrifices for a sister and her children, or a man so generous, either.

But he wanted children, and Lauren didn't know if she could have children, so she had to close off her growing feelings for Griff, or be vulnerable to the agony she had dealt with once before. Sadness swept through her. She toyed with her food as her appetite went south.

"Want a doggie bag?"

"I'd never feed such rich food to Spike."

"For you. Lunch tomorrow?"

The waiter stood by, awaiting her answer. She nodded.

Griff shot her a warm smile. "Dessert? Coffee? They have an amazing chocolate cake with peanut butter frosting."

Her stomach churned. One look into his dark brown eyes, and she began to lose herself. Her body grew warm as her private parts tingled. *No, no, no. You can't. Don't do it.* She shook her head, and he shrugged. "You go ahead. I couldn't eat another thing," she said, attempting to smile.

"Brandy?"

"I'm fine."

"Do you mind if I do?"

"Of course not. Go ahead." She chewed her lip.

After Griff placed his order, Lauren stood up. "Excuse me." She made her way to the ladies' room. It was elegant with real, cloth towelettes. She doused one with cold water and held it to her forehead then her cheeks. Some deep breathing calmed her. She resolved not to fall for him and definitely not to sleep with him. Her decision boosted her confidence, and she returned to the table. Griff was sipping his brandy, but stopped to rise from his chair.

His gallant gesture surprised her. With a lock of dark hair falling over his forehead, broad shoulders, wide chest, and a gleaming, white smile, he was irresistible, melting her resolve. She slid into her seat, trying to quiet the fluttering in her heart and between her legs.

"You know all about me. Now, how about your story?" He leaned back, turning his attention to her, narrowing his eyes.

"Not much to tell. Not very pleasant. I'd rather not."

"Hey, wait a minute. You can't do that. Strip me bare and stay dressed."

"Please. I don't want to. There's nothing to say. Some bad things happened to me. On top of that, my father's dying, and that's that."

His smile dissolved at her words. "I'm so sorry to hear about your dad. Isn't there anything they can do?"

"I'm afraid not. He's been sliding downhill for a while. Now, time is running out."

"What about your mom?"

"She's living on the West Coast with some younger guy. They've been divorced for five years."

"Wow. That sucks."

"Yep. That about says it."

"And the other stuff?"

She sensed blood rushing to her face. "I'd rather not. Please don't push." Her gaze rose to meet his.

He held up his hand. "Okay. You win. Silence, it is."

Relief flooded through her. She didn't think she could explain one more time that her brief affair with Bob had been only his way to get back at his ex-girlfriend. After a mishap with a broken condom, Lauren had found herself pregnant. Bob had stepped up to the plate, and they had married quickly at City Hall. Then, before her first trimester had passed, Lauren had miscarried.

How could she tell Griff, this amazing man, the truth? How could she admit that when she had asked Bob to try again, he'd refused, saying they'd "dodged a bullet." A month later, he had requested a divorce. She couldn't stand the pity she'd see in Griff's eyes, knowing he'd think her a pathetic loser, unable to bear a child, deserted by her husband. The humiliation would be too great. She'd hold on to her secret, opening up only to Don and her support group.

All her dreams and plans for the baby she'd happily anticipated had vanished in one bloody afternoon. Then, she had been tossed aside like a pair of old galoshes. Rehashing the feelings brought bitterness to her throat. She took a gulp of water to wash it down.

"You okay?" Griff asked.

"Super peachy keen dandy," she said.

He laughed. "You're one strange chick, ya know that?"

"Chick?"

"Excuse me. Beautiful woman."

The heat generated by his lusty stare went straight to her core. Desire bubbled up through her veins. *To be touched by him. Bet he's a great lover.* She shifted in her seat, uncrossing her legs. Lauren tried to tear her gaze from his, wondering what it would be like to lose herself in his arms. *No more men. What if I get pregnant? What if I miscarry again? He wouldn't hang around. I can't live through that twice.*

Emotion clutched at her stomach. She returned to the ladies' room and threw up.

A woman combing her hair at the sink turned to Lauren. "Pregnant, honey?"

Lauren laughed bitterly. "Nope."

"Hope you're feelin' better real soon." The woman left.

Crouched over the bowl, Lauren cooled her forehead on the porcelain tank for a moment. A rueful chuckle escaped her lips when she thought about all the expensive food she had just upchucked. She washed her mouth out at the sink, popped a mint, and took a deep breath.

When she returned to the table, Griff was signing the check. He took a last gulp of brandy then stood. "You don't seem well. Let's get you home."

She smiled in relief. He guided her toward the exit with a large, strong hand on her lower back. The warmth of his touch made her shiver. They rode the familiar roads in silence. Lauren eased back into the comfort of the luxurious seat and stared out the window. They drove past The Savage Beast. Twenty-somethings spilled out the door onto the sidewalk, drinks in one hand, cigarettes in the other.

"Have you ever been to that place?" she asked.

Griff's head jerked back. He stared at her. "The Savage Beast? Why do you ask?"

"No reason. Looks like a busy place. Do they have great burgers or something?"

"Been there a few times. Yeah. The burgers are great. Especially the bleu cheese."

"I'll have to try it some time."

Griff swallowed. He turned into the driveway before she could ask any more questions. She opened the front door, Spike's signal to start barking. When he recognized them, the pug ran in circles, not knowing which one to greet first. He finally settled on Lauren, jumping up on her leg, trying to lick her face. She crouched down, laughing, to allow the little dog to slurp her cheek.

"I don't know many women who'd let a dog lick 'em like that."

"I love Zan...Spike. He's my best friend." She straightened and stretched.

Griff patted the pooch and placed the doggie bag from the restaurant in the fridge.

"Thank you for the great dinner," she said, locking the door and turning out the porch light.

When she turned around, he was right behind her. She bumped into his chest, bouncing back against the door. Griff surrounded her waist with his arm, steadying her. She looked up. His breath had a slightly sweet, brandy scent, enticing her to taste the liquor on him.

He stared for a moment, before he lowered his mouth to hers. *Just a good night kiss.* When his soft lips touched hers, an electric spark passed between them. Her bones turned to liquid as he drew her into his embrace. Her brain shut off as need welled up in her. When the tip of his tongue pressed against the seam of her lips, she opened.

He slid his hand down her back to rest on her hip. He pulled her to him as he ravaged her mouth. Lauren wanted him, all of him. Every nerve ending fired away double-time. Her fingers clutched his muscular shoulders as he held her to his strong chest. Finally raising his head, his dark eyes searched hers.

Her breath caught in her throat, prohibiting speech. He released her to lean against the wooden door. She touched her mouth with her finger and took a deep breath.

"Good night kiss," he murmured.

"Really?"

He chuckled. "A great night."

"A great dinner. Thank you."

"My pleasure." Eyes glistening, he backed away. "I'll take Spike out." He plucked the leash and harness from a hook and whistled for the dog.

Lauren nodded. "Thank you."

"Hey, he's mine, too."

Preoccupied by the runaway beating of her heart, she simply smiled.

Then, she scampered up the steps before she threw herself at the handsome quarterback, looming large in the doorway, watching her. She opted for the safety of her room over a wild night with a hot man.

GRIFF SCRATCHED HIS face as he wandered through the darkness behind Spike. The pug pulled toward the street, obviously following some scent. He wondered what Lauren's secret was. It was obvious she was hiding something. He needed to know what had happened to her. *Must be pretty terrible.* Her face had become tight, her words clipped. She hadn't met his gaze. *Something awful she's embarrassed about. Humiliating.*

He shrugged, letting his mind wander back to their kiss. He hadn't meant for tonight to be a real date, but when she came downstairs looking like that, his libido had kicked into high gear. Sure, she was attractive, but tonight, she had been gorgeous. The kiss had been amazing, electric. He smiled at the memory of her, pliant and willing in his arms.

I could have taken her, pushed up her dress, and wham*! Right against the front door.* He grinned. *She's hot. And my landlord. Better keep my hands to myself.* Still, his fingers tingled at the idea of touching her bare skin.

Spike tugged on the leash, leading him farther down the road. *Better keep her away from The Savage Beast. If she meets Carla...fireworks!* Spike lifted his leg on a telephone pole then turned around to head for home. Griff walked behind the small dog, enjoying the warm breeze. He wondered if her fingers on his face would feel as good as the gentle wind. He chuckled. *All of her on me. Yeah.* He closed his eyes for a second, imagining her soft flesh pressing against him.

The house was quiet when he opened the door. Griff pulled his tie loose then slipped a treat to Spike. The dog took it in his mouth and trotted up the stairs to join Lauren. Griff hung up his suit, washed up, stripped off his underwear and shirt, and slid between the sheets. With the light out, he could see the full moon shining down on the back deck, coating the furniture and wood with silver.

Sleep came quickly.

The smell of brewing coffee woke him at seven. *She must have set up the timer last night.* He slipped his boxers on and opened his door. Lauren usually slept until seven thirty, so he didn't need to put on pants before he made his way to the kitchen, rubbing his stubbly face and yawning.

His eyes flew open when he almost bumped into her at the counter. She was wearing a sheer, pink nightie that didn't make it much past her rear end and nothing else. While the short gown wasn't quite see-through, it didn't leave much to the imagination.

"Sorry," he mumbled as his gaze zeroed in on her curves, his fingers combing through his unruly hair.

"Oh my God! I didn't expect you up yet." She turned her back to him.

A familiar twitch in his groin caught his attention. *Shit! I can't get hard here.* "I run in the mornings," he said, edging toward the hall.

"But not this early." She stretched the gown in a useless attempt to cover more.

"The smell of coffee woke me up. Guess I should have expected to find you here."

"Ya think? Spike can't work the coffeemaker."

"Yeah, but not dressed like...wearing...that." His gaze swept her form.

"If you weren't here, I'd probably come down naked." Her fingers covered her smile.

Griff stepped closer to her. "I can fix that with one hand." He gripped the bottom of her nightie. But he laughed and released the fabric when she squealed and charged toward the stairs. "Be careful, little girl. If you tease the quarterback, you might get a very forward pass."

She stopped and turned to face him. With a saucy look, she said, "And the quarterback might get a mighty kick in the balls."

He chuckled as she disappeared to the second floor. Stepping into a hot shower cooled him off. *Last night, I could have had her in a second. Today, the ice queen. Women. They don't know what they want.*

He threw on running shorts and shoes and headed for the front door, where he nearly collided with Lauren. She was dressed in a light pink suit and white, silk camisole. She looked stunning.

"I'm taking Spike for a walk then to the office. Maybe I'll get a project." She fidgeted with the leash, first staring boldly at his bare chest then averting her gaze.

He grinned, flattered to be the object of her attention. "Project?"

"I'm an interior decorator. But I work freelance for Annette Coombs. I lost a big commission when I took time off to get my dad settled into a nursing home. I need to work."

"That's too bad. I hope they have something for you," he said, holding the door open.

"Me, too. See ya later." She snapped the harness around the dog and headed outside.

He stretched his leg muscles then started out loping down the block. *She's had it rough. But what isn't she telling me? Losing that project isn't everything. I need to know.*

GRIFF HEADED FOR THE training room, his mind still trying to figure out Lauren when someone called his name.

"Griff Montgomery?"

He turned to see a young man, well built, with sandy hair and blue eyes. "Yeah?"

The stranger stuck out his hand. "Tony Hastings."

As they shook, Griff nodded. "Oh, yeah. My replacement."

"I'm not... No one could replace you, Mr. Montgomery." Tony blushed.

"Griff, please. I'm not your father."

"Sorry, sorry. Yeah. Griff," he said, rolling the quarterback's name off his tongue like it was gold.

"You're pretty hot stuff. From Kensington State?"

"Yep."

"I'm from Wellington."

"I know. Our biggest rival."

"Light years ago. Welcome to the team. Get your locker yet?"

"Yep. Thanks."

Griff slapped him on the back. "Come on. Let's see what you can lift." He opened the door to the training room.

With the light banter among the men in the background, Griff's mind focused on his future. Griff figured he'd have at least four more years before he was put out to pasture. That would give Tony plenty of time to get good enough to replace him. *What if he's better than I am?*

Doubts crept into his mind. Though it would be nice not to have to stay in a game when the Kings were way ahead, be able to hit the showers early, what if Tony was a star? Would Griff find himself playing less and less in favor of Tony? *If that happens, I'll quit.*

A touch of anger made him frown. Could he quit? He'd have to call his manager and go over the contract. And if he did quit, what the hell would he do? Art Neal, offensive coach, was already sixty-two, maybe Griff could take over his job if the guy retired. But the idea of coaching in his mid-thirties depressed him. He had the spirit. He was tough and wanted to play. Griff loved the challenge, the thrill of a great pass that scored a touchdown, of being at the top of his game and one of the best in the league.

Only one thing was missing.

He had been a role model for Joey and Missy. Not anymore. Sure, they'd probably watch the game, if they were home. Probably brag to their friends that their uncle was a winning quarterback. But it wasn't the same as coming back after the game, rehashing it with the kids, then slipping into a hot, herbal bath, prepared by his sister, to soak his aching muscles. He had been king of the castle and that had been the biggest thrill of all.

"Still living with the pug chick?" Buddy asked, curling a weight with his right hand.

"Boarding. Not living with."

"Yeah, right. You haven't made it with her yet?"

Griff shot him a dirty look. "She's my landlord, not my girlfriend."

"So, that means you struck out, right?" Buddy chuckled.

Griff put down his weight, wiped his face with a towel, and shot a dirty look at his friend. "You can't complete a pass you don't make."

"So, you didn't even try? And she's so hot. I almost believe you."

Griff sensed heat rising to his face. "Don't be an asshole, Buddy."

"How do you meet girls on the road? Are there special bars you go to?" Tony asked.

"I'm sure you can tag along with Griff. He knows every pick-up joint in every city."

"Like you don't, Buddy?"

"Hell, man. I'm way behind you."

"That's not what I heard when we were in Dallas. How many did you have at once?"

"Hey, I don't kiss and tell."

"Who's talking about kissing?" Griff said. "How many were there, Buddy?"

"A few." The wide receiver blushed.

Tony's eyes got big. "All at once?"

"Buddy doesn't like to waste time." Griff chuckled.

"Look who's talking?"

"I'm not into crowd fucking."

"That's not what Donna, Louise, and Joanne said."

"Bullshit!" Griff threw a towel at his friend.

"They're all talk," Trunk Mahoney piped up.

Griff and Buddy burst out laughing. Tony's blush deepened.

"They're showing off for your benefit, Tony. Don't fall for it."

"Hey, at least we're single," Griff said, eyeing Trunk.

"Don't go there," Trunk responded.

When the workout was done, Griff hit the locker room then the shower. He noticed Tony's locker nearby. The star quarterback didn't want Tony tagging along like a baby brother. *Train him, my ass. Let the coaches train him.*

As he was walking out, Tony stopped him. "Let's grab a beer."

"Why not?" *Don't want to look unfriendly.*

"Me, too?" Buddy requested.

"No date tonight?"

"Resting up for the weekend." He chuckled.

"Where do you go in this town?" Tony asked.

"We hang at The Savage Beast."

"I saw that place. Great. Let's go."

"I'll meet you there in an hour," Griff said.

"Gotta go home to the little lady?" Buddy snickered.

Griff threw a towel at his friend. "Shut up, asshole."

Griff walked to his car, uncertain what he'd learn at the bar, but knew it would be best to keep an eye on Hastings. He sent a text to Lauren.

Business dinner tonight. Don't cook for me. See you later.

Chapter Seven

LAUREN OPENED THE DOOR of Designs by Annette. Spike trotted ahead of her, leading the way to the cubicle she shared with the other freelancers. There was a small dog bed under the desk. The pug circled it a couple of times then settled down for a nap.

Lauren strolled into Annette's office. She was on the phone, but signaled for the brunette to sit down. Lauren wished she was established enough to have her own design studio.

"Well, how are you?" Annette sat forward, removing her reading glasses to study Lauren's face.

"I'm okay."

"How's your dad?"

"In a safe place, holding his own, for now."

"I'm so sorry, Lauren."

"Anything come in?"

"I know you need the work. I mean with Bob gone, I'm sure your finances aren't what they used to be. I don't have anything now, but keep coming in. You never know."

"Thanks." She sighed and returned to her desk. The soft snore of her pug made her smile. Her cell rang. It was Marnie, her friend from the support group.

"Sam's out of town on business. How about dinner?"

"I'm watching my expenses."

"My treat."

"You don't have to do that."

"I'm celebrating."

"Oh?"

"Yeah. Turned the stick pink."

"You're pregnant? That's fantastic! Congratulations."

"So, come eat with me. We'll toast with lemonade."

Lauran laughed. "Perfect. Where?"

"Any suggestions?"

"I understand the bleu cheese burgers at The Savage Beast are terrific."

"Sounds good. How about six? I'm always starving early."

Lauren closed her phone, woke up Spike, and drove home. She changed into jeans and headed for the grocery store. Feeding an athlete would be new to her. She figured healthy food and lots of it. The bill was high, but she had enough to cover it.

After lugging the bags to the kitchen, she began to unload. Finding enough space for the pile of steaks and a whole, large chicken was a challenge. As she was making room for three gallons of milk, her phone signaled the arrival of a text.

She closed the fridge and read the message from Griff.

"Perfect timing. I can go out without making dinner for him. Works for me." She finished putting away the groceries then stretched out on the sofa with *If I Loved You,* a new romance book. Spike jumped up, settling behind her knees. He rested his chin on her leg and closed his eyes. After an hour, the warmth of the dog and the restless night she'd had trying to forget Griff's kiss got to her. She closed her eyes.

The sound of the key in the lock woke Lauren. She yawned. Spike gave a half-hearted bark and opened his eyes to check out who was entering the house.

Griff lingered for a moment in the doorway, leaning against the jamb, filling the space with his trim, muscular body. Lauren's gaze connected with his, then slid over his frame, making her pulse jump. "No work today?" he asked, closing the front door and putting his gym bag down.

"Nope."

"I need to talk to you about our schedule."

"Oh?" She sat up, rubbed her eyes once, and swung her legs down from the sofa.

"Yeah. Training camp starts in a couple of weeks."

"What does that mean?"

"Means I'll be gone all day and won't be able to walk Spike in the afternoon. Can we switch? I'll take nights, if that's okay."

"Sure. What's training camp?"

"Don't you know anything about football?"

"Not much. Used to go to my college games."

Griff plopped down next to her. "Training camp is where we run plays, scrimmage, work out, fix strategies, and stuff like that."

"What's a scrimmage?"

"Look it up."

"How long does this last?"

"We had a good season last year, so we're only doing it for three weeks this time."

"Are you going away?"

"They're having it at Kings' Stadium. So, I can come home every day. We report on July twenty-fifth, and it's done by August twentieth. Two weeks before the season opener."

"When's that?"

"Right after Labor Day."

"Guess I'll have to increase the amount of food in the house, then."

"Probably. Plenty of protein. Steaks, chicken, fish, that stuff."

"Got it. Bet you eat like a horse during the season."

"I can pack it away."

"I bought groceries today. Tell me what you can't eat, don't eat, or are allergic to."

"I eat everything. But I like to eat healthy on season. No chips or ice cream type of deal."

"Fine by me. I eat that way all the time."

"I can tell."

She sensed his gaze gliding up her body like a warm hand. She fidgeted, opening and closing her book.

Griff pushed to his feet. "Sorry about the last minute notice about dinner. Going out with a new member of the team."

"That's business?"

"It is when Coach tells you to train the guy."

"I get it. No problem. Saves me the trouble, 'cause I'm going out with a friend."

"Oh?" He cocked an eyebrow at her.

"You're not the only one who has friends." She petted Spike, slipped her bookmark in place, and stood. "Time to change."

"Going out fancy? With just a friend?"

Is he jealous? Do I have to report on my social life? What social life? "Not fancy. But not in an old T-shirt, either. With a member of my sup—uh...my book club."

"Oh. Have fun." He turned and headed for his room.

Lauren put on a grass green tank top. She loved the way the color highlighted the emerald of her eyes. After running a comb through her hair, she grabbed a long sleeve, cotton shirt, in case The Savage Beast had mega-air conditioning. She fed Spike and called out a goodbye to Griff as she left the house.

While she drove to the bar, she smiled as she thought about Marnie. Her friend, who was a social worker, had suggested the group to Lauren. Marnie had had several miscarriages, but she was hopeful that the next pregnancy would hold. The group had been helpful to Lauren, and she was grateful to Marnie. The two women had grown close, sharing their experiences over glasses of wine, laughing and crying together.

Marnie was seated at a table near the bar when Lauren entered. "Sam said this is my last night out until my first trimester is over."

"I'm honored you chose to spend it with me."

"Who else? You so understand what I'm going through. But this time, I'm calm. I took a leave of absence from my job."

"You're going to rest."

"Rest, read, and remain calm. Think positive thoughts. In the meantime, I'm starving. All I could think about all afternoon was that bleu cheese burger you mentioned."

The waitress came over, raising a small pad and pen. "Hi, I'm Carla. What can I get for you today?"

The women ordered burgers.

"No drinks, ladies?"

"Just water. I'm pregnant," Marnie said, beaming.

"Better you than me," Carla responded, scribbling on her pad and heading back to the bar.

Lauren stared at her back. "That was pretty rude."

"I don't care. I'm happy. That's all that counts."

GRIFF PULLED INTO A spot right on Elm Street. Buddy and Tony parked in the lot behind the building. Griff waited at the door for them. A crowd was already gathering. He caught Carla's eye. She shot him a frosty look, and he shivered as the coldness of it chilled him to the bone. *She's not the forgive-and-forget type.*

The three men bellied up to the bar. Griff introduced his pals to Carla. She smiled flirtatiously at the two football players.

"She yours?" Buddy asked Griff quietly, who shook his head.

Not anymore.

"I've been wondering when you were gonna bring your teammates in. Seems like you picked the two best looking," Carla said, shooting a mean look at Griff.

He swallowed a mouthful of beer and shifted his weight. *This is gonna be bad.*

"I see your girlfriend here has good taste." Buddy took a gulp of his drink.

"Oh, I'm not his girlfriend. Lauren is." Carla glared at Griff.

Suddenly, the collar on his shirt got tight.

"Lauren? You know Lauren?" Buddy asked.

Oh, shit. Here it comes.

"No, but I'd love to meet her," she said, casting her gaze on Griff. "I've got a message for her."

Over my dead body. He let out a breath before he guzzled more beer.

"That's easy. She's sitting right there." Buddy pointed to Lauren and her friend, who were munching on burgers.

Griff turned to look and spat out his drink. *Holy shit.*

"That's Lauren? Griff's Lauren?"

"Yep, that's her," Buddy said, ignoring the kick from Griff. "Ouch."

Carla fisted a hand and rested it on her hip. "So, she's your girlfriend?"

"No, no, no way. She's my landlady. I'm renting a room with her while my house is being renovated." The words poured out in rapid fire.

"Even better." Carla licked her lips. "I'll bet she has no idea you're having sexual fantasies about her."

"I'm not. It was an accident," he hissed.

"Sure, sure. Keep telling yourself that. Wonder what she'd think if she knew?"

"Don't, Carla. Please don't. I'm begging you." Griff reached for her arm, but she shook him off.

Buddy faced the quarterback. "What the hell did you do?"

"You don't wanna know."

"Oh no. You didn't?" His eyebrows rose.

Griff nodded. "Guilty."

"Whoa, stand back, Tony. There's gonna be some fireworks in a minute." Buddy pushed Hastings to the wall.

"You wouldn't be lying, now, would ya?" Carla asked, directing her stare at Buddy.

"See for yourself." He gestured to the brunette at the corner table.

"Lauren!" Carla cupped her hands and yelled.

Lauren stood up, turning to face them.

"You Lauren?"

"Please, please, Carla. I'm sorry, so sorry," Griff whispered. "Don't do this."

"Yes? Lauren Farraday." Her gaze traveled from Carla to Griff.

No place to hide. This is gonna get ugly. Sweat gathered under his arms and on his forehead. His heartbeat doubled. He shifted his weight from foot to foot, trying to look relaxed under Lauren's scrutiny.

"I have a message for you," Carla called out.

"Carla, come on. After everything we've been through," Griff pleaded.

"You're right. Because of our history, I'm not gonna shout it out."

"Thank God. Thank you so much," he said, heaving a huge sigh.

"I'm gonna tell her soft and slow, right in her ear." Carla was heading toward Lauren before Griff could stop her. He tried to block her way, but she scooted to the left, giving him the slip. When she got to her destination, she bent down, cupped her hands, and spoke softly.

The room was so quiet Griff could hear a crow caw from a tree outside. The patrons in the bar stared at Carla and Lauren. A few looked at Griff and snickered.

"What?" Lauren straightened in her seat. "What? No. I don't believe it."

Carla leaned over and spoke again.

Lauren blushed pink then redder and redder. She shot a look at Griff. He stared at her, pleading with his eyes. She stumbled up from the table. "I'm sorry, Marnie. I've got to go."

"It's on the house," Carla said, returning to the bar. Her eyes glistened with malevolence as she glared at Griff.

"I can't believe you did that."

"Just be happy I didn't scream it out to the whole room." She returned to washing glasses.

"I thought we were friends."

"Yeah? Feel betrayed? Now you know how I felt, jerk."

Griff tossed some bills on the counter and left. He glanced up and down the street, but Lauren was nowhere to be seen. The last thing he wanted to do was return home, but he had no idea where else he could go. He got behind the wheel and drove, his sense of dread growing as he neared the old Victorian.

Lauren's car was in the garage, but the house was quiet when he slipped inside. The only noise was the *click click click* of Spike's nails on the tile floor of the kitchen as he trotted over to greet the quarterback. He bent to pet the dog.

"Do you always do that?" Her voice startled him.

"Do what?" he asked, his gaze focused on Spike.

"You know what."

"I don't. Why don't you tell me?" He glanced up to see her lips compressed into a thin line, her brows knitted.

"Call out the wrong name when you're having sex."

"Nope. Never done it before."

"Why did you call mine?"

He stood up. "How do you know it was yours?" *Best defense is a good offense.*

She placed her hands on her hips. "You know more than one Lauren?"

"Maybe I do."

As the idea clearly grew in her mind, a blush returned to her cheeks. *Now, she thinks I've got the hots for some other Lauren. Damn, she's gullible.* "If I called out your name, so what?" He shrugged.

"So what? It's a lot more than 'so what.'"

"Is it? What if I did have the hots for you? That's over now. One kiss. I'm satisfied." *What the hell are you doing?*

She averted her eyes, but he could see her blinking rapidly.

What the hell have you done, idiot? "Look, I'm sorry. I didn't mean to embarrass you. Hell, I was a whole lot more embarrassed when it happened, guaranteed. It's nothing against you."

"I thought it meant you liked me. Wanted me instead of her."

"And that'd make you mad?"

"No, but being humiliated in a bar full of strangers would. Is she your regular date?"

"Let's not talk about her. That's over now."

"Because of me?"

"Got any of that stew left over?"

"Trying to change the subject?"

He chuckled. "You noticed."

"I guess it's your turn to be embarrassed."

"The stew?" He sensed blood rushing to his face.

"It's gone, but I bought some steaks today."

"You got a grill?"

She indicated the back door.

"Awesome! Gimme. I'm a master griller." He motioned for her to hand over the food.

"Wine?" she asked.

"Beer." He snatched a bottle from the fridge while Lauren put the steaks on a platter. She fished a long fork from a drawer and handed everything to him. He headed for the back door. "How do you like your steak?" he hollered.

"Well done."

"Sure know how to ruin a good piece of meat," he called out, just before the screen door slammed shut.

WHILE GRIFF WAS PLAYING country music on the radio, singing along and grilling the steaks, Lauren called Marnie. After telling her exactly what happened, she asked for advice.

"That means he likes me, right?"

"Lauren, don't be an idiot. If a man calls your name at a...significant moment during sex, it means more than just he likes you."

"It means he wants to sleep with me?"

"Duh. I can't believe you have the sexiest man in the state in your backyard, grilling steaks and wanting to have you for dessert...and you're worried."

"I don't want to get involved. You know why."

"You're being ridiculous."

"You should understand."

"One miscarriage doesn't mean you'll miscarry every time."

"But if I do, he'd leave me, just like Bob. Griff wants kids. He said it was a deal breaker."

"Why don't you just go out with him? Sleep with him? You might not even like each other. You're projecting too far ahead."

"He told me things... He's an incredibly decent guy."

"So? There are lots of decent guys."

"Not like Griff."

"Can't you go on the pill and just have an affair with him? Probably do you good."

"I don't know."

"He's really gorgeous. How can you resist him? Does he walk around in a towel?"

"The bathroom is in his room, so no. But he's ventured out in his boxers."

"And you didn't attack him?"

"Get real."

"I would have."

"If Sam heard you talking like this…while you're carrying his child. Shame on you."

"I love to hear those words. Say it again."

Lauren grinned. "Carrying his child."

"I'm sorry. Am I being insensitive? Would you like to be carrying Griff's child?"

Lauren sensed heat in her cheeks. The back door opened, and Griff marched in.

"Gotta go." Lauren hung up.

"What's up? You're red as a beet."

"Nothing."

"Let's get one thing straight," he said, his legs spread wide. "You're a bad liar. I catch you every time."

"It's private. My conversation with my friend."

"The one at The Savage Beast today?"

"Yeah. Marnie."

"Okay, don't tell me. Do you have any steak sauce? Meat's almost ready."

Lauren ran her gaze over his biceps, shoulders, and chest, barely hidden by a sleeveless T-shirt. It clung to him, outlining his abs. A bit of dark chest hair peeked around the neckline. Her mouth watered, and her fingers twitched, aching to touch him. His jeans were tight, but not obscene. She licked her lips then swallowed as an image of him naked flashed through her brain.

"Earth to Lauren." He waved his hand in front of her face. "Do you have any steak sauce? I like to put it on just before the meat's done."

She forced herself to concentrate on his words. "Right here." She opened a cabinet and took down a bottle. His warm, rough fingers touched hers as he took it. She looked up into his eyes, sparkling with merriment. A shiver shook her.

He smiled. "You're not mad anymore, right?"

She nodded. "Right."

Fifteen minutes later, Griff placed the steaks, cooked to perfection, on the dining room table. Lauren had already set a plate of corn on the cob and a salad there. He refreshed her wine and took another beer. They sat down.

"We need steak knives. Do you have any?"

"In the silverware drawer."

She heard the clink of metal on metal as Griff searched for the sharp implements. She joined him in the kitchen to help.

He pulled out a baby spoon and held it up. "Hey, what's this?"

Lauren froze at the sight of a remnant from her pregnant days. *Bob swore he got rid of that stuff. What's it doing here?* Her breath came quicker, and she began to pant. Panic grew inside her. Emotion at the reminder of the baby she'd never have washed through her like a tsunami. "Where did you find that?" She could barely talk.

"In here."

"Throw it out. Throw it out." Her hysteria grew. "Throw it out!" she screamed at him.

"Okay, okay. Calm down."

Tears blinded her as a sob broke from her throat. She fled the room, running up the stairs. After slamming her door, she flopped down on the bed, sobbing. In a minute, she was spent. As she lay there, shame filled her. *When am I going to get over this? Women lose children every day. I'm not unusual.*

A soft tap on the door interrupted her thoughts. "Are you okay?"

"Fine."

"Lying again. Can I come in?"

He didn't wait for her answer, which would have been "no." He opened the door slowly and crept in. Lauren didn't move. She closed her eyes, burying her face in the antique comforter, not anxious to face him or explain.

"I threw out the spoon." He crawled up the bed to lie next to her. His big hand rubbed her back.

"Thanks," she said, her voice muffled by the quilt.

The warmth and motion of his fingers calmed her. She wanted more and turned on her side to face him. He inched closer, easing her into his embrace. Lauren snuggled into his neck and shoulder, snaking her arm around his middle as he held her. She inhaled his scent mixed with a hint of pine soap, which soothed and aroused her.

He rolled over, enabling her to rest her cheek on his pecs. Her eyelids fluttered. He hummed a tune she didn't recognize and continued to stroke her back. The vibration of his chest against her own was like a massage. Within a few minutes, she was sound asleep.

Chapter Eight

HUNGER WOKE LAUREN at nine o'clock. Clad only in her bra and panties, she threw on a short robe and crept downstairs, trying not to make a sound. Griff had wrapped a plate of food for her and left it on the kitchen table. She licked her lips as she uncovered the meal. The steak looked perfect. She pulled utensils out of a drawer and sat down. The meat was juicy, even though it was well done. She closed her eyes to savor the flavor of the fine sirloin.

A deep voice came out of the night. "It's perfect, right?"

Lauren opened her eyes as she jumped, rising two inches off her chair. "You scared me," she said, frowning.

He joined her. "Sorry. I heard a noise in here. Didn't expect you up."

"My stomach woke me. I'm starving," she muttered between large bites of the succulent steak. She kept her eyes on her food, trying to ignore the fact that he was only wearing jeans.

"Did you undress me?"

"Guilty. I stopped at decency, though how a woman could sleep wearing a bra is beyond me."

"Thank you." She tucked into her steak to hide her embarrassment.

"Well? How is it?"

"It's amazing." She snuck a glance at his amazing chest.

Griff chuckled. "I'm good at the grill."

"What else are you good at, besides grilling and throwing a football?"

"Do you want the PG version or X-rated?" He snickered, his dark eyes dancing with mischief as they skimmed over her skimpy robe, making her shiver.

She laughed.

Griff slipped his hand over her free one. "Or should I show you?" His gaze settled on her lips.

She finished chewing and sat back, checking him out again. His muscles were nicely defined, and the sprinkling of dark chest hair tempted her fingers. She ached to touch him, but resisted. *He's a womanizer. He'll leave you. He'll hurt you.* "Don't think so." She removed her hand to cut another piece of meat.

"Too bad. Tonight would've been perfect. You're already dressed for it." Again, his gaze swept over her, lingering too long on her breasts, making her cross an arm over them.

"Why?"

"Because the moon is full. It shines right through my window. Very romantic." He shook his head. "I hate to go to bed there alone."

"You hate to go to bed anywhere alone," she countered. But Lauren blushed as she recalled the allure of the moon. When she had moved into that room, the moonlight had mocked her, brought home her loneliness. With Griff sleeping there, the temptation to return was overwhelming. The image of staring up at it, snuggled in his strong embrace, gave her goose bumps. *I'd be safe.*

Feeling safe was a priority, but would she ever be with a man-whore like Griff Montgomery?

"It *is* beautiful. The moon, I mean," she whispered.

"Come. Share it with me," he said, his voice deep and seductive.

"Maybe...some other time." Her willpower was melting under the heat of his stare.

"You don't know what you're missing."

"I think I do. I'm sure you make love as well as you grill steaks."

"Better."

She laughed. "You certainly don't have a confidence problem, do you?"

"Hey, I can't cook, can't sew, not a great speller...but I shine at playing football, grilling, and making love."

"You sure about that?"

"If you won't come to bed, at least come to a game. See for yourself."

"I'd love to. But you'll have to explain it to me."

"My pleasure. Why don't we start now, in my bed?" He rose up and offered his hand.

"Damn, you're persistent. Why me? I'm not a great beauty, or very sexy." She put down her knife and fork.

"Are you kidding? You're damn sexy...and beautiful. There's something about you. I don't know. Something different."

"Great line, but I'm not buying." She plopped the last piece of steak into her mouth.

He sank back down into his chair. "That's not a line. Something sad about you. Like you need me to make you smile. You have an amazing smile."

She stopped chewing and swallowed, staring at him. *It shows that much? Damn.* "I appreciate your concern, but...I'm okay. I do like your jokes, I admit." She cast her gaze to her empty plate and toyed with the corncob there.

"What did I tell you about lying?"

When she looked up, she saw teasing in his eyes. "Nobody's happy all the time."

"You shouldn't be sad all the time, either. Bet I can find another way to put your smile back." He put his arm around her, drawing her closer.

The touch of his hand on her shoulder softened her will. She leaned into him, resting her head against his shoulder. Lauren sighed. *To stay like this forever.*

They cuddled together in separate chairs, listening to the ticking of the wall clock and Spike's soft snore. Her eyelids grew heavy as his pleasant scent and physical support comforted her. Then, she jerked her eyes wide. "Got to go back to sleep." She yawned.

"What's the rush?"

"Annette texted me. She might have a project. I need to go in."

"Tomorrow's Saturday."

"Oh, yeah. Still. I'm exhausted."

Griff released her. He smoothed her hair with his palm and gazed into her eyes. Lauren smiled up at him. He brushed his lips against hers.

"Goodnight, pretty lady."

"Goodnight." She wished she could overcome her doubts and trot off to bed with him. But she wasn't ready. *I hope he's still interested when I am. If I am.* She left him and climbed the stairs to her room.

THE SOUND STARTED OFF faint, but slowly grew louder and louder. Lauren tossed in her bed. She put her hands over her ears, but she could still hear it. What was it? A buzzing? No. It was strident. When it got louder, it penetrated her brain, her skin, her abdomen. A baby crying! It was definitely a baby.

Lauren sat up. She was bathed in sweat and sobbing.

"My baby. My baby," she muttered, confused, hugging her abdomen. "Where are you? Where are you?"

She threw aside the bed covers. She opened every door in the house, including Griff's. When she yanked open the closet in the kitchen, the crying stopped. She collapsed on the floor in a heap.

Griff entered, scratching his face. "What the—? What's going on? It's two o'clock." He rubbed his eyes.

Wiping her cheeks with her hand, Lauren looked up. Griff snatched a couple of tissues from the box on the counter and handed them to her. Then, he bundled her into his arms and carried her into his room.

He laid her gently on the bed and sat next to her. "What happened?"

"Nightmare," she said, in a low voice.

"One helluva nightmare. Geez. Are you all right?"

She nodded, stopped, and then shook her head. She swung her legs over the side, but they were too shaky to hold her.

Griff put his hand on her thigh. "Whoa. You're not going anywhere."

Her teeth chattered, and her heartbeat raced as she slid under the sheet and pulled the light blanket up.

"Do you want me to stay with you?"

"Please. I don't want to be alone."

He got in beside her and tucked her against his chest. She snuggled down.

"Look there," he said, pointing. "See the moon? It's full."

She nodded. He was lying behind her, his arm around her middle, holding her fast. Lauren laid her hand on top of his.

"I'm here. You're safe. Close your eyes. I'll be right here if you need me."

"Thank you," she whispered and brushed her lips against his arm. Griff kissed her hair and tucked his knees up under hers. The warmth from his body soothed her. Her muscles relaxed as she stared at the moon for a moment before falling back to sleep.

She tossed during the night as fragments of a bad dream disturbed her mind. When she jolted awake, a deep voice and gentle, warm hands calmed her. Lauren inched closer to Griff. He turned over on his back, opening his arms. She snaked hers around his waist and rested her head on his chest. She was back to dreamland in minutes.

Morning peeked through the sheer curtains, brightening up the room with sunlight. Lauren rolled over to find Griff on his stomach, sound asleep. She gently eased a lock of his dark hair off his forehead. His face was boyish, handsome, and adorable as he slept.

The sheet had fallen to his waist. Lauren satisfied her desire to look at him without his knowing. She ran a finger down his face, quickly withdrawing her hand when he shifted position and batted at her as if she were a fly. For a brief moment, she flattened her palm against his pecs, thrilling to the firmness that met her hand.

A glance at the clock told her it was eight. *He'll be up soon.* She eased out of bed slowly, leaving him sleeping soundly. Lauren went to work in the kitchen.

The smell of bacon cooking and fresh coffee permeated the house. *That should wake him up.* She mixed batter and greased the waffle iron. Pouring herself another cup, she sat back and sipped. When she heard his door open, Lauren's gaze was drawn to the doorway. Griff entered the room looking fantastic. He had combed his hair to the side and slipped on tight jeans.

He smiled at her then glanced at the stove.

"Coffee?" she asked. He nodded. She poured a mug for him.

"I thought I smelled bacon. Thank God I wasn't dreaming."

"Bacon and my secret recipe waffles."

"Bacon and waffles? My favorite." He grinned, took the cup from her, and sat down.

"My mother's special recipe."

"A special occasion I don't know about? A national holiday?"

"Just my way of saying 'thank you' for last night."

"Not necessary. Hey, what are friends for?"

Lauren opened the waffle iron and poured in some batter. "We're friends?"

"We're not lovers...yet. So, I guess that makes us friends."

"I like that." She closed the top and checked her watch. "Hmm, check in one minute."

Griff went to the cabinet and took down plates. Lauren plucked a small container of maple syrup from another. She removed the last of the bacon and put it on a paper towel to drain. While she waited for the waffle to cook, Griff came up behind her. He closed his fingers over her shoulders and bent to kiss her neck.

"Thank you for this incredible breakfast," he whispered, his lips brushing her ear, his breath caressing her skin. A shiver shot up her spine, and his soft chuckle let her know he felt it, too. "I guess you're not totally immune to me."

She laughed. *Immune? I'm putty.* "Waffle's ready."

Griff went to the table. Lauren placed a waffle on his plate, poured one for herself, and brought over the bacon. He dug in. The silence was broken by his "ums" and "ahs" as he chowed down on the special meal.

"I've never had waffles this good."

"I told you. Mom's special recipe."

"You could make a fortune selling these," he said, taking another mouthful.

When they finished, Griff shooed her out of the kitchen and cleaned up. Lauren took a shower. She needed time to think. Breakfast with Griff had been amazing. They were so comfortable together. The memory of sleeping in his arms aroused her. She wanted more, but fear stopped her. After she dried off, she called Marnie.

"I want to call an emergency meeting of the group. I need help."

"Okay. You got it. When?"

"This afternoon? Three? Griff usually works out then."

"Perfect. I'll get the phone tree going."

Lauren slipped a T-shirt on, pulled on jeans, and returned to the kitchen. Griff was finishing up. His presence filled the room.

"That was the best breakfast ever. Thanks again." He stepped up to her, gripped her shoulders, and kissed her. An electric spark ignited between them. A flush of heat swept through her veins.

She fought the magnetism drawing her to him and broke the embrace. "You're welcome. You were a lifesaver last night."

"You can come to my bed any night or every night." His eyes glistened with desire. Before she could respond, his cell chimed. He pulled it out of his pocket and answered. "Yeah. I'm in. Give me fifteen minutes."

Lauren steadied her breathing.

"Gotta go. Buddy and I run together. Then I'm throwing a few. See you later. We can pick up where we left off."

Before she could think of anything to say, he had disappeared into his room. She touched her lower lip and sighed. *He can add great kissing to his list of accomplishments.*

FUELED AND READY FOR action, Griff was energized. After a superior meal and the best night's sleep in ages, despite the interruptions, he was in top form. He met Buddy at the stadium, and they ran around the track, keeping a decent pace but not breaking any records. Then, he and Buddy practiced. Buddy ran, and Griff threw. Griff had a special ability to judge the flight of the ball and the speed of the runner.

As always, they were golden together. Buddy's instinct caused him to turn at exactly the right moment to catch Griff's pass, which was pinpoint perfect to the runner's location.

When they were done, Griff spied Tony Hastings watching from a bench. "The new guy is stalking me."

"Nah. Just trying to learn from the best."

"He makes me nervous."

"Relax. He can't touch you."

Griff smiled at his best friend and hit the showers. Then, he and Buddy went out to lunch. By the time he returned home, it was three thirty. He wondered at all the cars in the driveway. He met Marnie coming out of the house. "Another book club meeting?"

"Book club?"

"Yeah. Isn't that what this is?"

"Not exactly."

She tried to move away, but Griff blocked her path. "What exactly?"

"I suppose Lauren should tell you."

"Why don't you save her the trouble?" Griff asked, not moving out of the way.

"This is a support group for women who have lost a child."

Griff was struck dumb. He moved aside to let Marnie pass. Pieces started to fit together. *The spoon. The nightmare. How does Bob fit into this?* Anger at being lied to stoked his fire. He was determined to get at the truth.

At the front door, he stood by to let the women leave. Lauren was in the living room, cleaning up the coffee cups and cake plates. Griff leaned against the wall.

She turned as if she felt him standing there. "Hi. You're home early."

"Yeah. Just in time to see your book club leave. Seems like you meet often. For a book club, that is."

Lauren avoided his stare. "Well, sometimes a new book—"

"Stop lying, Lauren. I know it's not a book club. What the hell is going on?"

"Nothing that concerns you." She turned away from him.

Griff gripped her upper arm, hard. "I disagree. We're gonna talk. The truth. Now." He sat her down in a chair in the kitchen while he retrieved a beer.

"I don't see where you—"

"Last night gives me the right to know the truth. Talk." He offered her a beer, too, which she accepted.

"Okay, okay."

He straddled another chair, put his bottle to his lips, and eyed her. "Start talking."

She squirmed a bit, cast her gaze at the floor, and cleared her throat.

"At me. Look at me," he said, motioning with his fingers.

"All right..."

"You lost a child?"

"Sort of."

"What do you mean, 'sort of'?"

"Do you want to know?" She rose out of her seat. "Then, shut up and listen!"

He straightened up.

"About a year and a half ago, I started dating Bob. I had decorated his house. This house. That's how we met. We were friendly, but nothing special...at first. Then, he asked me out. I didn't know he was on the rebound. His girlfriend, Linda, had dumped him for someone else." She lowered her head as a blush stole through her cheeks. "Um, ah...a broken condom, and suddenly, I was pregnant."

"Did you love him?"

"No. And don't interrupt."

"Sorry."

"I wasn't in love with Bob, but I liked him. We got along well, had fun together."

"It was casual?"

"Will you shut the hell up?"

He raised his palms. "Okay."

"Where was I? Oh, yes. Pregnant. When I told him, he proposed. I accepted. We went down to City Hall the next day and tied the knot."

"Even though you didn't love him?"

"Right. I wanted the baby. Seemed like Bob did, too. I thought he'd be a good father. I didn't want to raise the baby by myself. I figured I'd learn to love Bob, especially after the baby was born. I was grateful he stepped up to the plate."

"Then what?"

She shot him an angry look, and he put his hand over his mouth and quieted down. "Before I hit three months, I lost the baby." Her voice faltered, and her eyes filled with tears. Griff stood, but she motioned him to sit down. Lauren grabbed a tissue.

"I'm so sorry," he whispered.

"Yeah. So was I. But apparently, Bob wasn't. Seems like after we got married, Linda decided she wanted him back. He had started seeing her...on the side."

"Did you know?"

She shook her head. "I had no idea. I was living in my happy bubble, so excited about the baby, preparing for his arrival. I bought a ton of stuff. Had his room painted. Everything. Then, one afternoon, it was all over." She gulped air.

He reached for her hand. "Then what?"

"Everything hit the fan. I became depressed. Bob kept seeing Linda. They decided they belonged together."

"How did you find out?"

"I asked him if we could try again. He said we'd dodged a bullet..." She paused to take a deep breath. "And no, he had no interest in trying again. In fact, he had no interest in continuing our marriage."

Silence hung heavy in the air.

"He actually said 'dodged a bullet'?"

She nodded. "So, I moved into your room." Emotion formed a hard ball in her throat, preventing speech. She shut her eyes tight to control the tears then opened them again.

Griff was staring at her, his face filled with sadness. "That's the worst..."

"Once the divorce was finalized, Bob and Linda took half the furnishings and moved to Los Angeles. And here I am."

Griff pushed to his feet. He engulfed her in a huge hug. Once in his arms, she broke down, sobbing into his chest. Her body shook, and her tears wetted his shirt. He rocked her, kissing her hair and rubbing her back. Finally, she calmed down, the weeping stopped, and she hiccupped.

"I'd never do that to you," he whispered.

"Never knock me up and leave me flat if I lose it?"

"Never."

"But you want kids. What if I can't have kids? What if I miscarry every time? Why would you want to get involved with a woman like that?

"You don't know if that's true. Besides, aren't you projecting a little far ahead?"

Her body stiffened. She pulled back, pushing away from his chest. "You're right. Who says we'd even be serious? You're busy sleeping around, and I'm plain not interested." She laughed. "That's almost funny."

"I told you I've changed. I want my own family."

"You did say that. Obviously, a woman who can't hold a pregnancy would never be the right one for you."

"I'll make that decision myself." He cupped her face with his hands and lowered his mouth.

She resisted for a moment then parted her lips.

He plunged in, taking her, demanding her submission. She softened against him, her body hip to hip, chest to chest, with his. His temperature began to rise, and heat flowed through his veins.

He wanted her.

Chapter Nine

EMOTION SAPPED LAUREN'S strength. His mouth worked magic on her, renewing her spirit, as desire flew through her body. Resisting Griff was out of the question. She ached for his touch. Weeks of watching his easy grace, as he moved about the house wearing only jeans or shorts, had captured her attention. Staring at his almost naked body day-after-day had made her beyond horny. She welcomed him, moaning when his hand slid up to cover her breast.

She flattened her palm against his chest. His fingers dipped under her T-shirt, spreading heat over her bare skin. He popped her bra open easily then circled around to close over her naked flesh. He caught her peak between his fingers and pinched gently. She caught her breath as the sensation zoomed down below her belly.

He moved his lips to her throat as he continued to massage her. The soft kisses made her breathe harder. She closed her fingers over his shoulders, feeling his powerful muscles. With a little push, he moved her back. He eased her shirt up and off then ripped his over his head and tossed it on a chair. Lauren couldn't wait to run her fingers through the dark hair lightly covering his pecs.

"You're beautiful," he murmured, scorching her skin with his gaze.

"So are you," she said.

He chuckled. "Nothing you haven't seen before."

She spread her fingers behind his neck and pulled his mouth to hers. She slipped her tongue over his. It was as if she had flipped a switch. He returned the favor, both hands massaging her breasts. When he stepped back, he picked her up and carried her into his room.

"I've waited long enough," he announced, reaching for the button on her jeans. In a second, he had stripped her pants down. She stepped out of them and reached for his zipper. He shucked his jeans then his boxers.

Shyness welled up in Lauren, standing in front of him in only red panties. She folded her arms across her chest. He sucked in a breath.

"Wow. You're amazing." His gaze raked her body.

"You, too," she said, eyeing his erection.

"Don't cover yourself." He eased her arms to her sides. "Let me look at you."

She sensed color heat her cheeks as he bent over, hooking a finger in each side of her panties and whisking them to the floor. She stepped back, leaving them where they lay. He stared at her.

"Better. Much better," he said, moving closer. "Stunning." He glided his hands down her hips and around to her rear end. She placed hers on his stomach and moved them up slowly. A tingle went from her fingertips to her sex. She pushed up on tiptoe to kiss his throat then suck on his earlobe. A hiss from him made her smile.

He moved his large hands over her behind, then inched them between her thighs. As the fingers that threw a football expertly touched her core, she jumped.

"Oh my God," she muttered, closing her eyes, frozen with need.

Griff stroked her then dropped his mouth to her shoulder. Lauren couldn't move, only feel.

"Griff," she murmured.

He raised his head. The tingles inside her had become fire, burning, making her squirm. He moved his hand around to the front, between her legs. She gasped as an orgasm began to build. He rubbed her faster and harder. She clung to his chest, muttering his name. Her knees wobbled until he snaked his arm around her waist, steadying her. She couldn't hold out any longer. Her muscles clenched then fluttered, as her release took over her body.

"Oh, God," she whispered, tucking her head into his shoulder.

His soft chuckle made her open her eyes. He kissed her, backing her up toward the bed. She went down when the mattress hit the back of her knees. He knelt beside her. His mouth sucked on her peak as his palm glided down her flat belly.

"You're magnificent," he said, then turned his attention back to her breasts.

She reached over and closed her fingers around him. He was hard as steel. "Wow. Impressive."

She saw him blush for the first time. He climbed up next to her, reached down for his wallet, and extracted a foil packet.

Lauren stiffened. "Condoms?"

"Unless you're on the pill?"

"Guess I didn't think it through."

"I've never had one break on me before."

"There's always a first time."

"Not necessarily. Don't worry. It'll be fine." He dropped the condom on the pillow, parted her knees, and inched down the bed. When his tongue touched her sensitive flesh, she bucked her hips. "I'm not gonna be able to do much if you keep movin' outta the way," he said, his eyes bright with mischief.

She giggled and stopped.

"Much better," he mumbled, as he continued his assault.

Lauren ran her fingers through his thick, dark hair. His hands gripped her thighs, and his tongue sent her to the moon. As the fire in her climbed, she began to squirm.

Griff was up in a flash, covering himself. "I want to be there for this one," he explained, pushing up. Glowing with lust, he stared down at her, before he entered her slowly.

She wiggled. "Hurry up."

"No way. I've waited a long time for this." He shot her a sexy grin as he pushed in farther.

She arched her back. "Oh, my God. Griff!" It had been months since she'd made love. A slight burn turned to pleasure as he filled her. She hiked her knee to her chest to enable him to move in all the way. He was larger than Bob, but fit perfectly.

Griff groaned and closed his eyes. "Lauren, baby. So good. So good." He dropped his forehead to her shoulder to plant a kiss.

He pumped in and out. The pressure of him inside her, the swipe of his chest hair against her breasts, the feel of his muscle and skin beneath her fingers shot her to her breaking point. A powerful orgasm ripped through her body, bringing pleasure to every nerve ending. Her hips undulated while he continued to push into her. A few seconds after, he came, thrusting hard once, and then stopping. He muttered her name as he balanced on his elbows and touched her face.

Lauren looked into his eyes. *Is that love, pity, or sexual satisfaction? Maybe all three?* She cupped his cheek and brushed her lips against his. Happiness flowed through her veins like adrenaline. Sweat beaded on his forehead and chest. His eyes, like pools of melted dark chocolate, stared into hers, questioning.

"What?" she asked.

"That was amazing."

"It was. Way beyond expectations," she admitted.

"Oh?" He cocked an eyebrow. "And what horrible thing did you expect?"

"I expected a self-obsessed lover who didn't care about me."

"Really? I gave you that impression?"

She nodded.

"And so?"

"I was wrong."

He bent over and kissed her. "So, what am I?"

She snaked her arms around his chest, hugging him to her. "You're just what you said. The best lover."

"And your experience is so wide? You've slept with so many men?" He pushed up, pulled out of her, and rested on his side.

"I've had my share."

He chuckled. "Nice save."

She smiled at him. "Unlike a man, a woman never tells."

Laughing, Griff headed for the bathroom. Lauren watched him. His back was broad and muscular. His waist was trim, and his butt, adorable. He was supported by long, strong legs with meaty thighs and tapering calves. She wanted to touch every inch. When he returned, she took her chance, running her palm along his chest and down his abs. He lay back as she explored his body. When she got to his arms, she asked, "Which arm do you throw with?"

"Right." He smoothed his hand down her back as she continued.

Lauren examined the muscles in his right arm. "Is that one more developed than the other?"

"I don't know. Never compared 'em."

She went back and forth between the two, trying to measure. "I think it is, maybe a little."

He wrestled her down onto her back and kissed her belly, tickling her. Lauren was lost in laughter, screaming and kicking. He subdued her legs with his, moving his thigh between hers. He slid it up against her. His eyes danced.

"More?"

"Hell, yeah." He reached down for another condom. "First one held fine, by the way."

She blew out a breath. He covered himself and was inside her before she could blink. He hiked her leg up, hooking it over his shoulder. She gasped when he plunged in deeper. His power and aggression thrilled her, sending sparks down her spine. He pumped hard and fast, making her come with him. His mouth captured hers, their tongues dancing.

Lauren arched her back and rubbed her nipples against his chest. They hardened immediately. She hummed a tune, like a purr.

"You're a special woman, Lauren."

"Yeah?"

"Sexy. I could make love to you all night long."

She giggled. "You're wearing me out."

"Already?"

"Umm hum."

He drew her close. She snuggled into him and closed her eyes. Griff pulled the sheet up. Within minutes, happy dreams filled her head.

AT NINE, GRIFF WOKE up, starving. *Missed dinner.* He tried to slide out of bed without waking Lauren, but as soon as he moved, she raised her head.

"Hungry?"

"Yeah."

She sat up. "Leftover meatloaf in the fridge."

"Cold meatloaf? Yeah!" He licked his lips. "Should I save some for you?"

"I'll have some corned beef."

He pulled up his boxers and offered his robe to her. It touched the floor, and he had to roll the sleeves up three times. She smiled as he threw his arm around her shoulder.

After their late feast, they cuddled up together in his bed for the rest of the night.

In the morning, Griff was whistling when he entered the locker room. Buddy was ready for his workout.

"A new tune?"

"Nope."

"Oh, yeah. I think someone got lucky, eh?"

Griff turned away to hide his blush, but Buddy wasn't deterred. He followed his friend.

"Man, you're red. Did you make it with that babe?"

"Butt out, Buddy."

"You did! Shit, you banged her, didn't you?"

"I said, shut up." Griff stuffed his bag in his locker.

"Really? How many times?"

"Shut the fuck up."

Buddy snickered. "Finally! Was she worth the wait?"

"I swear I'll take you out you if you don't shut your mouth." Griff raised a fist.

Buddy held up his palms. "No violence, please. Don't mess up this pretty face." He laughed.

Griff's frown broke into a grin. "Come on, asshole. Let's practice."

The two men continued teasing each other as they took the field. They did warm up exercises and ran on the track. Memories of Lauren in his bed invaded his brain. Buddy kept talking, but Griff wasn't listening.

"So, how was she?"

"Lauren's not a pick-up. Not some fuck buddy."

"Yeah, so? Tell me. Come on."

"Shut up." Griff pushed ahead, adding speed to avoid his friend's questions. Remembering the feel of her soft skin made Griff's fingers tingle. He couldn't wait to touch her again. She was sweet, loving, and wary. But when he got her going, she perked up, responding to his every caress. A twitch between his legs told him he'd better steer his mind in another direction, or he'd soon have a raging hard-on.

The two men stopped and emptied two water bottles. Griff tossed a few short passes to warm up. Then, the men got serious. Buddy ran and Griff threw for the next forty-five minutes. They stopped, grabbed more water, and headed to the workout room. Griff iced down his arm then showered at the stadium. He took care combing his hair, shaved, and slapped on an expensive aftershave in expectation of the night to come.

On the way home, he roared into town to do a few errands. When he placed the key in the lock, Spike's familiar barking greeted him. Upon Griff's entering the house, the pug jumped on him, trying to lick his face. A tantalizing aroma drifted to his nostrils and made his stomach growl.

Lauren sashayed out of the kitchen, wearing a simply stunning sundress in peach. The bodice hugged her breasts, attracting his gaze, tempting him. He licked his lips. Her dark, shiny hair flowed around her shoulders, ending in a loose curl or two. Her smile was broad, and her eyes sparkled. *A woman well loved.*

"For you," he said, offering her a dozen red roses.

Her eyes widened. "Oh my. Really? That wasn't necessary."

"I wanted to."

"They're lovely. I'll put them in water. What do you want to drink?"

"Beer? Something smells great. What's cooking?"

Lauren handed him an open bottle before arranging the long stem beauties in a vase. "Lasagna. My grandmother's recipe."

"My favorite." He put his hand on the small of her back as he accompanied her into the kitchen. Griff set the table while Lauren made a salad. "Wine?" he asked.

"Perfect."

Griff opened a bottle of Cabernet Sauvignon while she created homemade dressing and tossed the salad. The table was set. He retrieved the candlesticks from the dining room and set them down then struck a match.

"How romantic," she said.

He took the hot dish from the oven, placed it on a trivet, and then bowed low, pulling out her chair. She added the salad and took her seat. The candlelight kissed her face with its warm glow, making her eyes sparkle. He sat across from her. Griff hadn't seen such a beautiful woman off a movie screen.

As Lauren served the meal, he sat back, waiting for the piping hot pasta to cool. "Will you spend the night with me tonight?"

She shot him a sly look and grinned. "Guess where I was today?"

He shook his head and raised his eyebrows.

"At the drugstore. Guess who filled a prescription for birth control pills?"

He laughed and took her hand in his.

The next morning, Griff started training camp with a positive attitude. With a sexy woman in his bed and a hot meal waiting for him every night, his appetites were sated. He worked hard and drove home tired. Lauren remembered what he had told her about Kathy and every evening a hot, herbal bath was waiting for him.

He looked forward to the end of the day, returning to Lauren. It surprised him how comfortable he had become living with her and Spike. Sometimes in the car, as he sped toward the Victorian, he'd marvel that maybe he'd found a woman who captured Kathy's talents in the kitchen and bested Carla's in the bedroom.

Life was good, except for Sunday, when he called California. Most times, Joe and Missy were happy to talk to him. They filled him in on their school and sports achievements, bragging shamelessly, seeking his praise and approval. On the Sundays when they weren't around, he'd chat with his sister, then hang up, trying to forget the void in his life. He'd shut down, escaping for a run, a drive, or even a long walk with Spike.

Loneliness welled up in his chest, creating a hollowness inside.

When he returned, feeling guilty about abruptly taking off, Lauren was forgiving. She didn't mention it, but rather asked his opinion about something trivial or offered him a special snack. Gratitude flowed through him that she knew when to back off. Was it possible he was falling in love with the woman he accused, in open court, of being a dog abuser?

He pushed the idea aside and focused on training camp and enjoying his time with Lauren, ignoring the fact she was creeping closer to his well-protected heart. While he had decided he needed to get married, he still wasn't used to the idea of giving up bachelorhood and settling down. He wondered if he'd be able to make the switch from man-whore to husband material.

Part of him questioned if she was nice to him because he paid her thirty-five hundred bucks every month. *She could fool me in the kitchen and the living room, but never the bedroom.* He smiled to himself at the stupid idea that Lauren's affections could be bought.

When the game schedule was handed out, he tacked it up on the fridge and decided that out-of-town bed buddies had to become a thing of the past. Would he have the willpower to walk away from attractive, willing women when he was on the road? Time would tell.

LAUREN BUNDLED SPIKE into the car, fastening his leash into the seatbelt in the back before she slid behind the wheel. She was pumped up about her new assignment, decorating an entire house for a man who was in Europe. She breathed a sigh of relief he wasn't around, as she feared the same outcome as with Bob. *Something about decorating a guy's house makes you sexy to him.*

She chuckled. No need to hunt for a man. She had one available twenty-four seven, right in her own home.

Thoughts of Griff brought a smile to her face. Her nipples tingled at the memory of their lovemaking the night before. She admitted to herself that he was a masterful lover. Bob hadn't been inspired or inspiring, like the handsome quarterback. After she and Bob married, sex had become him rolling over a few seconds after getting in bed, two minutes of foreplay, and then *wham,* and it was over. She had settled for it because he was going to be the father of her child.

Now, her life was completely different. The breeze coming in the open window, caressing her neck as she drove, called to mind Griff's whisper-soft kisses. A twinge of soreness between her legs as she moved to step on the gas reminded her of his amazing stamina. A glance in the rearview mirror showed a happy face. Stress wrinkles between her brows had faded. Frown lines by her mouth, as well.

Anxiety had drained out of her body, leaving taut muscles relaxed. The occasional stomach cramps had gone away. Her shoulders now rested where they belonged instead of two inches higher.

Lauren parked the car and retrieved Spike. He took the opportunity to relieve himself before trotting alongside his pretty mistress into the office. She greeted Annette while Spike circled on his little bed then settled in for a nap. The decorator got to work, opening up drawings on her computer and fishing a book of wallpaper samples from her drawer. She sighed and smiled as she thumbed through design after design. Creating a beautiful living environment for people made her happy.

She hummed a love song as she made notes. Her cell rang. It was Marnie.

"Needing to go out to lunch."

"Can't today. I have a new project. Maybe tomorrow?"

"Works for me. How's your new boyfriend?"

"Griff? Fine."

"Are you madly in love?"

"Love? No way. It's an affair. That's all. I'm sure it will be over as soon as his house is livable again."

"Hah! I know you. It's love. I can hear it in your voice."

"Baloney. That's static. I'm in the middle of something here. Can I call you tomorrow morning for time and place?"

"Sure. Just don't lie to yourself, Lauren."

She closed her phone and tried to focus on the computer screen, but her mind wandered. *It's not love. I'd never be in love with a man who wants children. An affair. Wonderful for however long it lasts.*

Daydreams captured her attention. Exactly what would it be like to be married to Griff Montgomery? She pictured them in her house, cooking together, watching sports television, and in bed. Resting her chin on her hand, she propped up her head and closed her eyes.

A vision of Griff pulling her into the shower with him was followed by a chase through the house. She would escape to the bedroom, where he would catch up with her, throw her down on the bed, and make love to her. She would sigh when he called her "Mrs. Montgomery."

"He must be pretty special," a voice interrupted her dream.

Lauren's eyes flew open. "Who?"

"Whoever's got you sighing like that," said Annette, as she dropped off some sketches.

Lauren sensed her cheeks heating up. "Nothing. No one."

"Right." Annette chuckled. "Some hunk? A new guy?" She lounged on the corner of the desk.

"It's not important. Thank you for picking these up." Lauren took the papers one at a time and stacked them.

Annette shot a knowing smile at her. "Okay. If that's how you want to play it."

"I've got to talk to Harry." Lauren picked up her cell and searched the contacts.

"I can take a hint. But when you want to talk, I'd love to know all about him." Annette pushed to her feet and headed toward her office.

Lauren gazed out the window. *He's mine now. But for how long? Can I stay cool? Maybe it's already too late for that.*

Chapter Ten

GRIFF SUITED UP IN their colors and hit the field with the rest of the team. Half wore green jerseys and the other half, white. They divided into groups and lined up. Mac Jenkins hiked the ball to Griff, who spotted Buddy and sailed a pass right to his friend. Tony Hastings was the opposing quarterback.

When the defensive team took over, Griff, watched Tony and analyzed the young man's every move. He had his own style. When Tony's team lost possession of the ball, Griff trotted back out with confidence. With great protection from the offensive line, he connected with receiver after receiver. He was in the zone as his body performed perfectly, hitting target after target. He smiled and his satisfaction grew. *No way is that kid replacing me.*

He loved football, especially on the days when he could do no wrong.

Griff worked hard, the way he had every year. Always the first on the field for practice and the last one to leave the weight room, he earned a rep as workaholic. He didn't care because he reaped the benefits of all the hours he put in. His winning record spoke for itself—two Super Bowl victories and two losses, the latter by only one touchdown each time. Even making the Super Bowl was a victory in itself. That's what Kathy had said, and he agreed.

On top of that, he had been chosen top QB in the NFL for four years in a row by Sports News Digest, the top sports newspaper in the country. He had the loyalty of the team he captained to victory and socked away large bonuses every year. Glory wasn't the only reward.

The team owner upped the year-end loot by ten percent for each playoff game won. And Griff Montgomery ruled playoffs, motivated by the pressure and responsibility.

Practice ended at five thirty. The men hit the showers. Griff knew he'd pay for several idle weeks with sore muscles and couldn't wait to sink his sexy ass in a tub of hot water. He rinsed the sweat off and dressed quickly then called Lauren to give his planned time of arrival.

He grinned as he maneuvered his fancy car through winding streets home. A satisfying and regular sex life helped him maintain focus, relax, and not tense up on the field. He had Lauren to thank for that. He pushed the speed limit in anticipation of another delicious night in the bedroom, if he wasn't too tired.

He parked the car in the driveway and almost skipped up to the door. A spicy aroma and barking dog greeted him. His gaze caught Lauren bending over to pick up something in the living room. He ogled her nicely rounded rear. *Might want to try it doggie style.* He imagined grabbing her hips and plunging into her. The idea caused a tightening in his groin.

"You're home," she said, straightening up. "Right on time. Bath is ready."

"What smells so good?" He closed the door behind him.

"A new recipe for Jambalaya."

His mouth watered. "I'll make it fast."

She held up her hand. "Take your time. I still have to put on the rice."

He kissed her quickly before taking the steps two at a time to the larger tub in her bathroom on the second floor. Stripping off his running shorts and T-shirt, he eased down into the steamy water. The air was heavy and moist with a scent of vanilla and mint. The heat penetrated his aching muscles.

While he scrubbed his legs with the washcloth, he went over Tony's plays in his mind. *The kid is pretty good. Of course, that's not against a full line-up of heavy-duty defensemen. Still. He's pretty accurate.* He scrunched down to let the soothing water cover his chest. *He's not as good as I am. Not by a long shot.* Peace flowed through Griff as the herbs soaked the exhaustion out of him.

"Dinner in five," Lauren called up the stairs.

Griff rose to his feet and wrapped a towel around his waist. *A great dinner. Then Lauren.* He snickered to himself. *Am I too tired?* An image of her, naked, flashed through his mind. A chuckle, a snort, and his body's reaction convinced him he'd be in fine form to perform as well in the bedroom as he had on the field. He dried off, tossed on shorts and a T-shirt, and then descended the stairs, sniffing the enticing food.

When he entered the kitchen, he mentally stripped Lauren bare as she placed the dishes on the table.

After dinner, Griff cleaned up. They settled on the sofa to watch a movie. When the film finished, Lauren disappeared into her bedroom upstairs. He was tired. Practices at eight in the morning made him go to bed early. *Ten o'clock. Time to hit the sack.* He called to her, "Lauren, bedtime!"

She poked her head around the wall. "You go ahead. I'm going to sleep up here."

"How come? You mad or something?"

He watched a blush redden her cheeks. "No, it's just...well...not tonight. Tomorrow, either."

He cocked his head to one side. "I don't get it."

"I thought you had a sister," she said, exasperation evident in her voice. "No sex tonight."

"What am I missing here?" He scratched his scruffy face. "Do you want me to shave?"

"Sometimes you're really dense. It's my time of the month."

"Oh! Yeah. Got it. Okay." He finished cleaning up and went to his room. But he couldn't get comfortable in the empty bed. He rolled over, stretching out his arm, reaching for Lauren, but coming in contact with a cold sheet, instead of a warm body.

Griff slung his legs over the side, pulled up his boxers, and tiptoed upstairs. She was lying still. He couldn't tell if she was asleep or awake. Slowly, he pulled down the bedcovers.

She rolled over and gasped. "What are you doing?" She rubbed her eyes.

"The bed downstairs is empty."

"You missed me?"

"Yeah."

"But I said no—"

He put his finger over her lips. "I know. It's not about sex." He slipped in next to her.

She stared at him. "Then, what?"

"I like having you next to me. It's not like you've got a fatal, contagious disease. When we were kids, Kathy used to use it to get out of chores. Pissed me off."

She chuckled. "Not me. Never had a problem with it."

"Then, it's okay if I bunk in with you?"

"Sure." She smiled before she turned her back to him.

Griff scootched up against her, wrapping an arm around her middle. He rubbed the soft cotton of her nightgown between his fingers. Lauren pulled her knees up a bit, and he eased his behind hers.

"That okay?"

"Great."

"You don't have cramps or anything, do you? Need me to rub your stomach?"

She laughed. "I'm fine. This position is perfect."

He kissed her neck. "Goodnight, baby."

"Night."

The weariness in his body took over, and he was asleep in seconds.

AS USUAL, GRIFF HEADED to training camp before the rest. His muscles were still a bit sore from the day before. It worried him that he wasn't bouncing back as fast as he had in the past. Only two years ago, he could do training camp, hoist a few at The Savage Beast, and after only five hours sleep, still perform well the next day. Now, he needed eight hours, and he'd cut out alcohol. And still, his legs screamed at him during warm-ups.

Arriving early gave him time to stretch. He hit the weight room, did crunches and push-ups, and then squats until his muscles were warm. He joined the rest of the team for a run at nine. After, it was time for warm-ups on the field. Griff loved the physicality of football. Even the exercises made him feel good, once he broke through the initial stiffness.

At the lunch break, Buddy joined him. They stuffed themselves with sandwiches and washed them down with Gatorade. Griff massaged his calf and stretched while he digested.

"Sore?"

Griff nodded. "Didn't used to be."

"Getting old?"

"Nah. Just tight." He wasn't about to admit anything, even to his best friend.

"Don't worry. You're still the best," Buddy said, taking a bite of his second roast beef hero.

"I'd better be. Tony's here to take over if I'm not."

"Aw, come on. He's a rookie. Got a lot to learn. You're light years ahead of him."

"I hope so." Griff wiped his mouth after finishing the last of his food.

The men lined up to scrimmage.

"You got a big mouth, Montgomery," Trunk Mahoney said, squatting down into position.

"Remember, Trunk, this is just a scrimmage."

"No tackling. Touch only," the assistant coach hollered.

"Yeah, if you get taken out...now we got a replacement." Trunk shot an evil grin at Griff.

Glancing up, Griff spied Coach Bass up in the box with the owner. *Hope they're not just watching Tony.*

The ball was snapped, and the action began.

Out of the corner of his eye, Griff spotted Trunk coming for him. He slid down, hugging the ball.

"Lucky for you," the bruiser said.

"If you put me out of the game, Coach Bass will fire your ass so fast."

"Don't want to take you out, just make you feel the pain a little."

"Go fuck yourself, Mahoney."

"Like I did your mother last night?"

"Suck my dick, asshole."

"Why? You not getting any?" Trunk smirked.

Griff rifled the ball at Trunk's groin.

The linebacker doubled over. "I'll get you, fucker," he muttered, his face screwed up.

"Oops. Sorry. Meant that for Carruthers," Griff said, without a note of regret in his voice.

They lined up again. This time, Trunk managed to get through. He grabbed Griff by the facemask and pulled him down then kicked the quarterback in the stomach.

Griff couldn't breathe. He clutched his belly, gasping for air.

"So sorry," Mahoney said, bending down to whisper, "Never fuck with me again, asshole."

Buddy ran over and got in Mahoney's face. "You did that on purpose. You piece a shit!"

Trunk shoved Buddy in the shoulder, and he went flying, falling backwards over Griff, who was still prone. The assistant coach blew a whistle and ran over to the quarterback, who had moved up to his knees. The EMT's ran over to attend to Griff, who had regained his voice.

"I'm okay. But if that guy touches me again, I'll rip him apart."

The assistant coach chewed his pen. "Don't do that. He's a lot bigger than you, Griff."

"So what?" The quarterback pushed to his feet.

"You'd better go home and rest," the coach said. "Take the afternoon off. You're doing great. Missing this won't matter."

Griff headed for the locker room. One look back showed him Tony Hastings, putting on his helmet. *Fuck! Rookie is playing in my place.*

Trunk Mahoney gave Griff a half bow and the finger then turned back to the scrimmage.

Griff changed quickly. His belly hurt, so he drove slower than usual. When he arrived home, the house was empty except for Spike, who greeted him at the door, barking. He went right to the tub and turned on the faucet. A small packet of bath herbs sat on the counter. He dumped the contents in. Then, he found Spike and carried him into the bathroom.

The pug circled then lay down on the bathmat and curled into a ball, his big eyes focused on Griff as the quarterback slipped into the hot water. He rested his head on the back of the old-fashioned tub and closed his eyes.

"I hate Trunk Mahoney," he said.

Spike snorted.

Griff rubbed his own tender belly gently. "He's an asshole."

No response from Spike.

"Who do you like better, Lauren or me?" The quarterback cracked open an eye to glance at the bathmat.

The pug yawned and shifted position.

"Yeah, Lauren. I know. But you've been with her a lot longer. I'll grow on you. Trust me. *I've* already grown on her, haven't I?" He chuckled, his lips turning up in a sly little smile.

Spike snored.

"You don't have to admit it. She likes me almost as much as she likes you." He dunked a loofah then squeezed soothing droplets on the biceps of this throwing arm.

The only reply from the sleeping pooch was a soft snort.

"Okay, okay, maybe not almost as much. But I'm getting there." Silence.

"I get why you like her best. She's amazing, isn't she?"

The soft burr from Spike answered the question.

"Yeah. I know. And pretty. She's got the cutest little—"

A knock on the door made Griff jump and slosh water on the floor. He swore.

"Griff? Is that you?" a feminine voice called.

"Yeah. You're home early."

"Came home to start dinner. Who are you talking to? Are you in the bathtub with a woman?" Her tone became tense. He could visualize the red in her neck, her hands fisted on her hips.

"Are you crazy? No. See for yourself."

She threw open the door hard enough that it banged against the wall, waking Spike, who barked.

"It's okay, boy. She's just checking up on me." Griff chuckled, shooting her a flirtatious glance.

"You were talking to Spike?" Her eyebrows rose.

"I plead the fifth. And he's not talking, either." Griff stood up.

She burst out laughing. He followed her gaze to his groin. When she realized she was caught staring, a beautiful blush lit up her cheeks, and she threw him a towel.

"Cover up," she muttered, lowering her lashes.

"Are you sure?"

She shot him an angry, embarrassed look that made him laugh as he wrapped the cloth around his waist and stepped out of the tub.

"You're home early, too," she commented.

"That's a long story." He pushed his fingertips gingerly into his middle and cringed. The area was sensitive.

"You hurt?"

"It's nothing."

"Doesn't look like nothing to me."

"It'll be gone by tomorrow."

"Accident?"

"Accidentally on purpose."

She ran her hand gently over his belly then bent and kissed it. "That should make it all better."

Griff snaked his arm around her waist and pulled her to him.

"Now, something else needs attention."

TWO WEEKS OF TRAINING camp passed quickly. After one preseason game, the Kings prepared to hit the road for a week. Griff had a special suitcase he filled with toilet articles and underwear that was always ready to go. He took Lauren out for dinner, packed, and retired by ten.

The next morning, he left early. She awoke to an envelope with her name on it, sitting on the kitchen table. Dread lodged in her heart. *Is his house ready? Is he leaving now?* Her pulse kicked up as she opened it. There was a note from Griff wrapped around something stiff inside.

Been meaning to give you these. Bring Don and one of his kids.

Griff

She slipped her fingers under the flap and found three season box tickets. She wondered if they had been Kathy's tickets and if they were in the family box. A smile spread across her face. *Don will love it.* She picked up her phone.

"Guess what?"

"Dad passed?"

"No! What a horrible thing to guess! This is good news."

"Oh? What?"

"Griff gave me three season box seat tickets."

"You're kidding, right?"

"This is the real thing. Pick one of your kids and get your butt down here for the game a week from Sunday."

"Damn! I'm there. I'll bring Vinnie. Thank you, thank you, thank you."

Grinning, Lauren hopped upstairs to her closet. She tore through her wardrobe, searching for the right outfit. *Don't want Griff to be embarrassed.* The idea of meeting his teammates sent a thrill up her spine and anxiety to her stomach at the same time.

She stood back, shaking her head. None of her old clothes would do. *I haven't been shopping in an age. Not since I was buying pregnancy clothes.* A pain shot through her heart. *Stop thinking about that. Remember what the group said. Obsessing is not healthy.*

She took Spike for a quick walk then jumped in her car and headed for The Cottage, the stylish boutique on Main Street. Now that she had a little money to burn and was hanging out with a star athlete, she had to dress better.

Squaring her shoulders, Lauren walked into the shop, where she was greeted by a smiling saleslady.

"What can I help you with today?"

"I need a special outfit to wear to a football game."

"High school? College?" the older woman asked.

"Professional," Lauren said, a note of pride creeping into her voice.

"The Kings?"

"None other."

"Now, that's something to dress for. Come over here. We have a great selection of corduroy slacks and matching jackets. And we even have olive green. With your eyes, that would be perfect."

Lauren followed her to a rack by the wall and started sifting through the clothing.

"Do you mind me asking? Are you going with a friend?"

"My brother, actually."

"Oh." The saleslady's tone dropped, drawing Lauren's attention.

"But I got the tickets from my boyfriend, Griff Montgomery."

The woman's eyes widened. "You're Griff Montgomery's girl? Oh, my. A celebrity. Martha, Martha! The store owner is going to want to handle you personally."

Panic seized Lauren. *Why didn't I keep my mouth shut? What if Griff doesn't want anyone to know? Now, it'll be in the papers and everything.* Beads of sweat gathered on her forehead.

The manager—*Martha, apparently*—joined them.

"This young woman is Griff Montgomery's girlfriend. She's going to the next game."

"No, really, I'm not. We're just friends." Lauren bit her lip.

"Friends? With a woman who looks like you?" Martha cocked an eyebrow. "You're dating him, right?"

"Well, dating might be a stretch. You see, we live in the same house..."

"Oh my God! You're living with Griff Montgomery?" The manager's face lit up.

"No, no, it's not like that. We're roommates. We're sharing the dog, and the court said—"

"Are you engaged? Come on, you can tell me. You're going to be Mrs. Montgomery, aren't you?" Martha sidled up to her and elbowed her in the ribs.

The blood drained from Lauren's face. "Please, please, don't say anything. We're not engaged. Honestly. And if that appeared in the newspaper, Griff would bust a gut."

"Of course, dear. Of course. Your secret is safe with me. Now, let's find you the best outfit for that game. If—and I do say only 'if'—you're his girlfriend, you must look your best. I have some cashmere sweaters in the corner there. And I think I have the perfect color for you." The woman patted Lauren on the arm and led the way to a table in the back.

Lauren wrapped her fingers around the softest material she'd ever felt. She wondered what Griff would say if he touched her wearing one of those. A giggle bubbled up at the thought while an ache between her legs grew.

"Very sexy, isn't it?" the older woman whispered.

"Damn right. I'll take one. Which is the best color for me?"

Martha stepped back, narrowed her eyes, and selected turquoise. "Perfect with that olive green pantsuit, too."

"I'll take it."

"Wise choice, dear. If you're not engaged yet, you soon will be." The knowing smile on her lips raised a question Lauren had been avoiding. *He's not serious. Just this woman's idea. That'll never happen.* When she had herself convinced, she picked up her package and walked out of the store.

Chapter Eleven

LOS ANGELES, CA

Griff and Buddy had their own rooms on the road. They had a curfew, too, which made getting laid a bit tricky.

On the bus from the airport, Buddy turned to his roommate. "Got a date with Cheryl?"

"Haven't called her."

"How come?" Buddy's eyebrows rose.

"Not interested."

"Cheryl Charles's the hottest thing since the sun."

"Maybe." Just then, Griff's phone went off.

You're playing the Tigers this weekend. I saved Saturday night. Where you staying?

Cheryl

"Shit." Griff sent back the name of the hotel.

"Bad news?"

"Sort of. Cheryl."

"Sounds like good news to me. Somebody's gonna get laid."

"Not me."

"Why not?"

"Cheryl's too possessive. When she finds out Kathy's moved, she'll be pressing me to get married."

"And that's bad?"

"Hell, yeah. I don't want to marry her. Never have. She's boring as dirt. All she can talk about is celebrity gossip and clothes."

"Didn't know you two did much talking." Buddy snickered.

Griff punched his friend in the arm. "That's the point. Talking with her was a waste of time."

"New gal got you wound up, eh?"

"Shut the fuck up, Buddy."

The receiver laughed and went back to reading his newspaper. Griff stared out the window. *How the hell am I gonna do this? Don't want to hurt her.*

When they checked in, there was a message for him. Cheryl was waiting in the bar. Griff unpacked then joined Buddy.

"I can't believe she's downstairs." Griff shook his head slowly.

"How you gonna get around Coach? You know we're not supposed to go into the hotel bar."

"Better talk up here. I don't want to make a scene."

"Uh oh. Gonna be fireworks? Want me to protect you?" Buddy barely contained his laughter.

"Very funny, asshole." Griff returned to his room, whipped out his phone, and texted Cheryl his room number. In ten minutes, there was a knock on his door. He looked through the peephole. Cheryl wore a low cut dress. *Always a dress. Less to take off.* He sensed heat in his cheeks at how their relationship had gone. *Fuck buddies.* He cast his gaze to the floor, swallowed, and then opened the door.

"Hey, there, handsome. Long time, no see." She tilted her chin up to receive his kiss.

He dodged her lips and pecked her on the cheek.

Her eyes grew wide. "What the hell?"

"Sit down," he said, motioning her to a chair, not the bed. "Want something from room service?"

She shook her head. "Something on your mind?"

"Sort of." He paced.

"Well, spit it out."

He twisted open a bottle of water from the mini-fridge and took a long swig. "It's over between us." He'd planned to let her off easy, but the words were out before he could stop them.

"What?"

"We're done."

"But I thought...I mean, now that Kathy's moved out... I thought maybe I could move in."

"I don't think so." He took another slug.

Her face darkened. "You can't just brush me off like that."

"I can't? Why not?" He cocked an eyebrow. Griff knew he was being harsh, but couldn't stop himself.

Her eyes held fear. "Why don't we go get more comfortable?" She slipped off her shoes.

"I don't think so, Cheryl."

"Why not?"

"I've changed."

"Since Kathy left?"

"That's right."

They were silent. Cheryl reached for his hand, but he stepped away. Dread rose in his chest as he waited for the tantrum he expected next.

She looked at the floor before glancing up to meet his gaze. There were tears in her eyes. "You're everything to me, Griff."

He shifted his weight to the other leg. Cheryl pushed to her feet and moved toward him. She ran her hands up his chest and looked into his eyes. Her soft expression and exposed cleavage called to him. The pleading look on her face melted him a bit. He needed to put distance between them before biology took over. "Look, Cheryl. It's not you. It's not personal..."

"Not personal? It can't *get* much more personal."

"I'm someplace else in my life right now."

"So? I'll go there with you. I love you."

"Do you?" He stepped away. "What do you do for...uh, fun, when I'm back East? I seriously doubt you're home knitting sweaters for soldiers."

His comment brought a deep blush to her cheeks. "Same as you, I bet."

"How would you know? Love? No. Convenient? Yes. We share a great dinner and a bed when I'm here. It's been fun. You're great in the sack, Cheryl. But I'm not doing that anymore."

"Oh?" She raised an eyebrow. "Got someone at home already?"

Now, it was his turn to be embarrassed. He cast his gaze to the floor.

"Ah, now I get it. I see. You've found someone you're serious about."

"Not serious. No. I'm not."

"A fuck buddy?"

His cheeks heated.

"So, I'm out with the garbage. Replaced, like that," she said, snapping her fingers.

"It's not like that. I didn't plan this. I like you, Cheryl. I always will."

"Yeah? Big fucking deal. You like me? But not enough to give me a chance. I could sublet my apartment and quit my job. I'd give you great sex every night, Griff. Please. Let me move in. Just try it for...say, three months?" Tears spilled on her cheeks.

His heart squeezed. He hated himself for hurting her and hated her for begging. How could he turn her down? He shook his head, nonetheless.

"Come on. She can't be that great. What's she got that I don't?"

"I'm sorry, Cheryl. This isn't going to work."

She stepped closer and slapped him across the face, hard. He flinched, his hand flying to his cheek.

"You're a user. A fuck-and-chuck guy. You got what you wanted. Sex on demand. Now, you're taking off. Shallow, selfish creep. I don't know what I ever saw in you in the first place." She picked up her bag, swiped at the tears on her cheeks, and walked toward the door, her nicely rounded hips swinging, tempting him to change his mind.

"I'm sorry, Cheryl. I never meant to hurt you. If I had seen how involved you were getting..."

"What did you think? That I slept with you and it meant nothing?"

"We didn't see each other often. I had no idea."

"Then, you're as dumb as you are mean. Fuck you, Griffin Montgomery. Go to Hell." She slammed the door on her way out.

Griff checked his face in the mirror. There was a red spot, but it would fade. Heaviness hit his heart. She had treated him like a lowlife, and maybe he was. *Am I making a mistake? Was I a jerk?*

His stomach growled. Griff picked up the phone and gave the okay for the meal preplanned by the Coach to be sent up. Buddy arrived along with Griff's food. He lounged in an upholstered chair while Griff sat at the small table and chowed down.

"That was fast. A real quickie," Buddy said.

"An easy letdown that wasn't so easy." Griff cut off a piece of steak.

"You really broke up?"

Griff nodded while he chewed.

"Are you sure?" Buddy probed.

"No, but it's done."

His friend shook his head. "I don't know if you're a man of great willpower, or an idiot."

"Neither do I," said the quarterback.

Griff wasn't ready to face the fact that he was giving up good, steady road trip sex for a woman who didn't want to get married.

"How'd it go?"

"Not well," Griff replied.

"You survived."

"Barely. Good thing she wasn't armed." Griff leaned back and dipped his fork in mashed potatoes.

"Can you give me her number?"

Griff threw his spoon at his friend, for a direct hit. "Back to your own room, asshole."

"Hey, it doesn't hurt to ask."

"Yeah, it does."

Buddy sauntered over to the door. "Good night, Casanova," he said, before ducking out.

BEER IN HAND, GRIFF nudged the living room curtain aside and peered out the window. Lauren opened a package of small boxes and spilled them into a large bowl. He cast a disapproving eye toward her, his face stormy.

"Raisins?"

"They're healthy."

"Kids don't want healthy on Halloween. Sugar. Lots of sugar." He glanced around the room while she added another bag. His brows knitted when his gaze landed on the pumpkin. "You call that a pumpkin?"

"What do you call it?"

"I call it a disgrace. You should have at least two. One with a really scary face. Maybe two like that. This one is so happy, he's ridiculous. Silly. Stupid looking."

Her chest tightened, and her eyes stung at his blunt criticism. After a deep breath, she stared at him. "What's bugging you?"

"Your pumpkin. And no decorations. You don't know how to buy candy, either. No kid wants a box of raisins. You don't know shit about kids, do you?"

She sucked in air. "How could I? I don't have any." Her lower lip quivered.

"I'm sorry, Lauren, I didn't mean..." He reached for her, but she pulled away, upsetting the bowl and sending the little boxes scattering across the floor.

She shrank from his grasp and scooted out of his path and up to her room, slamming the door. Falling on the bed, she shed a couple of tears then stopped. *He didn't mean to hurt you.* She flipped off her loafers and sat up, cross-legged.

There was a soft knock on the door. "Can I come in?"

"I suppose," she huffed, swiping at the wetness on her cheeks.

He entered slowly, almost as if he was expecting her to throw something. "I didn't mean—"

"I know, I know. I'm sorry. I overreacted."

"I'm grouchy today. Guess I'm missing the kids."

"Were you around for Halloween?"

"Most times. If there wasn't a game. Sometimes, we were on the road. I hated that. Halloween is the best kid's holiday. Kathy took care of the costumes, and I did everything else."

"Like what? What did you do?" She slid over.

He joined her. "Carved the pumpkins. The kids would make drawings. Then, we'd vote on our two favorites."

"Didn't that cause friction?"

He laughed. "Yeah. They could be competitive. Missy was a better artist than Joey. Uh, Joe. So, we had a rule that you couldn't vote for two from one person."

"What else?"

"I bought the candy. The kids helped with that, too."

"And?"

"I decorated the house. We had little ceramic Jack O'Lanterns and ghouls and witches." His eyes grew distant. "Fake cobwebs. Sometimes, I'd even dress up. I got the scariest mask I could find. If you tell anyone, I'll deny it."

"Bet you scared the hell out of kids."

"Kathy made me stop after two years. Some of them cried." He laughed. "It was fun."

"Did you dress up as anything else after that?"

"The next year, I dressed as a clown, thinking it would make the kids laugh. But they were more scared of that than my monster mask." He chuckled. "After that, I settled for a pirate. The shadow on my face was my own."

"I bet you're one sexy pirate."

"Hmm." He lifted an eyebrow. "Never thought of that. Have to try that in the bedroom."

"With pantaloons, a sword, and a parrot?" She grinned.

"How about no pantaloons, and I bring my own sword? Forget the parrot."

"Polly want a cracker?"

"Maybe Polly wants something else." He leaned down and captured her mouth with his.

His tongue slipped over hers, his arm strong around her. Lauren closed her eyes and breathed in his scent, fresh lime soap mixed with his masculinity. Her palms pressed against his chest, feeling hard muscle as he pulled her closer. Her nipples tingled when his fingers closed around her rib cage. She wanted his touch.

As if he could read her mind, his hand slipped up over her breast, pinching the peak gently between his fingers. The sensation flew down to her core. She squirmed, itching to have him inside her.

As she opened the buttons on his shirt, the doorbell rang. She sighed. "Halloween, damn it," she muttered, leaning back.

He chuckled. "Hold that thought. I'll be back." He kissed her cheek before pushing to his feet. She followed him downstairs and into the kitchen, where he pulled out a bag out from the pantry.

"Where did you get that?" she asked, peeking inside, finding it overflowing with candy bars.

"I had a feeling you might not know what to get," he said, hauling the loot to the front door. "So, I bought these a couple of days ago." The doorbell sounded again.

Lauren laughed and shook her head. The doorbell rang a third time. By now, Spike was going bananas, barking until he was hoarse.

That was her last moment of peace for hours, as the kids of Monroe located Griff Montgomery, their hero, in his new home. She sat on the sofa and watched him give out almost as many autographs as he did Hershey bars. He talked with them, commenting on their costumes and answering their questions about football. She marveled at his patience.

He appeared relaxed and happy. *He'd make a good father.* A heaviness filled her chest at the thought of what it would be like to carry his child, and then lose it. She sighed. *He'd be as crushed as I would. How could I do that to him? He deserves to have kids.*

At ten o'clock, the doorbell was still ringing. Lauren yawned and headed for Griff's bedroom. She washed up, got naked, and slipped between the sheets. Even when they didn't have sex, which wasn't often, she liked to sleep nude, especially with him next to her.

The sound of the door opening woke her up. The bed creaked and dipped under the quarterback's weight. The room remained dark.

"Arrgh," Griff said in her ear.

Lauren jumped and giggled at the same time. She rolled over.

"I left me eye patch in me other pantaloons and me parrot on board me ship. Does ye fair lady fancy a tussle with ye old pirate?"

Lauren couldn't stop laughing. He put his hand on her waist and drew her up against his bare body. Lauren closed her fingers around his shoulder, tilting her head up for his kiss. He glided his palm up and down her body, creating heat.

"Where's your peg leg?"

"Right here, darlin'," he said, placing her hand on his erect shaft.

Lauren burst out laughing, burying her face in his shoulder as she gripped him. "Damn, you're hard."

"You do that to me."

Lauren hooked one leg over his waist, and he seduced her, first with his fingers then his tongue.

"Let this horny old sea dog have a taste of ye, lassie." He parted her legs and slid down her body.

"Oh my God." Lauren fisted the sheet.

They sailed away together on a ship called "pleasure."

THE DAY AFTER HALLOWEEN, Griff hit the road. Lauren worked on her decorating assignment from Annette, cooked lasagna and chili, and then froze them. *Time to begin plans for Thanksgiving.* She checked Griff's schedule taped to the fridge. His team was playing on Thanksgiving Day. The four o'clock game.

"Bummer." She sighed, pursing her lips. *His first Thanksgiving without his family. Damn. No turkey for Griff.* Her cell dinged. There was a message from Don.

Coming for turkey day?

She poured another cup of coffee and checked her watch. *I have an hour before my meeting.* She grabbed a piece of scrap paper from a drawer and began to make notes. When she was done, she sent a text to Don, packed up Spike, and headed to her office.

After dinner that night, she got a call from Griff. "We're in Cincinnati. Nothing to do here. Thought I'd find out what's going on at home."

"Nothing much. Spike and I are watching a movie."

"Buddy and I played cards. But strip poker's no fun without you."

She giggled. "Bull. You're probably watching some horror movie or porno."

"How'd you guess? I think it's Cindy Does Cincinnati."

She laughed again. "Good luck tomorrow."

"Thanks. I'm feeling good. Arm is loose."

They chatted for a while, bid goodnight, and ended the conversation. He called her every night he was away, always referring to the Victorian as home. When he said that, it gave her chills. Though it was only an affair, she'd never been happier. Sometimes they squabbled, but most of the time they got along.

And the sex was fantastic. She'd had to fake it from time to time with Bob. More and more, as their relationship deteriorated. But never with Griff. He made sure her needs were taken care of before his. Sometimes, she'd get turned on sitting at the dinner table, watching him chew, or brushing by him as she passed in the narrow pantry. Any touch from him ignited her fire.

The day he was due back, Lauren made his favorite—lamb stew. As it simmered on the stove, she finished up some important calls. She jumped as two large hands encircled her waist and lips tickled her neck. Griff's expensive aftershave, her favorite scent along with his own, wafted to her nose, mixing with the aroma of the mouth-watering stew.

She ended her conversation abruptly and turned. He kissed her hard, pressing up against her.

"Anything on the stove that can't wait?" he whispered in her ear, as he untied her apron and unbuttoned her pants.

"Nope." She reached behind to turn off the burner.

He stepped back, desire glowing in his eyes, and took her hand. She watched him yank his shirt from his pants and loosen his tie. By the time they reached the bedroom, Griff was already shirtless. He undressed Lauren quickly then picked her up and tossed her on the bed.

"No pirate today. Caveman." Naked, he crawled up to her.

"It's only been two weeks," she said.

"Seems like forever." He bent his head to kiss her while he cradled her breast with his hand.

Lauren didn't want him to know she'd been on pins and needles awaiting his return. A long, scented bubble bath while the stew cooked had gotten her in the mood.

"You smell good," he said, nuzzling her neck.

His knee parted her thighs and moved up to press against her center. She moved her lips to his neck and kissed her way down. When she got to his chest, she stopped, running her hands through the soft, dark hair for a moment before continuing. She closed her fingers around his erection and took it in her mouth. A loud groan from him made her smile. He combed his fingers through her hair as she stroked him up and down with her tongue.

Suddenly, he grabbed her arms and pulled her up, his mouth on hers, his hands under her rear end. He inserted one, then another, finger inside her. A moan from deep in her throat escaped as he pumped. His thumb circled her hot flesh.

Just before she came, he lifted her up and lowered her onto his hard shaft.

"Oh, God," she muttered, as he entered her.

"Damn." He closed his eyes for a second, grasping her hips and holding her still.

Lauren shifted her weight to her hands, resting on his shoulders. He slid one hand up to cup a breast and raised his head to kiss the peak. His tongue darted out to lick it, and Lauren thought she'd lose her mind.

"Go. Go," she said, straddling him and squeezing him a little.

He chuckled, his eyes staring through the darkness into hers. "I'm not a horse."

"Oh, sorry." She sensed her cheeks pinking.

He gripped her hips and moved her up and down on him. Lauren steadied herself with her hands, before lowering her mouth to his. He increased the pace, and she threw her head back as fire burst inside her, sending pleasure to every nerve, firecrackers to every inch of her body.

He raised both hands to her breasts and pinched the nipples, but not too hard. A tingle ran up her spine as her muscles continued to contract around him.

"Oh, baby." he whispered.

Lauren pushed down on his chest and pumped her hips up and down, increasing the pace until he began to moan. She watched his eyes squeeze shut, his lips draw back, showing his gleaming, white teeth. She moved harder and faster until he grabbed her hips, pushed down, and held her there. She loved to watch him in sexual delight, his face and neck flushed, his eyes closed. He blew out a breath and stroked her hair. She ran a finger down his rough cheek then kissed it.

He smiled up at her. "Crap. I've missed that."

"Rooming with Buddy isn't the same?"

"Hell, no. He'd never...well, besides, we don't share a room."

She grinned, delighted to see him embarrassed. It took a lot to make him uncomfortable. "I forgot," she said, dismounting.

"Com'ere," he ordered, sliding her across the smooth sheet and into his embrace.

"I thought men didn't like to cuddle?"

"Who told you that?" He wrapped his arms around her.

"Common knowledge."

"Liars. The hard part is taking my hands off you, not putting them on."

She snuggled into his chest. He was the first tall, muscular man she'd been with, and she liked it, liked the way he protected her. His skin on hers warmed her, as the air cooled with the night. *My own personal heat machine.*

He wrapped himself around her, his hands caressing wherever they landed. "Goodnight, sweetheart," he murmured in a lazy whisper.

"'Night, handsome prince." But he was already asleep.

Chapter Twelve

THANKSGIVING DAY—MORNING

Lauren tiptoed out of bed first, leaving Griff sleeping. He didn't need to be at the stadium until noon. Shivering, she grabbed her chenille robe and wrapped it around her slender body. Checking the thermometer outside, she frowned when she read thirty-seven degrees.

It's going to be cold for Griff's game today. Relief washed over her that she wouldn't be sitting in the stands, freezing for hours, to watch him play. Then, sympathy for him entered her heart. Cold played havoc with a quarterback's muscles, sometimes interfering with his ability to throw, as well as the receiver's ability to catch and hold on to the ball.

She prepared coffee and sat at the window, watching squirrels gather whatever they could before winter snows made the task harder. It was eight o'clock, and she felt good.

The slap of bare feet on tile drew her gaze. Griff entered, yawning, scratching his chest, and raking his fingers through his unruly hair. He wore plaid boxers and pulled a T-shirt over his head as he approached her.

"You're up early." She pulled down another mug.

"Might as well. I need to eat before I go."

"Pancakes?"

"And sausage, bacon, eggs. The whole thing."

Lauren put down her coffee and poured for him before tying her apron around her waist.

"How late will you be at your brother's house?"

"I don't know. Not late. We usually start Thanksgiving on the early side."

He grunted, scowled, and his shoulders slumped a little.

"I'm sorry you have to miss this," she said.

"You're sorry? Sorry isn't the word for it." He took a sip and leaned on the counter.

She laid her hand on his arm. "You must miss the kids."

"You might say that." He ducked his head, focusing on his mug.

"Does it interfere with your game?" Her brows furrowed.

"Nothing interferes with my game. I love football. I'll be in the zone. Totally focused."

She blew out a breath. "Good."

"It's after the game when things...uh, sort of fall apart." He turned his gaze to the window, spying several birds eating their fill at the feeder.

"I bet you'll win." She sidestepped his comment.

"I have no doubt. As long as the offensive line does their job and Buddy stays on his feet, I'm good."

Lauren mixed the batter and put up the bacon. Griff set the table then hit the shower. He always showered before a game. It seemed to boost his confidence. When he was done, the spread was ready.

He smiled as he lowered himself into a chair. "Looks great."

"Enjoy."

"You're not eating?"

She looked away, embarrassed.

"Oh, yeah. I forgot. You're having a big meal later." He looked down at his food.

Lauren wanted to touch his shoulder, to comfort him, but she refrained. Instead, she got busy cleaning up.

He looked up. "Hey, I'll do that."

"It's the least I can do today."

He sighed as he picked up another piece of bacon. "Thanks. Appreciate it."

She washed the bowls then joined him at the table.

"Have a pancake. This stack is too big, even for me."

They ate in silence. Before long, he kissed her goodbye, petted Spike, and was out the door. From the window, she watched him drive away. Her heart was heavy, knowing the sadness he felt.

She blew out a breath and went to work. Pulling down several bowls, she gathered flour, canned pumpkin, a fistful of spices, and two pie tins. She sat and cut up stale bread, mushrooms, and onions. She put them in a pan with a ton of butter and set it on the stove over a low flame while she prepared the crust for the pie and then the filling.

With a push of her finger, she added rock and roll to the room. Lauren sang along to her favorite songs while she whirled around the kitchen like a tornado. She manned the stuffing, the pie, and put yams in the oven.

Happiness bubbled up in her chest as she prepared one of her favorite meals. She flicked on the television and danced back and forth between the kitchen and the living room, so she could watch Griff play while she cooked. The house warmed with the oven on, and delicious aromas of baking yams and pumpkin pie mixed with the tangy scent of onions and the rich smell of mushrooms. Her stomach growled in anticipation of the excellent food to come.

THANKSGIVING DAY—AFTERNOON

Griff put his uniform on. A last minute pep talk from Coach Bass helped him get in the zone. He focused his energies on visualizing completed passes and touchdowns. Buddy joined him as their team ran out on the field. Because it took place in Monroe, the cheering was deafening. Home games buoyed Griff's spirits. He smiled at the fans and raised his helmet, which made them go wild.

He put his hand over his heart and sang along with the national anthem. His parents had been adamant about him singing at games. They had said it made people like him more and showed respect for the game and his country. The song had become ingrained in his brain and linked to football. It got him in the mood.

When it was over, the crowd cheered, and he went for the toss. The ground was soft and slippery from the rain three days earlier. He hated playing in muddy conditions, but it was part of the game. He won the toss and elected to kick off now and receive in the second half. He paced and watched from the area around the bench.

They were playing the Delaware Demons, and he wanted to see if he could learn anything from their quarterback, Mark Davis. Davis was good. He had won the Super Bowl in his rookie year.

The Kings defense was in top form, and Griff was on the field before long. He called the first play. Buddy got free, and Griff threw a bullet right to his favorite receiver, who caught it and took it for a fifteen yard gain and a first down.

The next play, the Kings' offensive line screwed up. Griff ran a few yards then had to slide to avoid a tackle. A fumble recovered by the Demons meant a turnover, and the Kings lost the ball. Davis came back with a long pass that enabled them to score.

The Kings bounced back with impressive blocking from the offensive line. Griff completed a pass to Homer Calloway, who ran it in for a touchdown. The score seesawed back and forth. It was tied then the Demons inched ahead with a field goal. Griff and the Kings leapfrogged over that score with a touchdown.

It was close at half time. Coach Bass tried to buck up the men in the locker room, as the Kings were behind by three. When they got back on the field, they redoubled their efforts and squeaked ahead. The defense fought to hold the Demons back, but they eked out a field goal to tie the game.

A rough tackle sent Homer to the showers. The pressure was on Griff. One more field goal for the Demons meant that only a touchdown could win the game. Griff nodded. It was a signal that indicated the quarterback was about to fake to another receiver and shoot the pass out to Buddy.

Jenkins hiked the ball. The linebackers did their job, while Griff sidestepped toward the right. The defense shifted, following the quarterback and removing coverage from Buddy. He tore down the line. Griff stepped back and, turning at the last minute, rifled a bullet to Buddy, who was wide open on the left. He snatched the pigskin out of the air and ran like hell to score.

The Demon defense managed to block the extra point, but their team couldn't come back, even for another field goal to tie. The Kings won the game. After shaking hands with the Delaware team, they retreated to the locker room, jubilant over their victory.

One player dropped down to his knees and thanked God. The men, muddy from head to toe, ripped off their uniforms and scrubbed themselves clean as fast as they could.

Homer Calloway, shaken up on a play, slipped on his jacket. "Nothing my wife's fine turkey can't cure," he said.

Trunk Mahoney licked his lips. "Antoinette makes great pumpkin pie. See ya later."

Even Buddy had someplace to go. "Maybe my cousin's wife's got a friend. Then, it'll be a real Thanksgiving." He snickered, as he headed for the door.

Griff took his time, letting his teammates shower first. They had someplace to go, and he didn't. His heart got heavy. Sadness crept into his bones. His mind turned to the celebration on the West Coast in Kathy's house. He wondered if the kids had watched his game. Probably not. They had their own lives now, and Uncle Griff was a million miles away.

The locker room emptied out. Even Coach Bass was gone before Griff left. *No reason to hurry.* He ambled over to his car, turning up the collar of his jacket against the winterish wind. He picked up his pace, anxious to get to his vehicle and blast the heat.

Within a few minutes, the interior was toasty, and Griff thawed out. *Even Spike will be gone.* When he remembered his victory, a small smile graced his lips. *At least we won.* He pulled into Eve Lane, which was lined with cars.

A glance at neighboring houses showed bright lights and the silhouettes of people celebrating, eating, drinking, and being with loved ones. He raised his gaze to Lauren's house, which was dark and empty looking. He gave a deep shuddering sigh.

He parked and heard a dog bark. *Almost sounded like Spike.* Maybe she had taken pity on him and left the dog. He'd stocked up on popcorn and beer and planned to watch X-rated movies until Lauren returned. His shoulders sagged as he headed for the door.

When he opened it, he nearly had a heart attack as a group of people shouted, "Surprise!"

Lights were flicked on. The smell of something wonderful was in the air. He looked around and only recognized Lauren and her brother, Don.

"What the hell?" Griff backed up.

Lauren came forward and took his arm. "We wanted you to have Thanksgiving. So, we made a surprise dinner here for you. You remember Don? This is his wife, Connie, and their kids, Vinnie, Carl, Marissa, and Teeny."

Griff raised his hand in greeting. "You waited for me?"

"Of course," Lauren said. "Sure took you long enough."

Tears stung at the back of his eyes. *Quarterbacks don't cry unless they have broken bones.* "Be right back," he said. As his control slipped, he escaped into the kitchen, leaning against the counter and breathing hard.

Lauren followed. "Is something wrong? Are you okay? Are you mad? We watched the game, and you seemed to be all right, but it took you a long time to get home. Is this the wrong thing?"

"Fine. I'm fine." He panted, taking a deep breath, and blinked rapidly. Then, he turned to her and smiled. "You planned this?"

"Guilty as charged."

"And kept it from me?" He moved closer.

"Wouldn't be a surprise if I told you." She tried to step back, but was blocked by a wall.

He advanced farther. "You let me think I was going to be alone?"

"As I said…surprise?" She shrugged.

He was right up against her, hands circling her waist, drawing her into his chest. "I could kiss you." He did. "Thank you, Lauren. So much. How did you know?"

"Your moping around here all week was a dead giveaway." She chuckled, fastening her arms around his neck.

"Hey! No PDA. There are minors here. Besides, I'm starvin' and the turkey's gonna get ruined," Don said, invading the kitchen and breaking up their little make-out session.

"It has to sit for a few minutes more. But we can get the other stuff out on the table." Lauren broke away from Griff.

"What can I do?"

"Talk to the kids about the game. They have some questions. Lauren and I've got things in here under control. Now shoo." Don eased the quarterback out of the room.

LAUREN BLEW OUT A BREATH when Griff was gone.

Don turned off the heat under the boiling potatoes. "These are done."

"I can't believe we pulled that off."

"Good planning, sis." He emptied the hot water into the sink.

"He liked it, right?" She pulled a salad out of the fridge.

"Hell, yeah. The man's not stupid."

"Thank you, Don. Couldn't have done it without you."

Her brother picked up the masher and went to work on the cooked spuds. "Milk. Butter. Let's go here."

Lauren whizzed around the kitchen, giving Don what he needed, pulling the sweet potato dish out of the oven, and finishing the green bean casserole. She carried dishes out to the table. Voices of children, mixed with Griff's deep tones, drifted into the dining room. She smiled as happiness flowed through her.

Listening to the chatter from the living room, accompanied by laughter, reminded her of her childhood. Back then, before her father got sick and when her parents still loved each other, holidays were joyous times. With her four siblings, the family had created a warm atmosphere of love and support. Now that her dad was ill, her mother had moved on, and two of her siblings lived across the continent, holidays had become fractured times of wistful memories and too much quiet.

Don had folded Lauren into his family, with the support of his wife. While she was always welcomed in their home, she yearned for her own family, own children, own traditions. Looked like this year she'd get as close as she ever would to having it all. Making Griff happy pleased her. She pushed questions about how long this would last out of her mind. *I'm going to enjoy this holiday. Give thanks for all that I have.*

When she returned to the kitchen, Don was carving the turkey. Griff's face lit up when he spied the bird and the trimmings. After the addition of salt and pepper, the mashed potatoes were ready. She brought them into the dining room and called the family to the table. The kids came running. After all, it was eight-thirty, and everyone was starved.

Don placed the stuffing on the table and sat down at the head. Griff graciously deferred and took a seat next to Lauren. Everyone clasped hands while Don recited a blessing. Griff gave her hand a squeeze. When she turned her gaze to him, he smiled at her and mouthed the words "thank you."

As soon as the prayer was over, they passed around the food.

"How much do you eat after a game?" Carl asked, plopping a big spoonful of mashed potatoes on his plate.

"A lot."

"Like five steaks or something?" Teeny, the youngest, wondered.

He laughed. "Not exactly. Maybe one steak, or a couple pieces of turkey." He licked his lips.

"My sister makes a fine one," Don said, shoveling a forkful of dressing into his mouth.

Griff took a bite and looked around the room. "I agree."

"Were you worried when your receiver got hurt?" Vinnie asked.

"A little, yeah. You never want anyone to get hurt."

"I mean, about the game," Vinnie went on.

"No, no. We had it under control." Griff took a healthy helping of the green bean casserole.

"You just squeaked out a victory. You weren't worried?" Lauren piped up.

"When you have a team like mine, you know they can pull off great plays and win before time runs out."

Lauren sat quietly and ate, listening to the conversation and accepting compliments about the food. She marveled at the amount Griff ate. He obviously needed to recoup his strength. Between bites, he asked each of Don's kids about their school, what classes were their favorites, and if they played any sports. He bemoaned the fact it was too dark for a game of touch football after the meal.

Connie had prepared her special dessert, chocolate layer cake with peanut butter frosting. And there were the two pumpkin pies Lauren had made that morning. The children were instructed to clear the table. Lauren let Connie prepare coffee and serve the desserts.

Griff rubbed his stomach. "Don't know if I have room for cake."

"You have to. Connie's an amazing baker."

He patted his belly. "Well, in that case. I don't want to hurt any-one's feelings." Griff cupped her cheek. "You're something else," he whispered.

"Uh, oh. Dad, quarterback's about to make another pass," Marissa called to her father from across the table. "Are you living together, Aunt Lauren?"

Griff blushed. Lauren pushed his hand away and laughed. "No. We're roommates."

"Roommates with benefits," Vinnie, the oldest, snickered.

"You can't get away with anything with this family," she said.

"I see." His eyes glowed with something she hadn't seen before. *Maybe it's more than lust?*

Connie took dessert orders. Even after such a large meal, everyone made room for a slice of pie or a piece of cake. When coffee was served, the children retreated to the living room, each trying to claim the right to decide what to watch on Griff's huge, flat screen television.

"You watched *Miracle on 34th Street* last year."

"The Dog Show, it's recorded."

Lauren tuned out the kids' voices and sipped her brew.

"Connie, Lauren, that was a meal to be proud of. Fantastic. Thank you so much."

"You're welcome, Griff. It's a pleasure to finally meet you. I've heard so much about you," Connie said, eyeing the quarterback.

Griff's gaze drifted over to Lauren.

"I mean from Don," Connie added.

"Lauren is amazing." Griff wiped his lips with a napkin. "I'm lucky she opened her door to me."

Lauren rose and headed for the kitchen before the questioning started. Griff joined the clean-up. They stayed with it, dividing up the food, packing some for Don and Connie, and stowing the delectable dishes that remained. By eleven thirty, the Farradays were packed in their car, heading back to Rhode Island. Griff rested his hand on Lauren's shoulder as the two of them waved farewell from the door. Spike yawned.

"I'll take him," the athlete said, fastening the harness around the pug.

Lauren got undressed, slipping on her cozy, pink, chenille robe, and settled down in front of the dying fire. Griff returned with a bottle of fine brandy he'd bought. He plucked two small snifters from a cabinet and joined her.

Right as he sat down, his phone rang. It was Kathy. He got up and moved away to talk. Lauren watched his expression. She saw it change and assumed he was speaking to either his niece or nephew as his features softened and a look of joy settled in his smile.

This makes his day perfect. She rolled the smooth, light brown liquid over her tongue and relaxed back against the sofa.

A soft sigh and a sleepy grin grabbed Griff's attention when he hung up. "Fading on me already?"

"Long day."

"Me, too."

He took her hand and led her to the bedroom. She slid between the sheets while he got undressed. After flipping the light off, he joined her, sliding over to her side of the bed. He wrapped his arms around her and nuzzled her neck.

"Thank you for giving me one of the best days ever."

"I'd think your victory did that for you."

"Yeah, but this surprise Thanksgiving...wow. You have no idea."

"Maybe I do."

"I'm too tired to make love. I hope that's okay."

She laughed. "Me, too. Cuddling's the best."

She snuggled her back into his chest, feeling a slight tickle from his chest hair against her skin. His arm closed around her waist. He curled his fingers around her breast and sighed. A kiss below her ear made her tingle.

"You're amazing," he whispered, before his breathing became even and a slight snore joined Spike's louder one from where the pooch slept at the bottom of the mattress.

Comfort and protection surrounded her as she drifted off to sleep in the embrace of her lover.

Chapter Thirteen

LAUREN WOUND A WOOL scarf around her neck. Bundled up in a down jacket, her new corduroy pants, scarf and a hat, she was prepared to attend Griff's game. Don and Vinnie would meet her at the stadium. Singing along with the radio, she drove through the back roads where the trees were bare and the air winterish. Snug in her small car with the heat on, peace and happiness washed over her.

Life had been remarkably pleasant. New work was bringing in money she was saving for when Griff moved back into his place. His rent paid her bills, with a money left over. She had Spike to curl up with when she read. And then there was Griff.

Was she in love? Lauren had skirted the question for months. Finding a man had been put so far back on her list, she had forgotten about it. But life with Griff was great. No hassles, no commitment, no worries—fun for today and no expectations for tomorrow. *That's what I wanted, wasn't it?*

Don spread out the Kings blanket he had bought, and they sat down. Lauren kept her eyes trained on Griff when the team had the ball. She noticed his confidence, grace, and perfectly targeted passes.

"His completion record is amazing," Don said.

"I wouldn't know. But he seems to be getting the ball to a guy who can catch it a lot."

"That's a completion record." Don cocked an eyebrow.

"Who knew?" She shrugged.

"He's the leader in the division. Probably the whole NFL."

Lauren watched Buddy one time, then Homer Calloway the next, pluck the ball out of the air and race downfield. The Kings played the Nebraska Coyotes and won easily. She jumped up as the final whistle blew and cheered with Don.

Life was better when Griff won. They celebrated. He appeared relaxed and happy, unlike when the team lost. Then, he'd brood and spend hours in front of the big screen, watching the game over and over again to figure out what had gone wrong. He'd be short-tempered, stormy, and go off by himself. She hated it when they lost.

Don and Lauren hung back a bit after the game to congratulate the quarterback. They waited by the team's door. Lauren rubbed her gloved hands together to keep them from getting numb. It was the last day of November, and the cold had penetrated her clothing.

With a shiver, she turned to Don. "Wish Griff'd hurry up."

"So do I."

At the sound of footsteps behind her, Lauren whirled around. "You waiting for Griff Montgomery?"

"Yep. You a fan?" the stranger asked.

"You could say that. And you are?"

"Cheryl Charles. Griff's fiancée."

Lauren choked on her saliva. "What?"

"Yeah. No sense waiting in the cold for an autograph or asking him on a date."

"I'm living with him," Lauren defended, sticking out her chin a bit.

"Oh?" The redhead's eyebrows lifted. "Maybe you'd better make other plans. I'm going to move in with him. We've been together for a couple of years."

Lauren fisted her hands on her hips. "You're not moving into my house."

"Of course not. Into *his* house." Cheryl straightened up and stared at Lauren.

"This is all news to me. When did you make these plans?"

"When he was in L.A. I flew out here to be with him."

"He never mentioned it to me."

"Why would he? If you've got someone on the side, would you tell? I wouldn't."

"I wouldn't *have* anyone on the side if I was in a committed relationship."

"Neither would Griff. So, I guess that means he's not committed to you." A cruel smile curled Cheryl's lips.

No commitment. Remember. Didn't you say that to him? To yourself?

Lauren was silent. Before she could reply, Don tugged on her jacket and pointed. Lauren raised her gaze and saw Griff striding toward them.

He froze. His gaze hopped from Lauren to Cheryl and back to Lauren.

Cheryl was the first to speak. "Griff!" She ran to him, throwing her arms around him.

Lauren's heart rate doubled, and her mouth went dry. Her pulse drummed in her ear.

He put his hands on Cheryl's upper arms and pushed her away. He said something, but Lauren couldn't hear. Right after speaking, he looked up at her, his brow creased, his mouth set in a straight line.

"Shit. I'm outta here." Don turned to leave.

Lauren clamped a vise-like grip on his forearm. "You're not going anywhere."

"WHAT THE FUCK ARE YOU doing here?" Griff kept his voice low, but his grip on Cheryl's arms tight.

"We didn't part on good terms. I said some things...I regret."

Griff glanced up at Lauren. Their gazes locked. Her lower lip quivered. "Shit. You've ruined everything," he said to Cheryl, without looking at her.

Lauren's hand covered her mouth as she backed away. Her other fisted Don's sleeve and pulled him with her.

"Wait, Lauren!" Griff called, his legs too tired to run.

But it was too late. She turned toward the lot and sprinted to her car. Griff found the strength to follow, but she was inside with the doors locked before he could stop her. He pounded on the window. Her tear-stained face was only inches from his, yet she turned the key and started the motor.

"I can explain," he begged, knocking again.

She trained her eyes in front of her and threw the vehicle in gear. She roared away before he could stop her.

"Fuck!" he yelled at no one.

Don looked at him and shrugged.

"It's not what you think, Don."

"Doesn't look good, man." He raised his shoulders.

"I know. I'll explain at home."

Cheryl caught up. She smiled up at Griff, pawing at his sleeve.

He brushed her off. "What did you say to her?" He shifted his weight.

"Nothing...I..."

"You said you were his fiancée," Don piped up.

Griff's eyebrows shot up. "You lied to her?"

"It's not really a lie—"

"Yes, it is. We're not engaged. I never proposed. In fact, I broke up with you when I was in L.A."

"We didn't have much time together. I know if I had more time alone with you that I could change your mind."

"You can't, Cheryl. It's over between us. I tried to be nice about it. Maybe I wasn't. I'm sorry about that. But you and I are history, and no amount of alone time'll change that."

Her eyes welled up.

"Don't go there. You've tried tears on me before. I'm sorry if this hurts. But you've left reality behind if you think we were anything more than casual."

"But, Griff, I know I could make you happy."

"I am happy. And now, you've screwed it up."

"If you'd give me three months—"

"We talked about this. You and I are not meant to be. Please accept it. Move on. Find a nice guy who wants to commit. It's not me." He walked away, with Don trailing behind.

"Do you expect me to tell my sister about that little scene?"

"That would be helpful."

"I'm not gonna mess in this. It's between you two. I thought you were only roommates...with benefits."

"Maybe we started out like that. But it's changed."

"Crap. Good luck explaining to Lauren. Thanks for the tickets. If you want 'em back, I understand."

"Keep 'em. I've gotta get home." Griff raised his hand to Don and headed for his car.

He stroked his stubbly chin on the drive home. *I'll tell her the truth. I'm not guilty this time.* The house was quiet when he arrived. The slow cooker was working, and there was a distant bark from Spike. *She's upstairs.* Griff climbed the steps slowly, his heart pounding. He knocked.

No answer.

"Please, Lauren. Talk to me."

No answer.

"You've gotta let me explain."

No answer.

He sighed. "She was lying. She's not my fiancée. Yes, I dated her in California. But I broke it off on my last visit."

No answer.

He knocked again. *Connecticut Kings never give up.* "Come on, honey. Come out. Talk to me. Hit me. Do something."

No answer.

He combed his fingers through his hair and paced the hall. "I'm not leaving. So open the damn door!" He pounded once, hard.

The bedclothes rustled inside. A faint padding of feet on the floor brought a smile to his lips. As the knob turned, he stepped back in case she took him seriously about the hitting. The door opened six inches.

Lauren's eyelids were swollen, and her nose was red. She twisted a tissue in her hand as she leaned against the jamb. "What do you want?" Her voice was gravelly.

"I want to talk to you," he said, pushing the door open and grabbing her arm.

She gave him a steely stare. "So talk."

"Downstairs."

"No. Here." She sank down, cross-legged, on the carpeted floor.

"Okay, okay." He followed her.

"Are you engaged?" She shot him a suspicious stare.

"No. No way. Not engaged. Not even going steady with Cheryl Charles."

"Then, why did she say that? Are you dating her?"

"I don't know why she said that. No, we're not dating. I broke it off when I was in L.A."

Lauren chewed her lip and cast her gaze to the ground. "What was she doing here?"

"She was pretty upset. She said some harsh things. Guess she thought if she came here, she could patch it up with me."

"And did you...she...you...whatever?"

"No. I was probably a jerk the way I broke it off."

"Probably?"

"All right. Definitely. I wasn't nice about it."

"Did you sleep with her?"

"This last time in L.A.? No."

"And you were mean?"

"I could have been a little more...sensitive or something."

"And you were going to tell me about her...when?" Lauren raised an eyebrow.

"It was over. Nothing to tell."

"I guess there was something to tell, wasn't there?"

"Hey, look who's talking. You don't want any commitment. You've said so a thousand times. Why should I clear my decks—especially on the road—for you? How do I know who you're sleeping with when I'm away?"

At that, she burst out laughing. "Me, sleeping around? What a joke. You're the whore in the room."

"Nice."

"I'm not the one who's in the Guinness Book for the longest list of sexual partners in the most cities. I'm a one-man woman."

"Yeah?"

"Yeah. And after you, I'm thinking of becoming a no-man woman." She pushed to her feet.

"I haven't slept with that many women. It's all in your mind."

"Bullshit."

"Just because you say you're not with anyone else—" Her icy stare froze the words in his throat. "Cheryl is over," he managed to croak out.

"Why, all of a sudden, are you putting this filly out to pasture?"

"Because I don't need her. I have you."

Lauren's mouth opened, but nothing came out. She cocked her head. "What?"

"You heard me," he said, his tone softer.

"What do you mean, you have me?"

"I mean I'm getting a complete package with you. So, why would I need someone else?"

"Because you're alone on the road?"

"Alone? Nah. I have Buddy to talk to. I can get along for a week or two without sex. Won't kill me."

"Does that mean you're committed to me?"

He took her elbow. "Uh, let's not go there. Something smells good. Don't you want to check on dinner?"

LAUREN DIDN'T KNOW what to think. *Was that a compliment or an insult?* She descended the stairs slowly. When she arrived, he had the top off the slow cooker and was bent over, sniffing.

"Stew?"

"Lamb stew," she said, taking the lid from his hand and replacing it.

He grabbed her upper arms and kissed her. "Love your cooking." He released her and stepped to the cabinet. As he was pulling down plates, Lauren stole over behind him, reached around, and shut the door. He didn't turn around.

"I'm a replacement?"

"Not exactly." He still didn't turn.

"What am I, exactly?"

"You're you. Wonderful, smart, sexy...and a great cook." He folded his fingers over hers resting on his belly.

"And you're full of shit."

He did turn then, placed his hands on her waist, and inched her closer. "We have something great, Lauren. Let's not wreck it."

"Wreck it?"

"Over analyze it. Can't we just enjoy each other...the way we've been?"

Her gaze searched his face.

"I love living here. Best move I've made. Thank you for inviting me."

"I'm renting to you. You're a paying customer."

"Maybe. So. Forget that. We're a team, a pair..."

"You mean 'a couple'?"

"I guess. That's so formal."

"You don't want a commitment, and neither do I."

"And that's why what we have works."

"You mean, if we changed that, it would fall apart?"

"I don't know. And I don't want to find out."

"Somehow, you've insulted me in there somewhere."

"I didn't mean to. I meant to say, you're perfect. Why would I need anyone else?"

Her heart skipped a beat. *Perfect? Me? A perfect failure maybe.* But she kept her thoughts to herself. "Delude yourself all you want. I'm not giving you my share of stew...or of the apple cobbler I made to go with it."

"Apple cobbler?" She could almost see him drool.

"Yep." She pulled it out of the fridge and slid it into the oven.

"I don't know which is better—sex or your cooking."

She cocked an eyebrow at him.

"Okay, okay, but your cooking is a close second."

Dinner started out quietly. Griff appeared content to eat while Lauren explained how she was decorating the new house.

"Annette told me the guy's in London and won't be back for a month or more."

"Yeah?"

"Yep. But she told me what he likes. A lotta wood. Brown. Earth tones. He loves fall, she said. So, I'm making his house a little woodsy and a real *guy* kind of place."

"Like a man cave?"

"Nah. More classy."

"How?"

Lauren retrieved her briefcase from the front hall table. She plucked out wallpaper and paint samples. She had some fabric swatches, too. Griff asked questions, and she was happy to answer.

"I like the green for the den walls."

"You're so interested in this. It's like it was your house."

Griff coughed. "Just taking an interest in what you're doing. By the way, no guys like yellow." He screwed up his face and shook his head.

"Say, when is your place going to be ready?" She put a piece of lamb in her mouth.

"Anxious to get rid of me?"

"Just thinking maybe I could decorate your house, too."

"Sounds like a good idea." He shot a sexy glance her way as he pushed his empty dish away.

"Like it here?" She stood up.

He sidled up to her and snaked his arm around her waist. "Are you kidding? With you in my bed and me in your kitchen...heaven." He bent down to run his lips up her neck.

Lauren shivered. "Okay, Mr. Sexy. Time for the dishes." She stretched her arm, reached the sponge, and dumped it in his palm.

Griff laughed. "It's the least I can do after that fantastic meal."

Lauren skipped upstairs and changed into a rose-colored, velour lounging robe. She curled up on the sofa, spread a small throw across her knees, and turned on her e-reader. *If I'm reading, I'm not thinking. Don't wanna think. Let it alone. Enjoy it while it lasts.*

Twenty minutes later, Griff strolled into the living room, rolling down his sleeves.

"Done?"

"Yep. Reading?"

"Yep." Lauren dropped her gaze back to her book.

"Me, too." Griff plucked a novel out from several standing together on the mantle.

"You?"

"You think I'm illiterate or something? I read."

"Could've fooled me," she mumbled. "What are you reading?"

He took the book, checked the spine, and then turned to her. "Vince Lombardi on Football."

She nodded, suppressing a grin. "Football. How unexpected."

Griff frowned. "You got something against reading about football?"

"Just thought you might have greater literary aspirations."

"Oh, like your book club, which isn't a book club? It's a support group."

Lauren's mouth hung open.

"Yeah. One of the women told me. So, don't be so high and mighty." He slumped down on the other end of the sofa.

"I need that group."

"Never said you didn't," he said, leaning over to take her hand. "Just don't go makin' like a literary snob or something. Reading is reading."

"It is." She smiled at him.

He opened the book and tried to get comfortable.

She peeked at him above her reading device. "A problem?"

"If you would scoot down," he said. "And settle right under here, I could get comfortable."

Lauren slid over and let him tuck her into his embrace. She rested her head on his chest and raised her e-reader. Griff closed his arm around her, shifted his position, sighed, and smiled. Spike jumped up and snuggled in-between. He snorted then closed his eyes before a quiet snore escaped him.

"This is the way I like to read."

"You've got a point."

The room grew silent as the pair turned their attention to their books.

Chapter Fourteen

LAUREN FOUND HERSELF humming a Christmas carol in the car. Just a few weeks until the celebration that included a big meal with Don and his family. She'd invited Griff's father to come for the holiday as a surprise. A little thrill shot up her spine at the thought of how happy Griff'd be to see his dad.

After a quick lunch at the diner, Lauren headed home. Her lasagna was ready to go into the oven. Griff would be home from practice in half an hour, hungry as hell for a solid dinner, with her for dessert. She turned on the bath that would soothe his sore muscles.

Returning to the kitchen, she popped the pasta in the oven. While shredding lettuce for a salad, she almost jumped out of her skin when two strong hands gripped her from behind.

"You like?" He nuzzled her neck.

"I like." She closed her eyes and eased her head back so he could kiss her throat.

He moved away from her to set the table. "I'm going on the road."

"What?" Her eyes wide, she snapped to attention.

"Yep. Road trip."

"But it's Christmas." She plucked utensils for two out of a drawer.

"Not yet. Besides, we play through December." Griff put down dishes.

"Don't you get Christmas off?"

"Christmas Day, yeah. Gives you a chance to miss me."

She made a face and picked up a knife to cut the lasagna.

"What's this?" he asked, turning an envelope in his hand.

"I got one, too. Open it."

"Damn! From the judge."

"You have to appear and tell him whether I'm a good or bad mother to Spike."

"You going?"

"If I want to keep Spike, I have to."

Griff pulled out a chair for Lauren then sat himself. "Good thing it's on a Wednesday. Don't have to miss a game."

"Can you just do that? Miss a game?"

"Nope. You get fined. I don't want you to lose Spike."

"You were the one to cause this stupid misunderstanding in the first place." She glared at him.

"Me? I'm not the one who left the dog out in the cold." He ate a forkful of pasta.

"It wasn't cold. And I didn't leave him anywhere. Damn. Let's not go over this again." She took some salad.

"Your attitude is ruining this great lasagna. I'd swear you're Italian."

"Got the recipe from Connie. *She's* Italian."

"Aha! Can't fool me. I know what's authentic."

"What attitude?"

"Skip it."

They finished the meal, trading bits about their day.

"Let's read in my room tonight."

Lauren arched an eyebrow at him.

"How 'bout it?" His fingers played with hers.

She nodded, snatched her e-reader from the counter, and joined her hand with his. He led them to the bedroom.

"What about your book?" she asked.

"I don't need it. I'll be reading your body, instead."

Lauren laughed, but stopped questioning him and followed along.

The next morning, she awoke brimming with energy and Christmas spirit. Always a fan of the holiday, she looked forward to making the Victorian house festive. She debated real versus fake garlands and opted for the real because she loved the scent. A fresh wreath for the front door and a tree were on her list. Standing in the seasonal section of The Beloved Knickknack in town, Lauren chewed her lip, trying to decide whether to put electric candles in every window or just the ones in front.

Will Griff want to decorate with me? Will we celebrate Christmas together? That's family stuff, and we're just...I don't know what we are. Pushing negative thoughts out of her head, she examined small, ceramic Santa's and reindeer for the mantle and mistletoe for over the front door. *Mistletoe? He doesn't need any help.* She chuckled to herself as she fingered the green leaves.

A saleswoman strolled by. "Does Mr. Montgomery need encouragement?"

Lauren turned wide eyes to the lady.

"Well, you are his girlfriend, aren't you?"

Lauren sputtered.

The woman patted her arm. "Don't worry, honey. Your secret's safe with me." She moseyed on to help another customer. *Can no one keep a secret in this town?*

Ten days later, at two o'clock, the sound of Lauren's cell broke the silence of the night. She grabbed it and slid out of bed.

Griff opened one sleepy eye. "Huh? Wazzup?"

"Sorry. I'll take it in the hall."

"Who's that?"

She rested her hand on his shoulder, kissed his cheek, and quickly padded out of the room, closing the door behind her.

ROLLING OVER TO FIND the bed empty woke Griff early. He stretched his arm out, but it didn't come in contact with any warm, soft, bare flesh. Cracking an eye open, he peered at the clock. It read six thirty. No Lauren. He smiled at the thought that she was in the kitchen, starting coffee and maybe rustling up some bacon and eggs. He eased the comforter over his chest and went back to sleep.

When the alarm went off, he lumbered out of bed, grabbed his robe, and headed for the kitchen. The lack of an aroma of goodies grabbed his attention. *No coffee. No bacon.* He frowned, scrunching his face up to look downright grumpy. *Where is that woman?*

He didn't find her, though he investigated the rest of the first floor. Spike followed him up the stairs. After checking all the rooms on the second level, Griff still couldn't locate his girlfriend. Finally giving up, he shrugged and returned to the kitchen. He put up coffee and slipped on jogging pants, commando, and a sweatshirt to take Spike for his morning walk. The pug circled by the front door and whined until Griff fastened the harness on him.

While he walked the dog, a vague memory of something the night before plagued his brain.

"That's it!" He snapped his fingers. "Her cell," he said to Spike. The pug looked up from sniffing a tree. He recalled the phone going off and her getting out of bed, but nothing beyond that. He'd gone back to sleep and had no idea what had transpired. Giving up, he hoped he'd know soon enough and headed for the gym.

He always left his cell in his locker when he was practicing or training. At the end of the day, he checked it first thing before hitting the showers. But this time, there was no missed call and no message from Lauren. He checked his watch. No time to investigate further, as he had to be at the courthouse within an hour. Griff showered, dressed, and headed for his car.

He turned up his collar against the bone-chilling wind whipping along the sidewalk. A quick glance at the parking lot didn't reveal Lauren's vehicle. *She's late. Not like her.* His brow furrowed.

He checked the time again then met his lawyer in the lobby. "Lauren still not here?"

"Let's go in. Maybe she slipped by when I wasn't looking."

The two men entered the large room where a trial was in progress. They found seats in the back and sat quietly as the opposing attorneys argued their cases. Griff's gaze searched the area, but no sign of Lauren. He spotted her attorney, who acknowledged him with a brief nod.

Shifting in his seat, the quarterback gazed out the window. A crease formed between his eyebrows as worry about Lauren grew in his heart. *I hope nothing's happened to her.* He smiled at his foolish anxiety. *Nothing ever happens to people. Probably a new assignment, and she got busy.* The bailiff interrupted his concern by calling his case.

"Where's your client, Ms. Chase?" the judge asked.

"Her brother called. Seems there's been a death in the family."

Griff's breath caught in his throat. "Her father?"

"I think so," Marcy said.

"Well, we can proceed, anyway. The court would like a statement from you, Mr. Montgomery, on Ms. Farraday's fitness to own Spike."

Griff stated that he thought Lauren treated the pug extremely well and should keep Spike. The judge ruled in her favor. After a quick handshake with his attorney and a few autographs, the quarterback headed for his car. He sped to the highway heading north.

Once he got to Providence, he pulled over to send a text to Don. He got a response right away with the address he needed. He drove slowly to the grassy hill, where a woman in dark clothing sat in a folding chair. Two burly men shoveled dirt into an open grave while she watched. She was alone. Griff crept closer, quietly. He heard her soft cries and watched her twist a handkerchief in her ungloved hands.

"Lauren?" he asked, gently.

She turned abruptly, staring at him with full eyes.

"You okay?"

She shook her head.

Griff was beside her in a second, yanking her up and into his embrace. He hugged her hard, holding her against him. A sob broke through. Her body trembled against his as she cried into his coat. He stroked her hair.

"I'm so sorry. So sorry. I didn't know. You didn't text or leave a note or anything."

She wiped her eyes and blew her nose. "There wasn't time."

"The call last night?"

"Yeah. Don said to come quickly. Dad was fading fast."

"Did you make it?"

"Not by much. Maybe five or ten minutes before he passed."

"Baby, are you okay?"

She simply snuggled into his chest.

He palmed the back of her head and kissed her hair. "The judge decided in your favor."

"Oh my God. I totally forgot. Was he mad I wasn't there?"

"Your lawyer explained. That's how I found out. Then, I gave you the thumbs up."

"Thank you." She clung to him. "And thank you for coming."

"Of course. What can I do?"

"You're doing it."

GRIFF MET BUDDY ON Saturday morning. They took a run around Monroe high school's track then headed toward Main Street to do some shopping. Christmas was in the air. The street, running through downtown, was decorated with garlands and tiny, white lights. Stores had holiday windows—some with miniature towns, some with Santa Claus and other holiday scenes.

Griff's favorite store, The Beloved Knickknack, had the model train set-up they did every year, with little towns, people, houses, and the sound of a train whistle every couple of minutes.

"Gotta get something for my mom," Buddy said, stopping to look in The Cottage's window.

"Yeah? Like what?"

Buddy shrugged.

"Are you buying something for Christy?"

"I have to. She'll probably get me something. Let's go in there. I'll get her one of those sweaters," Buddy said, pointing to the display.

The men entered the shop. A middle-aged woman met them and steered Buddy to the angora sweaters he had seen.

"What size do you need?" the saleslady asked.

Buddy made a gesture toward his chest with both hands cupped then blushed. Griff cracked up.

"Oh, my. I see," said the woman, turning an attractive shade of pink. "Perhaps large, then?"

Buddy nodded. "I like the black one."

"Shall I giftwrap it?"

"Please." Buddy drew out his wallet and handed her his credit card.

"Remind me never to go shopping with you again," Griff muttered, pretending to look at some nightgowns on a rack.

"Well, how the hell do I know what size? They're big. I guess 'large' is the right word."

The woman returned with the package wrapped and sitting in a colorful shopping bag. "If the size is wrong, she can return it, Mr. Carruthers."

"Thank you. I'll tell her." He took the purchase and headed for the door. Griff followed behind. "You're not buying anything for Lauren?" Buddy turned to his friend.

"Yeah, but not there."

They continued to walk, stopping to look at windows and talk about presents. Griff bought his father a book about the history of football at The Beloved Knickknack. They strolled along, discussing where to have lunch. Griff stopped in front of Solomon's Jewelry. Right in the window, he saw the perfect gift for Lauren. They went inside.

"Well, well, Mr. Montgomery. Griff. How nice to see you in our store," Hal Solomon said.

"You put that in the window just for me, didn't you?"

The jeweler laughed.

"I'll take it, but I want something added."

"Of course."

While they talked, Buddy roamed. "Hey, Griff! Look at this. Mom's birthstone, emerald, in earrings, necklace, and matching bracelet."

Griff finished up his conversation and joined his friend. "Get it."

"I will. She'll flip. She manages my money. When she sees this come up on my card, she'll think I'm getting engaged."

"Will she be pissed off when she finds out you're not?"

"Nah. This present oughta make up for it. I'll take it, all of it," Buddy said, turning to Mr. Solomon.

"Wrapped separately or together?"

"Separately, please." Buddy tossed his credit card on the counter.

"The engraver is working on yours, Griff. It'll be ready in a minute."

Fifteen minutes later, the men left the store, their shopping completed.

"Let's go to The Savage Beast."

"It's only two," Griff replied.

"Come on. I need a beer. Don't usually spend this much money in one day."

"You're a fucking tight ass, Buddy. Know that?"

"Yeah. So what? I'll have plenty of money to retire when my knee blows out."

Griff shook his head as he slipped behind the wheel.

The sign read "Closed" when they pulled up. Griff opened his door.

"It's closed," Buddy said, placing his hand on his friend's forearm.

"But I see Carla inside. She always opens up for me."

"Yeah, I get it. But the bar's closed." Buddy snickered.

"Mind in the gutter," Griff admonished, easing out of the seat.

"Right next to yours!"

They ambled to the front door. Griff knocked.

"Can't ya read? We're closed!" came the reply.

"It's me, Carla."

After a few moments of silence, the sound of feet shuffling in their direction made Griff smile.

She opened the door, an unfriendly expression on her face. "What do you want?"

"Can we get a couple of your great burgers and a beer?"

"One beer? Two straws?"

Griff grinned. "That's my girl."

"I'm not your girl and never have been. Can't turn away hungry football players. Come on in." She stepped back and moved toward the bar. The men followed, Buddy closing the door behind him. She plopped two menus down on a table close by. "I don't have to walk so far."

"Hard night?" Griff cocked an eyebrow at her. A frown claimed his lips.

"Wouldn't you like to know? Hard enough, playboy. What'll it be?"

They ordered blue cheese burgers, fries, and beer.

When she left, Buddy lowered his voice. "I thought she used to be your chick here at home?"

"Used to."

"Oh, yeah. That name thing. You'll never do that again. Lauren's pretty hot."

"Lauren's a nice person. She's sweet."

"And hot."

"I don't need you to tell me that."

Carla set two beers down on the table and returned to the kitchen.

Buddy took a drink. "Carla's hot, too. How'd you choose?"

"Choice isn't always mine, dumbass."

She returned with two plates filled with hot food.

Buddy licked his lips. "Looks great, Carla."

"Thanks."

"So do you." His gaze slipped up her body. She arched an eyebrow. "Busy tomorrow night?"

"Workin'. Besides, I've sworn off football players."

"Who's your new guy?" Griff asked, raising his burger to his mouth.

"None of your business. He's a manager, in a big store. Huge. No more athletes."

Griff laughed. "Can't blame you. Hope it works out."

"It's workin' out fine." She winked at him and sashayed out.

Buddy's gaze followed the swing of her hips.

"Stop staring," Griff said.

"It's a better view than your ugly mug."

"Asshole."

"Jerk."

Silence prevailed as the men tucked into their food. The only sound was faint laughter seeping in from the kitchen.

Griff's phone rang. It was Keen Barstow, his agent.

"Hey, Keen. What's up?" Griff lounged back in his chair.

"You've had a great year."

"Thanks."

"So, I thought I'd start negotiation on your contract early."

"But it's not up until June."

"Strike while the iron's hot."

Griff smiled. "And?"

"They want to talk. Looks like another three years and a twenty-five percent raise."

Griff whistled. "That's fantastic."

"Keep it up, buddy. It depends on how you finish out the season. So focus and kill it."

"This is great news. Thanks."

"Gotta keep you big boys happy. I'm not finished, yet. But it's looking good."

"Great."

"Just don't fuck it up."

Griff laughed and ended the call.

"You like him?" Buddy asked, taking a bite.

"Yeah. He's partners with Faith Brecken at Brecken and Magic."

"They any good?"

"I think so. He's already started negotiating my new contract. Old one isn't up till June."

"That's pretty good."

"He always gets me a sweet deal."

"This time, too?"

"Yeah." Griff extended his long legs. "Changes everything. Three more years. Guaranteed."

Chapter Fifteen

"THE SWEET MAGNOLIA? Are you celebrating?" Lauren fastened a diamond earring in her ear.

"Sort of. My agent's started contract negotiations. Looks good. More money and three more years."

"Congratulations." She freshened her coral lipstick, smoothed down her black velvet jacket over matching skirt, and looked up.

"Thanks. You look beautiful." Griff's gaze perused her, lingering a bit too long on her chest and the gold camisole she wore. His stare started a tiny shiver up her spine. Her skin tingled, and her nipples hardened. "Gorgeous," he muttered, as he opened the door for her and they headed for the car.

The maître d' showed them to a quiet table in the corner. Griff held out her chair then ordered his favorite champagne, *Moët et Chandon*. They sat quietly while the server poured then returned it to the ice bucket.

Griff raised his glass. "To three more years of healthy football with the Kings."

Lauren touched hers to his then drank. The bubbly tasted exquisite. "Maybe more than three years."

"One contract at a time. Let's talk about us."

Lauren choked on her beverage. The waiter stopped by with a glass of water and menus. They ordered, and then Lauren sat back. "Us? Is there an us?"

"That's what I wanted to talk about. I like what we have. But, well, I'm ready for more."

Her eyes got wide. "More?"

"A commitment. I want to know when I'm out of town, that you're not dating anyone else."

She looked at him, not daring to hope she'd heard correctly.

Griff took her hand. "Lauren, we're good together."

"What about you?"

"I'm willing to make that commitment, too. When I'm out of town, I'll be a good boy. What do you say?"

"I don't know what to say."

"Come on. We get along so well. You and me." He leaned over and kissed her.

Love. I'm not hearing the word "love." "I don't know, Griff. I've told you I have no intention of getting married."

"This isn't a marriage proposal..."

She moved away a few inches. "We get along great?"

"Yeah. Something wrong with that?"

"You make it sound like a business arrangement."

"Hey, okay, I'm not good with words." He looked at his hands.

"You're missing one important thing."

They sat quietly while the server placed plates with artfully displayed slices of beef tenderloin, tiny fingerling potatoes, and haricots verts in front of them. The tempting aroma made Lauren's stomach rumble. *This gorgeous man is asking for a commitment, and I'm thinking about food? Really?*

"What do you want me to say?" He picked up his knife and fork.

"Nothing. Not if you don't feel it." She speared a bean.

"Oh, I get it. I can be dense sometimes. You want me to say I love you?"

Her eyes filled. "Gee, isn't that romantic? I don't want you to say anything that isn't true."

"I thought that was obvious." He put a piece of beef in his mouth.

"Wrong. It's not love for you, it's convenience. I'm there. I'm willing." Her throat closed for a moment. She blinked rapidly, took a deep breath, and let it out slowly.

"I wanted this to be a special dinner. Romantic. And now, you're pissed and crying, and I don't know what I did." He shrugged.

"You didn't do anything. That's the point."

Griff put down his utensils and skidded her chair across the floor, up against his. He leaned over and kissed her, hard. "I love you," he whispered.

Lauren caught her breath.

"Guess I needed to say it. Thought you'd have figured it out."

"No one figures that out. It needs to be said."

"Okay, so now it's your turn."

"Do you want me to say it because it's my turn?" She moved her chair back and resumed eating.

"Of course not. I want you to say it because you mean it."

She ate in silence.

"So, you don't?"

She glanced up in time to see hurt flash across his features. She folded her fingers over his. "Of course, I love you."

"Do you? Why?" He narrowed his eyes.

"Because you're funny, sexy, handsome, smart, good to me...do I need to go on?"

He grinned. "Hell, yeah. Lovin' this."

She chuckled. "Okay, because you respect me and my house. And, finally, you love my dog."

"That last one is true. I do love Spike."

They ate in silence for a while. The waiter brought a lit candle to their table, refilled their flutes, and then disappeared. Soft music came on, and the lights dimmed.

"This is beautiful. Romantic." *Is it the champagne, the music, or Griff? Maybe all three?*

He took her hand with both of his. "That's what I want. Romantic. With you. Say you'll give exclusivity a try."

She laughed. "I'm already exclusive."

"You are?" He lifted his eyebrows.

Lauren leaned over, kissed him, and whispered, "I love you means I don't want anyone else." She peered up through her blackened lashes at him.

His eyes glowed in the dim light. His smile grew brighter, as he clasped her hands. "Baby, you make me very happy." He kissed her palms.

The clearing of a throat called their attention to the presence of the server. "Dessert?"

"Share?" Griff looked at Lauren. She nodded. "You pick."

"The chocolate lava cake, of course."

The waiter nodded, bowed, and then disappeared. About five minutes later, he returned with the amazing sweet.

Griff scooped up some of the warm cake and liquid filling on a spoon. He dabbed it in the whipped cream and served it to Lauren. She slipped the confection off the utensil with her lips then licked it, all the while staring up into Griff's dark eyes. Her pulse quickened as desire swept over his features.

They took turns feeding each other. Every bite, each lick, took on another meaning as their gazes held and the chocolate inspired their passion. People at other tables were staring, but Griff and Lauren only had eyes for each other. When the dessert was gone, Griff dropped a bunch of big bills on the table, and they left. He raced home, surpassing the speed limit. They hurried into the house, toeing off their shoes at the door.

Griff grabbed her. With their lips locked, he pushed her back up against the front door, slamming it, while he pushed off her jacket and pushed up her camisole.

Lauren fumbled with the buttons on his shirt, finally spreading it open, laying his chest bare to her touch. She heard him hiss as she ran her palms up his skin. He cupped her breasts, bending to kiss her neck. Heat flew to her core when his thumbs found her peaks. She thrust her hips up against his as her need for him grew. He gripped her rear end and pressed his erection into her.

"Perfect fit, top and bottom," he said.

Feeling his desire growing ramped up hers. Raising her chin, she accepted his hard kiss. When he demanded her full surrender with his mouth, Lauren's insides became liquid. Dampness between her legs, and the itch to have him fill her, inspired small moans from her lips.

"Want me?" he mumbled before nibbling on her neck.

"Oh, God, Griff. Yes, yes...let's—"

Before she could finish, he snaked his hand under her skirt and ripped her panties off. Spike barked, but they ignored him. Griff pushed the garment up. Lauren grasped his shoulders as he lifted her, her back leaning against the door. She squeezed her hand between them, unzipped his pants, and released his hard shaft from the confines of his clothing. Closing her fingers around him, she guided him to her center.

"Damn, woman," he muttered as he eased into her.

"Fuck," she said softly, her eyes closing as he rammed her down on him.

"Ooooh, she talks dirty," he whispered, moving her up and down.

She arched, pushing her breasts into his chest. Speech escaped Lauren. Her senses ruled her mind and body. Need rose up as he took her, stroke after hard stroke, until a strong orgasm contracted her every muscle. She screamed his name as her hips moved on their own.

Opening her eyes, she saw lust in his. His gaze studied her face, drinking in every aspect of her release. Totally naked, body and soul, with him, love shot through her like never before. All pretense washed away in that raw moment when the lovers were ruled by their animal passions. She wanted him. She needed him. And now, she had him.

Griff closed his eyes as he increased the pace. Her breasts rubbed against the hair on his chest, making her nipples hard again. She folded her fingers over his shoulders and lowered her head to lick and suck his neck. He groaned as she went to work on him.

"Fuck, you're killing me," he moaned, but she didn't stop.

He tightened his grip on her, slammed her down on him hard, and held her there. A loud sound from his throat, that ended with her name and his closed eyes, spelled his climax. She wound her legs around his waist as he clung to her. They lingered in the embrace. Lauren buried her face in his shoulder and sighed. His scent and his aftershave teased her nose.

With one hand under her rear and one holding her back, he slowly lowered her to the floor. Spike broke the spell by licking Lauren's bare leg. Her knees wobbled like jelly. She leaned against him, and he supported her.

"I've never done that before," she said, reaching down to pet the pug.

"What?"

"Not been able to wait to get to the bedroom."

He chuckled. "Me, neither."

She raised her eyebrows. "You haven't? I thought you'd done everything there was to do."

"Not by a long shot. That was amazing."

She slid her hands up his chest and looked into his eyes. "Thank you for dinner. It was great."

He combed his fingers through her hair and kissed her nose. "You're welcome."

The dog barked and jumped up on them. Lauren pushed her clothing down. Griff buttoned his shirt and zipped his pants. She fastened the leash on the wiggly canine, and Griff took him for his nighttime walk.

Lauren was in bed when he returned. She stretched her legs then her whole body, fisting her hands and reaching for the headboard. A purr of contentment bubbled up inside. Happiness mixed with satisfaction in her veins. She scooted over to make room for her lover.

Griff stretched out and opened his arms to her. Lauren cuddled into his shoulder. Resting a palm on his chest, she sighed.

He leaned over and kissed her hair. "Thank you for an amazing night. Sleep well, beautiful."

"You're the best," she replied.

As their body temperatures returned to normal, the chill in the air caused Lauren to pull the comforter up to their shoulders. When she heard his even breathing, she twisted away a bit, turned on her side, and gazed at the face of the naked, handsome man in her bed. His mussed up, straight hair shone blue black in a narrow beam of moonlight. Scruff shadowed his face, emphasizing the planes of his cheekbones. His lips were sensuous, sending chills down her spine when she recalled their soft feel and what they could do.

Lauren combed her fingers through his hair gently, so as not to wake him. But he was roused anyway, taking her hand, kissing the palm, and trapping it over his heart. She snuggled up to him. *Committed to the sexiest man in football. Can he really commit to me? Think I should give him a chance.*

Afraid to examine her luck too closely, Lauren closed her eyes, allowing sleep and contentment to take over.

ROLLING OVER AT SIX, the darkness seduced Griff into staying under the covers. December and January mornings were the hardest ones for him to push himself up and out to get to the stadium on time. It was only practice this morning, but Coach Bass was strict about starting time. He had two hours before he had to be there.

The quarterback slid back a few inches and turned his attention to the woman in his bed. Her dark hair tangled on the pillow, and her long, black lashes fanned out beautifully on her cheek. He wanted to kiss the tip of her small nose, but held back, afraid to wake her. His gaze traveled down her long, graceful neck to her chest.

He eased the covers down a bit to reveal her breasts. God, how he loved those. They fit his hands, which itched at the idea of squeezing the soft flesh. A warm feeling emanated from his heart. Was it love? Probably. He hadn't been over-the-moon, crazy in love since he was twenty. His emotions brought a smile to his face. He wanted to squish her against him, make love to her forever.

He'd found what he was looking for. She'd agreed to commitment, surely she'd agree to marriage. That pesky thing about miscarriages? *Crap. Silly shit.* He'd joke her out of that worry. Peace blended with anticipation. He'd found his soul mate, the woman he wanted to talk to almost as much as he wanted to sleep with. She took good care of him, and he'd return the favor, forever. He chuckled to himself. *Guess I owe Spike for bringing us together.*

Griff stretched as quietly as he could, but Lauren rolled over anyway. He had it all now. A winning season, a new contract in the making, and the love of his life made his dreams come true. *Does it get any better than this?* He didn't think so. She continued to sleep, so he slipped out of the quilt and padded toward the kitchen. *I'll make breakfast for her this morning.*

He whistled as he put up coffee. Opening the fridge, he rummaged through the contents, until he found the ingredients for a mushroom and spinach omelet. He sliced the mushrooms while butter melted in the pan. Although he was no cook, he'd watched Lauren make these a hundred times, so he knew what to do.

While the spinach and mushrooms cooked, he dug out a couple of pieces of ham.

"Perfect," he said, his stomach growling in anticipation. He switched the flame on under another pan and tossed it in.

"What are you doing?"

Griff jumped straight up in the air. "Creep up on a guy, why don't ya?" He turned to find Lauren, wrapped in her robe, yawning.

"I'm sorry. I smelled the coffee and something else. Couldn't place it, so I got up."

"Butter. Maybe mushrooms?"

"That's it. What's going on here?" She approached the stove, but Griff grabbed her waist and pulled her away.

"I'm making breakfast for you."

"You are? Why?"

"Because I love you. Now go. Get some coffee and leave the master chef alone." He gave her a gentle shove toward the coffeepot and patted her behind.

"Early practice?" She filled the mug on the counter.

"Yep. Big game tomorrow night."

"Who are you playing?"

"Nevada Gamblers."

"Are they good?" She added a touch of sugar and milk then stirred.

"Yeah. Big, too. Linebackers are fucking machines."

She sat down and watched him add eggs to the pan. "Machines?"

"Yeah. Known for mowing down quarterbacks."

"Aren't there penalties for that?"

"Unnecessary roughness? Sure. But by then, it's too late."

"They won't hurt you, will they?"

He loved the note of concern in her voice. "Nah. My guys are the best. I'm not afraid. We've played them before."

"Good." She blew out a breath. "I was worried for a minute."

"About me?" He ambled over to the table where she sat, sipping her coffee.

"Of course."

"How come?"

"Because I love you, and I don't want you to get killed." She pushed up to a half-stand to kiss him.

"They won't lay a finger on me, honey," he whispered. Her words warmed his heart.

Griff finished his omelet, which turned out surprisingly well considering it was his first effort. When the meal was done, they held hands over their beverages. Griff was reluctant to leave her, though he needed to dress and go.

He washed up and threw on work-out clothes. As he was heading for the door, Lauren put her hand on his arm.

"I have an early Christmas surprise for you."

He raised his eyebrows.

"Your dad is coming. He arrives tomorrow."

"My dad?"

"Yep. I sent him the ticket."

Griff picked her up and twirled her around. "That's awesome, baby. I haven't seen him for a year. Thank you." He set her down.

"You're close?"

"Always have been. He coached me, trained me, and encouraged my love for football. Went to every high school game. Gave me good advice. He's always been my biggest fan."

"I can't wait to meet him."

"He'll love you." After a goodbye kiss, he was out the door, humming.

LAUREN PACED. GRIFF had insisted on flying his father to the small airport forty minutes north of Monroe. She went to pick him up while Griff was going over plays with Coach Bass and working out.

Finally, the flight was announced. She fluffed up her hair, refreshed her lipstick, and plastered a smile on her face.

A tall, rangy man with steel gray hair walked through the doorway carrying a small duffel bag. He wore glasses and a well-trimmed, full mustache. Dressed in a sleeveless parka and a flannel shirt, Hank Montgomery was a good-looking man, by any standards, even at sixty. Broad shoulders, long legs, and narrow hips, like his son, allowed Lauren to identify him instantly.

The resemblance between Griff and his father was unmistakable. Gave Lauren shivers to think how good Griff was going to look when he got older. *Will I be around then?*

Hank approached her, his brows knit. "Miss Farraday?"

"Lauren, please," she said, extending her hand.

He shook it firmly without crushing it. "Pleasure to meet you." She saw his gaze travel over her body in the wink of an eye. "My boy always had good taste."

Lauren sensed color flooding into her cheeks. She didn't know how much he knew about her relationship with Griff. "Thank you. The car's this way." She turned her back to him, hiding her embarrassment, as she headed for the parking lot.

Hank settled into the front seat.

Lauren put the car in gear and opened the conversation. "Did you play football, too, Mr. Montgomery?"

"Hank, please. Yep. Quarterback, just like Griff."

"That's how you knew how to train him?"

"Yeah. But he was a natural. Took to it like a duck to water. Pretty soon, he didn't want to do anything but play."

"How'd you get him into college?"

"His mother, God rest her soul. She took him in hand. Sat with him while he did homework. Coached him on his weaker subjects. He's smart. No doubt about that."

"Are you retired?"

"I work part-time. I'm a carpenter. Do you work?"

"I'm an interior decorator. Just finished a big house. Now, I'm waiting for my next assignment."

"Paint, wallpaper, and that stuff?"

She laughed. "Yep. I try to make a comfortable, pretty home for people."

Griff was back by the time they arrived. He greeted his father with a big bear hug. He offered the older man a beer then sank down on the living room sofa to catch up. His dad quizzed him on the new contract, asking detailed questions.

Lauren slipped into the kitchen to prepare roast duck, Czechoslovakian style, like her mother used to make. Listening to the cadence of the deep, male voices from the next room soothed her. She smiled as she peeled potatoes. By three o'clock, she was almost finished.

Apple pie? Of course! She pulled out the flour canister.

"I'm taking dad to the stadium. I'll pick up an extra ticket for him for the game on Sunday."

"Don't. Don can't come. I'll give your dad his."

"You don't mind me running off with him, do you?"

"Go ahead. I've got plenty to do."

"What about work? Will you be here?"

"I forgot to tell you. I finished the house yesterday. I'm free until Annette gives me a new job."

"Fantastic. We'll be back. When's dinner?"

"About six thirty."

"Got it."

Lauren dumped apples in a stainless steel bowl, grabbed the peeler, and headed to the living room. She put in a Christmas movie and began removing the apple skins as she watched. Her cell rang.

"Hey, Marnie, how're you doing?"

"Getting bigger every day. Oops. Sorry. I didn't mean to…"

"No problem. I'm fine. I'm glad you're doing well. Do you still go to lunch? I've got some free time now."

"Why not? Haven't seen you in a while. Still with that gorgeous quarterback?"

"Yep. Things are good. Better than good. We're committed to each other."

"Committed? Like engaged?"

"In a monogamous relationship."

"So, maybe marriage is next?"

"Trying to take it one step at a time."

"Thought you didn't want to get married?"

"I don't. Didn't. I don't know. I'm trying not to think about it. Marriage. Pregnancy. Miscarriage. Ugh. I just want to be happy now and worry about tomorrow when it comes."

"The group would approve."

"I've learned from them. I'm leading exactly the kind of life I want right now. Your due date is almost here, right?"

"End of January."

"How are you feeling?"

"Huge."

The women arranged a date and time to meet for lunch before disconnecting. Lauren finished preparing the fruit. She put the pie together and slid it in the oven, right underneath the duck. Soon, the smell of cooking apples would blend with the aroma of roasting poultry.

She poured a mug of coffee and padded to the living room again. A small tree stood in the corner with a couple of bags of ornaments and lights. After putting on Christmas music, she tackled the decorating, singing along.

The tree was finished when the men returned. It didn't have much, as Lauren had never had one of her own before.

Griff tried to stifle a chuckle. "Charlie Brown would be proud," he said.

She swatted at his shoulder. "Thanks a lot."

"But dinner smells great."

"What are you making?" Hank asked, hanging his coat in the front hall closet.

She hooked her arm through his and escorted him to the kitchen. "Roast duck. Wanna peek?"

"I thought you'd never ask." The older man grinned.

The food was delicious. Lauren ate quietly, listening to the men banter and exchange stories. Hank brought Griff up to date on all his old high school chums and people in the little town of Adams, Indiana. She saw the small town boy emerge from inside Griff. He had always displayed the sophisticated outlook of a wealthy man to her. But she was intrigued and charmed by his boyish humor and interest in his hometown.

When the meal was finished, the men took over the clean-up. Lauren made a point of yawning and stretching and wishing them goodnight. She traipsed up to her room and shut the door. Lying in bed, her arms above her head, she wondered what Griff had been like as a child.

A knock on the door drew her attention. She cracked it open. Griff pushed, and she let him in.

"What the hell? What are you doing up here?" He asked.

"Your dad is here. Right across the hall."

"So?"

"I don't think we should be sleeping together with him in the house."

Griff laughed. "You think he's a prude? You think he doesn't know? Of course, he knows. And he's been single now for four years. He's probably got a ton of women in and out of his bedroom."

"That's none of my business. It's just…"

"You're embarrassed. That's it. You're embarrassed, aren't you?"

She nodded.

"That's ridiculous. I have a game tomorrow. I'm not sleeping alone. You have a choice—either come down to my room, or I'm sleeping here…and making you scream so loud my old man'll be jealous as hell."

"Griff!"

"He knows me. He'd think it weird if we were in separate rooms."

"What did you tell him?"

"Nothing. It's my business. And he wouldn't ask."

"I don't know." She cast her gaze to the floor.

Griff stepped up and took her in his embrace. "Come on, baby." He rubbed his hands up and down her arms. "Never had to beg before."

She giggled, sliding her palms up his bare chest. "An offer I can't refuse."

"Downstairs. More privacy."

"I thought you didn't care?"

"I don't. Don't want to rub his face in it, either."

She chuckled, pushed away from him, and slipped a robe over her nightgown.

"You're not sleeping in that, are you?"

"We'll see."

"Yeah. We'll see it hanging on the bedpost, beautiful," he whispered, taking her hand and leading her downstairs. She suppressed another giggle as she tiptoed soundlessly down the carpeted steps, feeling like a sixteen year old.

Once she got behind his closed door, Lauren was grateful he'd convinced her to join him.

Chapter Sixteen

IT WAS COLD THAT DECEMBER day, a week before Christmas. Griff put on a long sleeved thermal shirt under his uniform. He grabbed his cap, gloves, and jacket, too. He needed to keep his throwing arm warm, which would be a challenge.

He peeked out toward the stands and spied his father and Lauren, their legs wrapped in blankets. She held a cup in her hands. He'd bet it was a hot drink. At least he'd be moving some of the time today, not sitting still. *Damn hard to stay warm in the stands.*

The sight of his dad and his girl together swelled his heart. His life was coming together. After this game, he planned to propose to Lauren. The stupid commitment idea was a weak step in their relationship. Why bother with that, he told himself. Just go right to the big question. His confidence grew. Having the girl he wanted and his biggest fan rooting for him today, how could he go wrong?

He went out to warm up with Buddy. They tossed the ball back and forth. Griff's arm was strong, his eyesight clear, and his passes pinpoint accurate. The Nevada Gamblers were warming up on their side. Darvin Sweetwater was good, but Griff knew he was better. The wind had died down and was no longer a factor in getting the ball to his target. He thanked God for that break.

The teams ran out on the field and stood for the national anthem. Adrenalin kept him warm. They lost the toss, and the Gamblers elected to kick off. Griff didn't mind. He'd be getting into the action sooner, keeping his body limber. Rumor had it that the Gamblers had the biggest defensive line in the league—average weight two hundred thirty pounds. That didn't scare Griff. He had a strong offensive line to protect him.

With Bullhorn Brodsky leading the front line, Griff dropped back to search for an open man. Homer Calloway had two men on him, but Buddy Carruthers was alone. Griff rifled one to Buddy, who plucked it out of the air with ease. The brutes on the Gamblers took him down, holding the Kings to a fifteen yard gain. Griff was pumped.

Next play, Griff again dropped back. Buddy was covered by two men and Homer by one. Griff's blockers accidentally created an opening. Griff scrambled through and hightailed it for the first down. A huge defenseman flew at him. Griff slid, as if running for home plate in baseball, but the big man was already in flight. He landed smack on top of Griff. Ribs pushed into the ground, his body seemed to compress for a split second then bounce back.

A penalty was called for "unnecessary roughness." Bull offered Griff a hand. He pushed up and sprinted back to position.

The next play was a diversion. Griff faked a hand-off to Buddy on his left, but really slipped the pigskin to Caleb Turner on his right. He took it for eight yards before they brought him down. Griff noticed Bull was still on the ground. Time out was called, and the Kings' trainer ran onto the field. The team stood around, watching Bull hug his thick ankle.

Nothing ever happens to Bullhorn Brodsky. He's fine. But the trainer signaled for the cart while Bull was helped up by two of his teammates. Griff touched helmets with the big man as they took him away.

"It's only a flesh wound," Bull kidded, locking eyes with Griff.

"Fuckin' better be. Then, get your ass back here. I need you," the quarterback replied.

Lawson "The Kid" Breaker ran out onto the field. He was Bull's backup. Griff swallowed. Lawson was called "The Kid" because he was twenty-two. He had been acquired in a special deal Lyle Barker, the owner, had cut with the Delaware Demons. The Kid was as green as they come. Griff looked at the bruisers on the Gamblers' front line. He uttered a silent prayer and went into the huddle.

Play after play, the Kings marched downfield. They scored. Then, it was the Gamblers' turn. Darvin Sweetwater threw well, but the Kings defense cut them off. They charged down to the thirty yard line, where the Kings' stopped them with an interception, taking possession of the ball.

At half time, the score was Kings, twenty-one, and the Gamblers, seven. Griff checked on Bullhorn.

"Twisted. I'm out for today, but I'll probably be able to play next week."

"You've got to be okay for the playoffs," Griff said, staring at the trainer, who was rewrapping Brodsky's bad ankle.

"I will. Just make sure we get there."

Griff checked the stands and nodded to his father and Lauren. She waved. Strength oozed through him. He flexed his arm. The muscle was warm and feeling good. He was ready to start the second half.

Not long after the second half kick-off, the Kings recovered a Gamblers fumble. Griff trotted out to take command. He kept his eye on The Kid, the weak link in the front line, but so far, he was holding strong.

Then, it happened. Two defensemen blitzed Lawson Breaker, and he went down. Griff spotted Homer and was taking aim. The two men barreled forward, rushing through the line. Griff saw them out of the corner of his eye, but chose to fire off the pass anyway. They leapt at him as he let go of the ball, taking him down sideways, piling on top. He heard the crack seconds before pain seared through him and everything stopped.

The stinging agony rocketed through him so strong it took his breath away. He saw stars then everything went white. Closing his eyes, he lay still, because it hurt like hell to move. *Oh shit, oh shit, oh shit.* His body froze in position. From far away, he thought he heard a whistle.

The two enormously heavy bodies were lifted off him. Still, he couldn't move. Tears from the intensity of the agony formed. He blinked them back.

He didn't want to open his eyes. *This is a bad dream. It's not happening. I'm going to wake up any second.* But he didn't. He didn't hear any noise and again thought he was dreaming. But dizziness made him nauseous, so he was forced to open them or throw up in front of everyone.

The normally boisterous crowd was silent. Voices called his name. The moment the trainer tried to turn him on his back, sharp, stinging pain ripped through his torso, making him gasp.

"LOOK OUT, GRIFF!" LAUREN screamed, but it was too late. The noise in the stands was deafening, and he wouldn't have heard her anyway. She gripped Hank's arm with all her might as she watched two brutes sweep the rookie lineman out of the way and charge toward Griff. He wasn't looking. Lauren bit down so hard on her lip that it bled. She was bouncing up and down, hollering to Griff, but in a flash, it was too late.

She watched him go down hard with two giant defensemen toppling over on him. The big guys rolled off, and Griff lay still. She fisted Hank's sleeve. He covered her hand with his. The referee blew the whistle to signal the play was dead. The audience quieted down instantly when the quarterback didn't move. Lauren jumped up and screamed his name. Hank gasped. He immediately hit the stairs, taking them two at a time.

She waited, her eyes wide, her pulse racing. Adrenaline pumped through her body, raising it to high alert. Still, Griff didn't move. Two trainers raced out onto the field. They bent down. She couldn't see what was happening. Pushing her way through the throng, now on its feet, she made it to the stairs and flew down, following Hank. Her feet moved so fast she could hardly feel them.

Once she got to the field, she still couldn't see what was going on. Fear raced through her. Slipping past security, she snaked her way through the fans, getting as close to the bench as possible. Buddy turned and spied her standing there. He shook his head. Griff still wasn't moving. Tears clouded Lauren's eyes, and she couldn't stop the flow.

She spotted Hank, who came over to her.

"I'm gonna go with him."

She cocked her head. "Can I come?"

"I'm sorry. Family only." He put an arm around her and squeezed.

Suddenly, Griff's helmet moved. With help from the trainers, he sat up. The crowd roared and clapped. Two more men came with a stretcher. Griff waved them away. They helped him to his feet, and he slowly walked off the field. The spectators chanted his name as he disappeared into the locker room.

Lauren went to the door, but was shoved aside by trainers and medics.

"I'll let you know what happens," Hank said, patting her shoulder.

In that instant, that very moment, Lauren knew exactly how she felt about Griff Montgomery. She loved him with all her heart. Her stomach knotted, and her chest tightened. He was the most important person in the world to her. She knew then she had to marry him. *Damn the consequences.*

It didn't matter what happened with a pregnancy, or if he left her. She had to be with him, for however long. Being shut out hurt as much as if someone had punched her.

The guard stepped in front of her. "Family?"

She shook her head. "Girlfriend."

"I'm sorry, miss. I can only admit immediate family."

She nodded her understanding. She'd be family. She had to. Whatever happened to Griff, she wanted, needed, to be there with him, helping him. And nothing else mattered.

She waited outside the locker room. An ambulance arrived.

Griff walked out wearing his jersey and sweatpants. "No ambulance."

"It's the rules, Griff," the man standing next to him said.

The quarterback turned, raising his gaze to hers. Emotion rose up, trapping words in her throat, but tears poured down her face.

He took her hand in his. "I'm okay. Probably just a broken collarbone. Go home. Take it easy. Dad's coming with me." She nodded. He swiped his fingers over her cheeks. "Don't cry, baby."

"I'll be home. Waiting."

He tried to bend down to kiss her, but grimaced when he changed position.

"Come on, Montgomery. Gotta get you some serious pain meds."

Griff cupped her face, handed her his car keys, smiled, and was gone. His dad climbed into the ambulance next.

She got in his car and sat for a moment, with the motor running and the heater going full blast. Deep breathing calmed her. She dried her tears and put the vehicle in gear. *What does this mean for his career? For us?* Questions swam through her mind as she drove slowly home.

She parked and entered the house. Spike was at the door, barking and jumping up to kiss her with his puggy tongue. She smiled to see him. He needed dinner so she fed him and poured herself a generous brandy. After turning on the television, she watched the news about Griff. There was no information she didn't already have.

Sudden hunger gripped her belly. She heated up some leftovers and flipped channels until she found a romantic movie. Then she ate, sipped, and cuddled up with Spike and a crocheted throw. Lauren decided it was time to face life and stop running away. Making a decision calmed her heart, but worry about Griff still nagged at her.

She dozed in front of the television, only to be shaken awake by Hank at two o'clock.

"Talk later," he whispered before hiking up the stairs to the guest room. Lauren yawned and headed for Griff's room. She stripped off her clothes, lifted Spike up under the quilt with her, and fell into an exhausted sleep.

WHEN SHE DRAGGED HERSELF out of bed at eight o'clock, Hank was nowhere to be seen. Neither was Griff's car. Lauren was miffed he didn't wake her and tell her what was going on.

I'm just his son's friend with benefits. I don't count. She set her jaw, fished her keys out of her purse, walked Spike, and then headed to the hospital.

At the desk, she was denied access to Griff's room. She argued and pleaded, to no avail. Then, she spied Marnie coming down the hall. "Hey, Marnie! Help me, please. They don't believe I know Griff. They think I'm some crazed fan. Could you tell them the truth?"

Marnie put her arm around her friend. "Is Griff here?"

Lauren's voice shook. "He was hurt yesterday. They won't let me in to see him."

Marnie turned to the nurse in charge. "Grace? My friend, Lauren, is living with Griff Montgomery. I think he'd want to see her." The woman in white cocked her eyebrow at Lauren and frowned. "Well, if Marnie says...but I'm not sure about this."

"This is legit, Grace, honest."

"Room 126, down the hall, on the left."

"Thank you." Lauren hugged Marnie then practically ran down the hall. She stopped to take a deep breath before pushing open the door.

The small room was stuffed with people, including a doctor, another man talking to him, Coach Bass, who she recognized from the games, Hank Montgomery, and Griff, in bed wearing a special collar and a sling. The men were talking and arguing. Lauren managed to slip past them. Griff smiled at her.

"How are you?" She touched his arm.

"I don't know, yet. I have to have surgery, then heal, then train my ass off. I'm thirty-three. I don't know if this is the end of my career." The crease between his brows deepened.

"Come home. I'll take care of you..." She took his hand.

"It's not like a bowl of chicken soup will make this all right. I'm not coming home."

"What?"

"I'm going to New York for surgery then back to Indiana with my dad. We'll have to take a break." He eased away to adjust the sling.

"Why? Come back to my house."

"Actually, mine is ready. I'm going there tonight. Then, we leave for Manhattan."

"What about us?" Lauren could barely choke out the words.

He took her hand, kissed the back, and laced his fingers with hers. "I need to get well before there's an *us*. I may not have a job. I need to know where my life is going before I make anything...uh, permanent with you. Do you understand?"

"I don't care about that stuff."

"But I do. I need to focus on getting my career back. That has to come first. I have nothing to offer you now, but an injured athlete. One who might never play again."

"But...I..."

He put his finger over her lips. His eyelids fluttered.

"Excuse me. Excuse me, people. Everyone out, please. My patient has to rest." The doctor opened the door.

Reluctantly, she was swept out with the others. Hank was the only one to remain. She drove home, wondering what had just happened. When she arrived, Spike was barking, and there were several cars parked in front of her house.

Buddy Carruthers approached as she put the key in the lock. "Hey, Lauren. How you doin'?"

"Been better, Buddy. What's up?"

"Hank asked a few of us to come over and get Griff's stuff. He's moving back to his place."

She stopped to stare at him for a moment. "Oh. Sure. Okay. Come in." She threw the door open. A few other teammates exited their cars and followed Buddy. Lauren spent the next hour gathering his belongings. The big men hauled clothes, books, and his television down to their vehicles.

Lauren felt like she was going through another divorce. But the men were nice and polite. She even saw a touch of sympathy in Buddy's eyes.

He patted her on the shoulder. "It'll all work out. You'll see. Here's my cell, just in case."

She nodded, even though she doubted what he said. Holding Spike in her arms, she waved goodbye as the three cars pulled away from the curb. A heaviness in her chest spread sadness and emptiness through her gut. Her footsteps echoed down the hall as she marched into his room. Lauren stripped the bed, bundled the sheets, and threw them in the washer. The space looked sterile, unoccupied, like a hotel room when the occupant has checked out.

She fell down on the mattress, pulling the pillows to her chest, and cried. Spike jumped up and licked her face.

She opened each dresser drawer. In the bottom one, there were two items. One was a rectangular package wrapped in red paper with a gold ribbon. The tiny card said it was for her from Griff. The other item was a pair of brand-new running shoes, still in the box. She slipped his present under her small tree, picked up the ones she'd bought for him and his dad, and got in her vehicle.

One call to Buddy gave her Griff's address. Shock hit her when she pulled into the driveway. Buddy opened the door. The men from the Kings were still in the house, drinking beer.

"Welcome, Lauren. Come in. Have a brew."

"No, thanks. This is really Griff's place?" she asked, putting down the box of shoes.

"Hell, yeah. Whoever did this did a great job," Buddy said, looking around.

"I did this."

"You?" He turned to stare.

"So, Griff was the mystery client?" She shook her head and smiled.

"This is awesome. Would you do my place, too?"

"Let me show you around." She led the men through the house, from the home gym in the basement, to the living room done up in fall colors. The den had a wild feel to it, with jungle wallpaper and a grass rug. His master bedroom, with a king size bed, had a deep pile rug, perfect for bare feet, and was decorated in shades of blue and silver.

All three teammates took her card.

Lauren pulled Buddy aside. "What's going to happen to Griff?" She chewed her lip.

"Hey, it's a long road back, but he can make it, if he tries hard enough. He's out now, but should have enough time to be in shape by training camp next summer."

"Do you think he can?"

"I think he can do whatever he makes up his mind to do. He's that kinda guy. He'll be back, Lauren. Don't worry." He gave her a hug then they descended the stairs.

Mac Jenkins hooked up the huge flat screen television.

"Any good games?" Another player said, rooting around in Griff's stash.

Lauren slipped out quietly. *He hired me anonymously to do his house?* The generosity of his move overwhelmed her. *Of course, he got a great house that all the guys envy, but still. He didn't have to do that. He could have hired anyone. I hope he likes it.*

She returned home to eat leftovers again with Spike. Her heart ached, and the quiet was deafening. She hadn't realized how much vitality, energy, and noise Griff Montgomery brought with him. Now that he was gone, his absence made her shiver, like lack of heat in a cold house.

GRIFF GRIPPED HIS FATHER'S arm as he climbed the front steps of his place. He had returned several times, on the sly, to check Lauren's progress. Each time, he was more in love with the warm, masculine home she had created. It had no tchotchkes or clutter. That's the way he liked his life—clean and orderly. He'd lived that way for so long, compartmentalizing his existence.

Then, he had met Spike and Lauren, and it had gotten messy and out-of-control.

"Wow. You weren't kiddin' when you said you were redoing the place."

"Lauren did it."

"She did? She sure knows you." Hank guided his son into the living room.

"Actually, she didn't know it was for me."

"You paid her?"

"She needed the money. Besides, it's her profession." Griff sank down onto the sofa, hissing with pain.

"Paid her rent. Paid her to redo this place. She's one expensive woman." Hank switched on the lights.

"It's not like that, dad."

"Then, what is it like? You shack up with this chick. If she's so great, why don't you marry her?"

"She doesn't want to get married."

"Did you ask?"

"She told me before I asked."

"Never met a woman who didn't want to get married."

"Well, now you have." Griff pushed to his feet, with help from Hank.

"How come?"

"It's complicated." The quarterback headed toward the kitchen. "Hungry?"

"Starving."

Hank opened the fridge and some cabinets. "Not much in here. There's soup. Chicken noodle or beef barley?"

"You pick. Call The Savage Beast. Carla'll send over some burgers and fries."

Griff handed his cell to his father before he eased himself down on a stool. The pain broke through his meds, and he shut his eyes to gain control.

"Here. Time to take these." Hank shook two pills out of a plastic container into his palm, and filled a glass with water. Griff swallowed them while his dad dialed the bar. After the order was placed, he took down a can and rooted around, looking for a can opener.

Griff's gaze perused the kitchen. With barley-colored walls, black cabinets, and stainless steel appliances, the room had a sleek, modern feel. "Nice. She's good. Very good."

"Got your style exactly, huh? Without even asking you? Pretty neat trick."

"Yeah, she's pretty amazing."

"I never shacked up with your mother, you know."

"Uh, TMI, dad?"

"When you find a good woman, the right one, you marry her," Hank said, pouring the soup into a pot.

"The lady has to be willing." Griff pointed to the cabinet where he kept bowls.

His father turned to stare at him then threw up his hands. "None of my business, I guess. But you young people today. Damn, you make an easy situation so much harder."

Griff laughed. "So, you approve?"

"Doesn't matter what I think, does it?" Hank ladled soup into two bowls and put one down in front of his son.

"Not really. Well, maybe. A little."

"Don't know the lady. I'll go along with whatever you decide." The doorbell rang. Hank went to answer it then returned. "Right now, seems to me you've got a career to save," the older man said, opening the bag and removing the Styrofoam containers.

Griff picked up a burger and took a big bite.

"You come home with me after the surgery, and I'll get you back into shape."

"You're a slave driver."

Hank chuckled. "Damn right, I am. That's what got you to the Kings in the first place."

"That and a shitload of talent, maybe?"

"That, too." Hank smiled and picked up his burger. "This looks good."

"How long do you think it'll take?" Griff asked, before shoving two fries in his mouth.

"Don't know, son. Depends. On a lotta things. Let's get through the surgery first."

"Then, I gotta lie around for six weeks. That might be the hardest part."

"I doubt that." They both laughed.

Griff called Lauren.

"I'm going to New York early tomorrow. Surgery is scheduled. Christmas in the hospital."

"Oh, no. I'm so sorry. Damn, Griff. I was counting on being with you. I hope you'll be okay."

"As long as they don't fuck up the procedure. Dad's gonna get me in shape."

She chuckled. "Probably just what you need."

"I don't know how long it'll take. I hope you understand."

"I do."

"I'll be gone six, maybe seven, months. It isn't fair to ask you to wait for me."

There was silence.

Finally, she spoke. Her voice was husky. "Doubt I could replace you in seven months. Call me when you get back. I'll still be here."

"Yeah? I hope so."

"Of course, if you meet some small town beauty...well, I'll understand."

"Will you?"

"Not really. But I had to say that. Say...that's some surprise you pulled on me. Your house, all along."

"You really didn't know it was me?"

"If I had suspected, I'd have said something."

"True. You're not shy about speaking up."

"Thanks for having faith in me."

"The house is great. You did an amazing job."

"Thanks."

"You're blushing, aren't you?"

"Probably. Can I see you in the hospital?"

"Sure. I'll have dad call you when the surgery is over."

"I love you, Griff."

"I love you, too, beautiful."

"Good luck."

"Thanks. I'll need it. Bouncing back won't be so easy."

"You can do it."

"I hope so."

He hung up. *She's not going to be around seven months from now. Beautiful women like Lauren don't stay single for long.* The heaviness in his chest centered around his heart. His dad was talking, but Griff, staring out the window, was miles away. He pictured a honeymoon suite on a tropical island, alone with Lauren. No clothes, no inhibitions, no people. A sigh escaped him. A song title came to mind. *The Impossible Dream.*

Chapter Seventeen

GRIFF'S SURGERY WAS done on December twenty-fourth. Hank called Lauren to tell her it was a success. Don and his family were coming for Christmas Eve instead of Christmas Day. Griff was in recovery, and Hank urged her to stay home. She planned to visit him on Christmas Day, regardless of Hank's words.

By six o'clock, the house was filled with noise and bodies rushing around. The activity cheered her. Lauren had lost her taste for living alone. Don made a fire while Connie heated lasagna. The kids set the table and retrieved the salad and garlic bread Lauren had prepared. They ate quickly then opened gifts.

With her new earnings, Lauren had splurged. The kids fell on their presents like hungry wolves on an unsuspecting fawn. Soon the living room floor was covered with bits and chunks of wrapping paper.

They watched a movie, ate popcorn, and enjoyed Connie's special Christmas Coconut cake. By eleven, the brood was on the road. Exhausted, Lauren summoned the energy to take Spike out for his walk. The neighborhood was silent. Colored lights blinked in windows, around doors, and on bushes and trees. The icy wind whipped her scarf up, into her face. Spike, wearing his little coat, shivering by a fire hydrant.

Once inside again, Lauren finished cleaning up the kitchen and made a hot toddy. She curled up with Spike on the sofa, listened to Christmas music, and watched the fire burn down. She refused to think about her future, instead insisting on celebrating each day as it came.

The evening had been fun. She didn't know what she'd find when she saw Griff in the hospital. But she'd deal with whatever came along.

Thoughts of her first Christmas without her father weighed heavy on her heart. Sad and weary, Lauren rested her head on a cushion. The soft snore of her pug soothed her. After the last sip of her drink, she drifted off on the sofa, hearing "Silent Night" playing in her head.

The morning was quiet. Lauren arose feeling achy from sleeping on the narrow couch. She walked Spike and fed him. Heating up a bowl of oatmeal, she dug out the box from Griff she had found in the bottom drawer. She loaded up the cereal with butter, milk, and brown sugar then sat at the dining room table. She slipped the ribbon off and tore the paper. Carefully, she pulled the top off. Inside, nestled in snowy white cotton, gleamed a gold chain.

She lifted it out. *A charm bracelet!* Putting down her spoon, she fingered each charm. A tiny football, a football helmet, a pug, an artist's palette, a book, a little football player, and so on. The fourteen-carat gold trinkets depicted their time together. At the end, there was a heart. On one side was etched *Griff,* and on the other, *Lauren.* Tears welled up in her eyes. She turned it around and around. The sentimental present choked her up.

She fastened it on her wrist, checked the time, and jumped in the shower.

Lauren didn't expect the train to be packed with people going to see the sights in New York City. She arrived just as it did and almost didn't find a seat. Alighting at 125th Street, she descended the station stairs and caught a taxi to the hospital. She got Griff's room number and walked through the long, winding hallways to find the right elevator. He was in a private room. The door was open. Griff was in the bed, asleep. Hank dozed in a chair by the window.

She stopped to gaze at her lover. It was a bit shocking to see such a strong man look fragile, pale, and innocent. The neck collar forced him to sleep sitting up. The thin, off-white blanket rose only to his waist.

His hair went every which way, and his face was scruffy. He looked adorable. Wishing she could cradle him in her arms, she tiptoed closer. *He's too big to put in my lap.*

Sleepy eyes cracked open. His parched lips moved, but no sound came out. Lauren slipped into a seat close by. She picked up a Styrofoam cup of water with a straw in it and held it to his mouth. He was wan, looked tired, and his eyes reflected pain. While he drank, she combed his hair back from his forehead with her fingers. She whipped a ChapStick out of her purse and rubbed it over his lips.

He smiled. "Is it you, or am I dreaming?"

"Merry Christmas, Griff." She leaned over to kiss him gently.

"The Christmas I'll never forget." He laughed, until the vibration brought pain.

A nurse entered. "Time for medicine," she said, handing him a tiny, paper cup with two tablets in it. Lauren held the water for him. "Haven't had anyone famous in here for a bit. He's calm for a celebrity."

"Is he a good patient?"

"So far." The woman stuck a thermometer in his mouth then held his wrist while she checked her watch.

By now, Hank was awake. He stood up and stretched his lanky frame. "How's he doin'?" He nodded at Lauren before turning to the nurse.

"Fine. Dinner will be here at five thirty."

"Any food restrictions?" Hank asked.

"Today, he has to eat what we serve, but if he's doing well, tomorrow, he might be able to bring in some food from the outside. Mr. Montgomery, anything you need?"

Griff shot a look at Lauren then shook his head.

"I see." The woman chuckled. "You have everything you need right here."

After fifteen more minutes of conversation, Griff began to fade. Hank suggested Lauren join him for a bite at the hospital cafeteria.

They closed the door, leaving Griff nodding off, and found their way downstairs.

Settling at a table near a corner, Hank brought his gaze up to meet hers. His eyes were questioning, probing, his brows knitted. "Why won't you marry my boy?"

"What?"

"Griff says you won't marry him. Says you don't want to marry anyone. You gay?"

Lauren choked on her coffee. "I beg your pardon? How is that any business of yours? And, no, I'm not gay."

"You're shacking up with my son. But you won't marry him?"

"He hasn't asked me. And I don't see how that concerns you. Really, Hank. This is hard enough without a third degree from you."

Hank took a bite of his sandwich, chewed, and swallowed before responding. "I'm sorry, Lauren. I want to see the boy happy. And tom-catting around doesn't cut it. Know what I mean?"

"You'll have to ask Griff what he wants. At this point, I'm not sure he knows."

"You got that right."

"Tell me how you plan to train him, bring him back to where he used to be."

"All depends on how well he heals," Hank said. He sipped his drink then cracked a smile.

As he spoke, Lauren could see that he warmed to his subject. *His chance to help his son.*

"Once he gets the okay from the doc, we're heading out."

"To Indiana?"

"Yep. Driving him in that fancy car."

"Doesn't look too comfortable."

"It's fine. Besides, all the flights are booked."

"Why don't you stay in Monroe? His house is plenty big enough."

"Got the training stuff in my basement."

"Griff has a gym in his basement, too."

"That's just a gym. He needs special stuff. I got it at home."

Sensing she couldn't win, Lauren clammed up. *Go ahead. Take him. Take him away from the big, bad, loose woman.* Checking her watch, she realized she'd only have time for a quick goodbye, if she wanted to make the five o'clock train. Spike was at home, waiting for dinner.

Griff was awake when she popped in. Hank waited in the lounge, giving them some privacy.

"Thank you for the bracelet. It's beautiful. I love it," she said, swishing it so the gold charms clinked together.

"There's one missing. It's at the engraver. Guess it'll have to wait."

"Did you get my gift?"

"The sweater? Yeah. It's great. Perfect for an Indiana winter. Thank you."

Hissing with pain, he pulled her closer to plant a kiss on her lips. They spoke in low tones and kissed again, longer this time. The clearing of a throat brought their attention to the door. Hank stood, shifting his weight from foot to foot and gazing at the floor.

Lauren stood, shook Hank's hand, and blew a kiss to Griff before leaving for the station. She gazed out the train window on the gray, cold December day, slightly cheered by colored holiday lights in windows. She fingered the chain on her wrist, convinced she had seen Griff Montgomery for the last time.

AT GRIFF'S INSISTENCE, Lauren and Don continued to attend the Kings' football games. They bundled up more and more each week as the thermometer plummeted, but no amount of clothing or blankets enabled them to stay beyond the third quarter. Even then, it took Lauren ten minutes to thaw out in a warm car.

Tony Hastings took over as quarterback. Lauren tried to get into the spirit of the game, but every time she looked at Tony, she wished he was Griff. Her lover's record got the team into the playoffs. He was pleased. Sadly, the Kings lost in the first round to the Delaware Demons.

January turned into a busy month. Annette called to give her the good news—she had a bunch of new clients. Several of Griff's teammates had hired her to do the same for them.

"Can you do two at once? Buddy Carruthers is first, but then Max Jenkins wants his done right away. Is this too much to ask? Should I give it to someone else?"

"Didn't they ask for me?"

"They did. But we have other talented people, too."

"Those are my clients, Annette. You can't do that."

"This is my company. I can do whatever I want," she huffed.

Lauren called Griff. Since he was still sitting around recuperating, he had plenty of time to talk.

"Fuck her. Start your own company. The guys'll go wherever you go, baby. Screw her. Why should she get anything? She didn't bring in that business. You did."

"You're right. They're my clients."

"You've got the talent. Don't let that bitch steal your thunder. Hang out your own shingle."

"I could do it. I've inherited some money."

"Go for it, baby."

Lauren grinned. "Thanks. Your support means a lot."

"I'm proud of you. Wish I could be there for you."

"Get better. And come back to me."

"I'm tryin.'"

After exchanging "love you," they hung up. Lauren called Marcy Chase, the lawyer she had used to defend Griff's old charges of animal neglect, and started her own company. Once she began the process, her life became one giant, never-ending, to-do list. Papers to sign, bank account to open, office space to find, and bills to pay was the easy stuff. She also had to forge relationships with a truckload of retailers.

Between the driving, planning, looking at paint and wallpaper samples, and making drawings, Lauren barely had time to eat and sleep. She opened accounts with the hardware store, paint and wallpaper companies, and local furniture outlets. She attended art gallery openings and hawked small gift boutiques for just the right decorative pillow or candy dish.

One day a week, she hit the road, meeting antique dealers at auction houses across the state. She'd pack up Spike, find a modest motel, and drop in on shops. Spike was so friendly that he broke the ice for her.

Long phone conversations with Griff became a luxury. It wasn't that she didn't want to talk to him, but she got caught up in the insanity of opening a new business. She tried to focus on his words, but sometimes her eyes would begin to close. Other times, she'd return home too late to call. Her star athlete was an early riser.

Mostly, she missed him at night. She'd throw off her clothes and slip into bed, alone. Pillow talk, snuggled up against Griff's chest, was her favorite way to catch up on their day. She missed their lovemaking, but even more, she missed those cuddles and confidences shared when the lights went out. Then, she could tell him anything, from how much she loved him to the dumb things she had done at work, without embarrassment.

After spending her day on her cell, chasing down deliveries and ordering fabric, the last thing she wanted was to be on the phone. Daily talks with Griff dropped off to every other day then three times a week. His absence became a small ache inside that never left. Talking alone wasn't enough to lift the sadness from her heart.

She sank half of the money her father had left her into the new business and rented a small, two-room office in town. She set up a desk and used the other room to store all the samples she needed. Spike had a bed there, too.

Every morning, she bundled up the pug and drove into downtown Monroe. Days were filled with creative decisions and digging, searching for the right antique table or fireplace equipment. Nights were spent going over her books, sending out invoices, paying bills, and watching movies with Spike.

She stopped sleeping in what had been Griff's bed, because it simply made her miss him more, and returned to her own bedroom. When Griff started his training, seven weeks after the surgery, the phone calls ceased altogether. It took Lauren a few days to notice. She figured he was busy, and she was too swamped to worry.

Sometimes, late at night, when she awoke from a bad dream or was restless, Lauren stood at her window, looking down on the street. It was now March. There was snow on the ground. Ice, lining even the tiniest branches of bare trees, glistened in the moonlight. It was cold and beautiful.

She missed Griff. She remembered the feel of his strong arms around her. She longed to cuddle with him under the comforter on a chilly night. But then, those memories faded. With her days so full, it was as if her life with Griff had never happened.

Was what she'd had with Griff Montgomery real, or had she made more of it than it was to get through those tough first six months of being divorced? Still, he was a man like none other. When she had time to pause, she'd ask herself if she'd ever have a permanent relationship. After a sigh, she admitted that she might not. Griff Montgomery was the gold standard. And there weren't any more around like him.

AS SOON AS THE DOCTOR gave him the green light to work out, Griff's dad got him started exercising.

"Have to build you up. Get you used to moving around again," Hank said, massaging his son's calves. "Running first. Then weights."

"I need to get my arm moving."

"Yeah. I've got you set up to work out with the Adams' Football Juniors squad."

Griff laughed. "Little kids?"

"Some of 'em are pretty big. Junior high."

"Better than nothing."

The Football Juniors outfit was thrilled to have a famous quarterback working out with them. They arranged publicity. The story appeared in the local newspaper and was picked up by the Indianapolis Star. The Associated Press splashed his picture on the sports pages of newspapers across the country. Hank fielded tons of calls for interviews. And his son didn't miss one. He needed to stay alive in the minds of his fans.

In the pictures, Griff was flanked by some of the football juniors and a few cheerleaders. He wondered if Lauren had seen any, and if she was upset about the girls. He called three times, but the phone went to voicemail. He shrugged. *She'll just have to trust me.*

Griff was lonely. He had been to a bar once with his dad. Women crawled all over him. His will to resist slipped a bit. No sex was making him a horny and desperate man. But he'd made a commitment. Perhaps going out wasn't a good idea. He flirted and joked with his admirers, but went home alone.

Hank stepped up Griff's schedule. Running and working out then throwing with the football juniors in the afternoon. He kept himself safe from an affair by starting a backgammon tournament with his dad. They played every night after dinner, keeping Griff out of the bars. Determined, he swore to himself that he was going to reclaim his starting quarterback position and rekindle his romance with Lauren. By nine o'clock every night, he was exhausted and fell into bed, dreaming of her.

Day after day, his drive pushed him. His father controlled how much the quarterback attempted, careful not to overdo it and injure his son. Hank's life took on added significance now that he had become essential to Griff again.

Every week, he got stronger. The football juniors rallied and provided him with a long string of eligible receivers. They stayed longer and longer to practice with the star of the Kings. The whole town got behind Griff. Story after story hit the papers, following his progress.

A few speculated about his social life, but the quarterback knew enough to keep his mouth shut. He'd smile enigmatically and blush a bit, but never admit he wasn't dating. Finally, one reporter guessed he had a girl back in Monroe. When that happened, Griff was busted. He burst out laughing, turned red as a beet, and admitted there was someone he was anxious to see.

He hoped Lauren would see the article. He managed to connect with her on the phone from time to time, but she sounded preoccupied. *It's not you. She's starting a business. She's busy.* As often as he told himself that, still, he doubted her commitment. The more distant she sounded, the more convinced he was that she was seeing someone else.

Driven almost out of his mind by jealousy, he called Coach Bass and made arrangements for the team to provide a private trainer. He changed his plans, scheduling his return to Monroe earlier than he had anticipated. Hank didn't agree and tried to stop his son.

Griff pushed past his father, ripped his suitcase down from the closet shelf, and began packing.

"What? You're leaving now? When you're just getting started?"

"I'm not just getting started, Dad. I've made a lot of progress. I'm ready to go to a regular trainer." He opened the top bureau drawer.

"You're doing so well here."

"I need to get back to Monroe." Griff grabbed everything and threw it in the valise.

Hank paced. "What about the football juniors?"

"They're a great group of kids, but I'm done. They'll do fine without me."

"Come on, son. Hang here for a while. There are some great gals down at Bernie's place," Hank said, stopping his son's arm.

Griff shrugged off his father's hand. "I don't care about the great gals at Bernie's. I have one of my own. At least, I did. I hope to hell I still do."

"You're going back for her?" Hank's eyebrows rose.

Griff's expression clouded. "Watch it, Dad. Watch what you say about her."

"A girl who won't marry you? Just wants to shack up? Doesn't seem like you've got much of a future with her."

"That's my business. Stay out of it. I'm going home." He threw the last drawer's worth of clothes in the suitcase and closed it.

Hank stepped back.

Griff let out a breath when he saw the sad expression on his dad's face. "I can't live with you forever. You've got to get your own life, Dad."

"I know. It hasn't been easy."

"Mom's been gone for four years." Griff folded his jeans.

"Sometimes, it seems like yesterday. Other times, it seems like a century." Hank dropped his gaze to the football in his hands.

"I'm looking for the same thing you had with mom. And I've found it. It's in Monroe."

"Lauren's the one?"

"I think so."

"How are you gonna convince her to tie the knot?"

"I don't know. I'll figure it out when I get there." He rested his hand on his father's shoulder.

"She's sure pretty enough. Seems nice. Seems like she likes you a lot."

"She does. I'm ready to go back now. And I have you to thank. I'll never forget what you've done for me." The two men stood facing each other, when son clasped father in a bear hug. "You're the best, Dad."

Hank sniffled. "You are. Good luck. I hope you convince her."

"Me, too."

Griff loaded his luggage in the trunk. He waved to his father as he roared out of the driveway and hit the highway. It would be a long drive, but he had a lot to think about. His life was back. He hoped for the best year yet. When mental pictures of Lauren, naked, horny, and laying across the bed waiting for him took over his mind, he depressed the gas pedal. He blasted the radio and sang along with the theme song from *Frozen*.

He was moving forward at lightning speed. On to a new life and to reclaim his crown as King of the gridiron, nosing Tony Hastings back to the bench where he belonged.

LAUREN QUESTIONED HER support group and her friend, Marnie, but no one had the answer. Was she still committed to Griff? Considering she hadn't heard from him in a couple of weeks, she figured maybe not. So when Marty, the new manager at Carson's Department Store, asked her to dinner, she agreed. Marty was nice enough. Attractive, but not handsome like Griff. Still, she was lonely.

Marnie wasn't so sure. "You're going out with that guy from Carson's?"

"It's been a long time. I'm tired of waiting for phone calls that never come. I want a man who's here." Lauren talked as she prepared dinner for Spike.

"I thought you didn't want a man at all?"

"I did. I do."

"But that guy?"

"What's wrong with Marty?"

"Nothing. Unless you have Griff Montgomery in love with you." Marnie's voice dropped an octave.

"Do I?"

"I bet you do."

"I can date Marty and not worry about him getting serious."

"Why's that?"

"Because I'd never get serious about Marty. He's nice. Pleasant company."

"Would you sleep with him?"

"No way!"

"Then, why go out with him?"

"Why not? It's just dinner. We've gotta eat."

"No sex?"

"Marnie, come on."

"I mean, you've had quite a dry spell."

Lauren could feel herself blush. "This is a little personal."

"Only a little?" Marnie laughed. "Don't you miss him in bed?"

"God, do I."

"I thought so."

"This is an innocent date. I'm tired of being alone all the time."

"Go ahead. But I think you're making a big mistake. What if Griff finds out?"

"In Indiana? I doubt he'll know. Besides, we're just going out for a burger. To the Savage Beast."

"Good luck. I hear the baby crying. Gotta go."

Lauren picked up the noise in the background. It stabbed her heart. *Will I ever have that in my house? Probably not.*

She changed Spike's water and hit the shower. Though it was June, the evening temperature dipped below sixty. Her turquoise cashmere sweater and snug jeans lay on the bed. She slipped cute earrings in the shape of grapes on and decided to wear Griff's charm bracelet. *I'm not wearing it because I feel guilty. I'm only grabbing a burger with a colleague. It's not really even a date.*

She got in the car and hit the gas. When she arrived, Marty was already at a table. He rose from his chair and pulled out hers. *Well mannered.*

He took a sip from his beer. "You look amazing." His gaze lingered on her chest, while a touch of color stole into his cheeks.

"Thank you. What are you drinking?"

"Dark beer."

Carla arrived and took their order. Ordering the blue cheese burger reminded her of Griff. The pleasant clinking of the bracelet made her think of her quarterback more. Perhaps both were a mistake. She shifted in her chair, crossing and uncrossing her legs.

"You don't need to be nervous with me. I'm not going to jump you or anything," Marty said, chuckling. "At least not on the first date."

Her eyes widened. "Jump me? Not on any date."

"I didn't mean anything. It was a joke. A tasteless one, I guess."

She watched him blush and take a gulp of beer. *What am I doing here? Marnie was right.* "I think I should tell you, Marty, I'm not looking for a real relationship."

"Oh?"

"Yeah. I've been going out with someone, and he moved away temporarily, and, well, it's complicated."

"Dating almost always is. Then, why are you here with me?"

"I like you. Thought it would be just grabbing a burger together. Nothing formal or serious."

"Of course, it isn't serious. I hardly know you."

"Right. So. Hey. Why don't I just shut up now?"

Carla arrived with the burgers. Lauren picked hers up and took a big bite, relieved not to be talking. *You're assuming he likes you. Duh. Why would he be here if he didn't? Still. He's not that into you.*

They ate in silence for a while. Lauren looked up when she sensed his gaze on her. His light brown eyes paled when compared to Griff's dark ones. The quarterback's eyes got so dark when he was making love to her that they looked like two black olives. She shifted again and put her burger down.

"These chairs could be more comfortable."

I could be more comfortable.

"So, are you still involved with this other guy?"

Lauren paled as her gaze was drawn to the open door. Her mouth fell open.

Chapter Eighteen

GRIFF STEERED HIS SPEED machine onto the Merritt Parkway. June was the season of the Earth coming back to life, blooming, robust with color and renewal. He flexed his arm muscle and made a fist then opened his hand a few times. It was good, loose, comfortable, and no pain.

Bright colored flowers trimmed neat houses or growing wild in backyards smiled at him. The green of the lawns, the bright blue of the sky, and the blossoms cheered him. Power coursed through his veins. He was back. Back to being the best. He knew he could do it. *Thirty-three, injured, and not over the hill.*

Football had always been his first love. Now, it was crowded out of the top spot by a beautiful brunette. He could hardly wait to see Lauren. At a gas station, he dialed her number, trying to keep the excitement out of his voice. He planned to tell her he had a surprise for her. The phone rang and rang then went to voicemail. After a few frustrating tries, Griff gave up. He called Buddy instead.

"Hey, Buddy. I'm back!"

"Griff? Is it really you?"

"Yeah. I'm on the Wilbur Cross now."

"You're in Monroe?"

"Maybe forty minutes away."

"You son-of-a-bitch. Damn. Wanna grab a burger?"

"Sure. Meet me at The Savage Beast."

"You got it."

Griff steered back onto the highway. He turned up the radio and smiled. The car handled the curves like a racecar. He kept his speed under seventy to avoid a ticket, though it was hard. He was anxious to see his girl. It had been too long.

Since he had some time to spare, Griff pulled up to his house and dropped off his suitcases. He washed up, slapped on Lauren's favorite aftershave, changed clothes, and got back in the vehicle. *Boy, I'll sure be glad to stop driving.*

He pulled up to The Savage Beast and found a spot right in front. When he got out of the car, he stretched his long limbs. Buddy was coming down the sidewalk at the same time. They embraced for a moment then Buddy held the door open for his friend.

"So, your arm back to normal?"

"Damn right." Griff's gaze roved over the bar, as was his habit. He saw Lauren and did a double take. *No. Couldn't be.* His feet froze while he stared. He wasn't there long before she raised her eyes to meet his. She paled, and her mouth opened slightly.

"What the fuck?" he muttered under his breath.

Buddy stopped and turned. His eyes followed Griff's. "Uh oh." Buddy backed up and wrapped his fingers around the quarterback's biceps. "Don't do it."

"Do what?"

"Whatever you were going to do. Come on. Let's go to Bruno's." Buddy yanked him back toward the door, but Griff shrugged the hand off his arm.

"Why would I want to do that? I'm here now," he said, advancing toward Lauren's table. He stopped, looming over her. "Lauren. How nice to see you." His tone could freeze meat.

"Griff! How wonderful..." her words trailed off, her gaze bounced from Griff to Marty and back again. "This is Marty. Marty, Griff."

"Say, aren't you the quarterback for the Kings?" Marty extended his hand.

Griff took a breath, trying to control his temper. *Do I shake, or toss this guy out the window?* He took the proffered hand, briefly, and then lowered his voice. "Lauren, could I speak with you outside?"

He didn't wait for a reply. He closed his fingers around her upper arm and lifted her out of the chair to her feet. "Sure, sure. If you wanna talk. Fine." She nodded.

Griff kept his tight grip on her until they were outside. "What the hell? Who is that? Better be another brother or your cousin."

"He's not. He's a guy I work with. We're just grabbing a burger."

"Oh?" Griff arched an eyebrow. "Looks a lot like a date. What the fuck, Lauren? I thought you were waiting for me? I thought we were committed?"

"In the hospital, you said maybe we shouldn't be. You said you didn't know what was going to happen. You didn't know for sure that you'd be coming back. I waited for a long time. Haven't heard from you. You never even told me you were coming home." She poked her forefinger into his chest, her eyes blazing.

"The minute I'm gone, you're cheating."

"Cheating?" Her eyebrows rose. "I haven't heard from you in weeks! You've got some nerve."

"Maybe that's harsh. Still, I haven't had one, single date. In seven months. A record for me."

"Well, whoopee, give the man a trophy. Aren't you Mr. Perfect?"

"This better be your first date," he said, his face clouding over.

"It is. Not that you have a right to say anything."

"I thought we were on the same page. Guess I was wrong." He released her arm. "You're free. Go date whoever you want."

"What?"

"You heard me. Go to Smarty Marty, whatever the hell his name is. With my blessing. I'm done." He turned his back to her.

"Wait a minute. Wait!" But he was moving around to the driver's side of his car and didn't stop. "Griff! Stop! Don't go. Can't we talk about this?"

He planted his feet and raised his gaze to hers. "What's to talk about? You prefer to date other men. That's obvious. I prefer to be with someone who can be faithful. Let's agree to disagree."

"It's not like that. I don't even like him."

Griff cocked an eyebrow. "Didn't look that way to me."

"Well, you're wrong. I know, no one tells the fantastic star quarterback he's wrong, but you are." She plunked her hands on her hips.

"Then, what were you doing here?" He stood still, jingling his keys.

"I was lonely. He asked. I figured it wouldn't hurt."

"Are you sleeping with him?"

"Of course not! This was our first date."

"Were you going to?" He shifted his weight and tossed the keys from hand to hand.

"No way." Her tone softened.

"Why not?"

"I don't want to. You've ruined me. Ruined me for anyone else." Tears welled up in her eyes. She turned her head to the side, but Griff spied one on her cheek.

"How can I ever trust you?"

"You were gone for so long, it's almost like we never happened." Her voice was so low he could barely hear her.

"Saying you missed me?"

She nodded, still not facing him. She swiped her fingers across her face. His heart swelled. "Some days, I was so lonely. And the nights were even harder. Then, I'd hate you for making me love you and leaving. When I started my company, I was grateful to be too busy to think about you. Then, I kinda lost what we had. I couldn't feel you hugging me anymore."

Neither one moved. Emotion choked Griff, keeping his words trapped and his feet frozen.

"I saw pictures of you with those cheerleaders, and I thought maybe you'd moved on. Maybe I was holding a torch, but the flame was only burning on my side. Not yours. And then, I didn't know what to think. Why didn't you call?" She looked up, her tear-stained expression so hurt, so innocent. He could barely keep from folding her in his arms.

"They didn't mean anything. Just publicity. I did call you. But it always went to voicemail. And you never called back."

"By the time I found your calls, it was too late. You'd have been asleep."

"So? Wake me up." He stepped back toward the sidewalk.

"And interfere with your training? Hank would have my head." She smiled briefly.

People leaving The Savage Beast pushed past Lauren.

Marty strolled through the doorway. "Can I assume our date is over?" His angry eyes stared at her.

"Yeah. Sorry, Marty."

"Don't be sorry. You did me a favor. Cheating on this guy while he's away? I don't need that in my life. Good riddance."

Griff was on the sidewalk in a heartbeat, grabbing Marty's shirt. "How dare you talk to her like that?"

"It's the truth."

"You don't know shit. Yet, you judge her?"

"As I said. It's the truth. Now, let go."

"Apologize."

"I'm gonna call the cops," Marty said.

Lauren tugged on Griff's forearm. "I don't care what he thinks. Let him go."

Griff released the other man and stepped back.

"Some role model. I hope you lose every game this year," Marty mumbled.

Griff's eyes widened. The quarterback took a step toward him and raised a fist. "Someone ought to teach you a lesson."

Marty cringed, drawing back in fear.

"Don't worry. Not gonna be me. Don't want to break my hand for a tool like you."

"Tool? Is that the best you've got?" Emboldened by Griff's pledge not to hit him, Marty straightened his shoulders and stepped forward.

"Shut the fuck up and get outta here, before I forget what I said." He knit his brows and shoved Marty's shoulder. The smaller man scurried inside quickly. Griff laughed. "Coward."

He took Lauren by the elbow. "We can't talk here. Come to my house." She moved with him. He opened the car door for her then slid behind the wheel.

Once inside the foyer, she smiled. "I've been in this place so many times. I can't believe I didn't know it was yours."

"I'd sneak over here sometimes and check it out. I love it. Now the only thing it needs is you."

"Me? I thought you couldn't trust me."

"Your explanation makes sense. But it'll take me a while to get past Marty."

"I wasn't going to sleep with him. Was it so wrong just to want company for dinner?"

"How about female company?"

"I did that. For six months."

He hung his head. "I don't know what to think, Lauren. If this asshole Marty was nothing, then where do we go from here?"

"That's not my decision alone." Her gaze traveled down his chest to his hips and back again.

"You say you don't want to get married, but you want me to wait for you? What are we waiting for? Are you committed?"

"I am. Are you?" She shifted her weight and inched closer.

"Of course."

"Then, how about a proper hello first?" Lauren raised her chin. Her green eyes sparkled. He took her in his arms, holding her up against his chest, and then closed his mouth on hers.

LAUREN MELTED INTO his embrace. He tasted of minty toothpaste. His aftershave mixed with the essence of Griff acted like an aphrodisiac, raising heat in her veins. His fingers pressed into her back, keeping her flush up against him. She could feel his response growing. The knowledge was heady, sending a zing straight to her center.

When they broke, she stared into his eyes, black with desire. Happiness welled up inside her. His touch was like a magic wand. It soothed, comforted, and aroused her all at the same time. *Yes. This is what I've been missing.*

"Better?" he asked, with a slow grin.

"Oh, God. Much," she replied, her arms still closed around his neck.

"I've missed this."

"Me, too."

"Do you still love me, Lauren?" His brow furrowed.

"Of course."

"I'm back into the game."

"That's wonderful."

He lowered his lips to her neck. He closed his fingers around her breast. The minute they found her peak, she felt him grow harder. Her breathing became ragged, and she ached for him.

"What are we doing out here? You have a fantastic bed upstairs," she breathed, barely able to talk.

He picked her up and took the stairs two at a time. He tossed her onto the mattress. She bounced up, laughing. Then, he was on her, ripping at her clothes. She yanked her sweater up and off. He unhooked her bra in record time then sat back, gazing at her chest. He lowered his lips to her peak this time, nipping and sucking. His hand squeezed her soft flesh.

She pulled at his T-shirt. With one hand, he tugged it off and threw it on a chair. Griff slipped his hand under her skirt. She gasped and closed her eyes as his fingers traveled up her inner thigh, slowly, his thumb caressing the soft skin. They dipped under the elastic of her panties, and she moaned.

She ran her palms up his torso. He groaned. Feeling him sent a tingle down her spine.

"Touch me. Oh God, touch me, baby." He closed his eyes as his palm covered her mound.

Lauren pulled him down on top of her and ran her nails up and down his back, making him shiver. His big hands closed around her hips, pushing up her skirt even more. She reached down and unbuttoned the waist. He unzipped it and slid it off before she could blink. His hands moved up her chest and closed around her flesh, kneading, pinching. Something animal let loose in Lauren. Pent up, frustrated desire burst forth, taking control.

She unbuttoned and unzipped his jeans, pushing them down over his hips. He shimmied out of them then ripped her panties down and off. He shoved his boxers to the floor and stepped out of them. When they were finally naked on the bed, they lay staring, drooling, feasting their eyes on each other.

Lauren snapped first. She arched up, her mouth searching for his. He came down hard on her, pinning her to the mattress while his lips ravished hers. His knees forced hers open, and he knelt between them. His erection poked her core, seeking entrance. She shifted, and he gave a strong thrust and was inside her immediately. She cried out, throwing her head back, letting go.

"Did I hurt you?" he whispered.

"Oh God, no. It's so good!" she breathed out, gasping for air. Her hips moved then she wrapped her legs around him. Basic urges took over. Lauren's mind turned off. She was a mass of feelings and sensations, as her hips undulated with his. Grunts slipped from her mouth. The faster he pumped into her, the louder she became. She dug her nails into his back until he groaned. Her teeth closed down on the flesh of his shoulder, her lips sucking on his tender, fragrant skin.

Sweat dripped off his body. Desire, building up for months, reached a crescendo, spiraling up, twisting inside her, turning until she could stand it no more. With a shout, a huge orgasm washed over her like a tsunami. Every muscle in her body clenched and released. She gripped him, squashing her breasts into him, her mouth open, her eyes closed as pure pleasure poured through her veins.

Opening her eyes, Lauren spied Griff's trained on hers. They held hers captive as they grew darker. The dampness between their chests made them slippery. He slid up and down, massaging her flesh in a new and arousing way. She took a breath then kissed him.

He pulled away, screwing up his eyes, making strange noises as he pumped faster. "God damn. Fuck, baby," he said, as he stopped for his release.

He lowered his forehead to her shoulder. Droplets dripped onto the bedspread. Lauren lay, spent, underneath him. Her fingers loosened their grip and caressed him. She leaned up and kissed his neck. His breath on her throat was warm. He nuzzled her, planting small kisses on the sensitive column.

"Lauren. Oh my God."

"Amazing." She closed her eyes and took a deep breath, inhaling their passion, their loving, and their heat. It was heady. She slid her palm down his back, resting it on his butt.

"Shit, Lauren. I can't go this long without you again. I came in about two minutes."

"So did I." She giggled.

He pushed up and looked at her. "You're beautiful." Then, he bent down and kissed her nose.

She combed her fingers through his hair. "I love you."

"Do you?" He rolled off on his side.

"Can't you tell?"

"If I could, would I ask?"

"I guess not. Yeah. I do. I love you, body and soul."

He laced his fingers behind his head. Lauren cuddled up next to him and rested her cheek on his chest.

"I'm sweaty."

"I don't care." She smiled, contented to be touching him.

"I love you, too. I've got something for you." He leaned over and snatched his jeans from the floor. Fishing around in the pocket, he pulled out a tiny envelope. "Here. This was supposed to go with the charm bracelet."

She still wore the chain, which had jingled like mad as they had made love. She opened the packet carefully and reached inside. There was a small, gold heart, like the ones with their names, but this one said "forever."

"Forever?" Tears clouded her eyes.

"Don't get upset. I'm not going to hold you to that. If you don't want to get married..."

"Who said I didn't want to get married?"

He bolted upright. "What? You've always said that."

"Maybe I've changed my mind."

She sat up and opened her mouth to speak further, but Griff held up his hand. "Hear me out first. I figured it this way. If something happened, and we couldn't have kids, we could adopt. After all, I spent the last ten years raising kids who weren't mine, biologically. And I loved 'em as if they were. Why not?" When he turned to look at her, tears were cascading down her cheeks. "What? What did I say?"

"That's so sweet," she said between sobs.

"It's you, Lauren. You. I want to be with you. Forever. We'll deal with whatever comes along. Okay? Marry me, honey. Make me happy."

"I love you so much, Griff. Yes, I will."

He grabbed her, squeezing her tight, a big grin on his face.

Lauren pushed away to breathe. "Yeah, I know, touchdown," she joked.

"Completed pass, first and ten, field goal, touchdown, safety, and extra point all rolled into one, baby." He kissed her.

Lauren snaked her arms around his chest and leaned in. She had waited so long for the chance to be close to him, and she wasn't going to waste another moment.

Griff pushed to his feet and retrieved a package from the top dresser drawer. "I was hoping for this. Here. This makes it official." He knelt down and opened the small box. "Will you marry me, Lauren?"

She gasped when she saw the four-carat, emerald cut, diamond. "Yes. I will," she repeated.

He slipped the ring on her finger, and they sealed the deal with a kiss. "No trades now. You're stuck with me."

She grinned.

"This is the best. I'm going to take back starting QB, and now, I've got the girl I want. And a gorgeous house. What more could there be?"

"Nothing. This is a win-win." She sighed, resting her palm on his pecs. She combed the fingers of her other hand through his dark chest hair and kissed his skin. Tucking her knees up, she snuggled into his shoulder. "Can we stay like this for a couple hundred years?"

"Whatever you want, babe. Whatever you want."

The extra training Griff had gotten helped him immensely. He was a star during training camp, easily earning back his post as starting quarterback. He and Lauren scheduled their wedding for after the Super Bowl, in case The Kings made it. Lauren was beyond busy planning the event and decorating the houses of Griff's teammates.

When he went on the road, Griff hung with the married members who weren't fooling around. He even managed to keep Trunk Mahoney from cheating. They played cards and watched porn.

Hank flew out for Thanksgiving. Griff again played a four o'clock game. Don, Connie, and their kids, along with Hank, helped Lauren cook a fantastic meal. Griff rushed through his shower and home to good food, and the people he loved.

The Kings lost the Super Bowl to the Delaware Demons. Everyone on the team was bummed, but vowed to win next year. Griff and Lauren took a vacation on St. Thomas for a week. Spike bunked in with Buddy. The couple stood on their balcony in the gentle, nighttime breeze. They sipped pina coladas and watched the sun set.

Griff inched up behind her, snaking his arm around her middle. He bent his head to kiss under her ear. Lauren shivered.

She smiled at him. "I'm so happy."

"We have it all. Almost all."

"Almost?" She cocked her head.

"When do you want to talk about having a baby?" He continued to brush his lips up and down her neck.

She frowned. "Do we have to discuss that now?"

"Don't get tense. I told you. We're not gonna stress about it. Let's just be natural. After we're married, let's throw away the birth control pills and see what happens."

"Really? That soon?"

"I'm not getting any younger, honey."

"If it's what you want."

"It's gotta be what you want, too."

"It is, but…"

"Don't you want to have a baby with me?" He raised his head and caught her gaze.

"I do. I do, so much. But I'm scared." She avoided his eyes.

"Whatever happens, we'll be together. I'll never leave you. You're the best. Best woman in the world."

Lauren leaned back against him. *Maybe this time, I have the man I've always wanted.* She took a deep breath and knew, in her heart, that Griff meant every word. His reassurance calmed her.

"How about a little practice before dinner?"

"Great idea." She turned and was in his arms instantly.

Epilogue

GRIFF HAD BEEN WALKING on air since Lauren had agreed to marry him. Even picking out flowers and being in on all the details of the wedding didn't annoy him. He went along with whatever Lauren wanted, grateful to have her become his wife.

The short honeymoon was just his kind of vacation—sex, meals, and long walks. He returned to Monroe, rested and ready to lead the Kings to victory.

Their first game was at home against the Montana Rams. Griff met Buddy in the parking lot. They walked to the locker room together.

"I can't believe you're a married man," Buddy said, shaking his head. "No more tomcatting on the road."

"Yep. Best thing ever. You should try it," Griff replied.

Buddy snorted a laugh. "Right. You've been married five minutes, and it's the greatest thing in the world."

"Yes, it is."

Coach gathered the team in the locker room half an hour before game time. "This year we've got our work cut out for us. Not just the usual with The Gamblers and the Demons, but L. A. has traded for some big guys for their defensive line. We can't afford any more injuries, so be careful out there."

Flanked by Max Jenkins, Bullhorn Brodsky, Caleb Turner, and Buddy, Griff jogged out to the gridiron. The team stood quietly. They held their helmets. He and Buddy put their right hands over their hearts, as they prepared to sing along with the national anthem. An announcement came on the loud speaker.

"Today, it's an honor and a privilege to welcome a fabulous new singer to do the National Anthem. We are honored to have Emerald with us."

The applause was deafening.

Buddy's head snapped up. He looked at Griff then at the singer. "What the fuck is she doing here?"

The End

Turn the page for Lauren's Lamb Stew recipe & the author bio.

Want to go on to the next story now? Click the link for Buddy Carruthers, Wide Receiver & go directly to Amazon.

Lauren's Lamb Stew Slow Cooker Recipe

Ingredients
3 lbs. lamb cut into chunks
2 medium onions quartered
1 bag of carrots cut into chunks
5 large red bliss potatoes, quartered
½ cup water
¼ cup red wine, dry not sweet
 Flour for dredging (about 1/4 cup)
 1 plastic food storage bag
Salt and a pinch of black pepper

Directions
Put flour into the food storage bag. Dump
half the stew chunks in the bag, seal and
shake until the pieces are lightly coated
with flour. Place them in the slow cooker,
then repeat with the rest of the lamb.

Place onion quarters in with the meat. Add
potatoes and carrots. Pour water over all
ingredients, then the wine. Add salt to
taste and a pinch of pepper.

Cook on high for one hour. Then switch to
low and continue cooking for seven hours
or until the meat is tender. Stir if you wish.

About the Author

Jean Joachim is a best-selling romance fiction author, with books hitting the Amazon Top 100 list since 2012. She writes contemporary romance, which includes sports romance and romantic suspense.

Dangerous Love Lost & Found, First Place winner in the 2015 Oklahoma Romance Writers of America, International Digital Award contest. *The Renovated Heart* won Best Novel of the Year from Love Romances Café. *Lovers & Liars* was a Rom-Con finalist in 2013. And *The Marriage List* tied for third place as Best Contemporary Romance from the Gulf Coast RWA. To Love or Not to Love tied for second place in the 2014 New England Chapter of Romance Writers of America Reader's Choice contest. She was chosen Author of the Year in 2012 by the New York City chapter of RWA.

Married and the mother of two sons, Jean lives in New York City. Early in the morning, you'll find her at her computer, writing, with a cup of tea, her rescued pug, Homer, by her side and a secret stash of black licorice.

Jean has 30+ books, novellas and short stories published. Find them here: http://www.jean-joachimbooks.com. Sign up for her newsletter, on her website, and be eligible for her private paperback sales. Sign up for her newsletter here: https://www.facebook.com/pages/Jean-Joachim-Author/221092234568929?sk=app_100265896690345

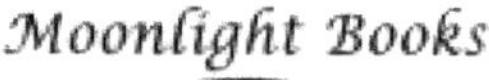

Moonlight Books

Don't miss out!

Visit the website below and you can sign up to receive emails whenever Jean C. Joachim publishes a new book. There's no charge and no obligation.

https://books2read.com/r/B-A-MDPF-HMUG

BOOKS 2 READ

Connecting independent readers to independent writers.